DEC _ 2017

D0443123

the day the angels fell

SHAWN SMUCKER

Revell

a division of Baker Publishing Group
Grand Rapids, Michigan

Published by Revell
a division of Baker Publishing Group
P.O. Box 6287, Grand Rapids, MI 49516-6287
www.revellbooks.com

Printed in the United States of America

Library of Congress Cataloging-in-Publication Data
Names: Smucker, Shawn, author.
Title: The day the angels fell / Shawn Smucker.
Description: Grand Rapids, MI : Revell, 2017.
Identifiers: LCCN 2017012124| ISBN 9780800728496 (cloth)
Subjects: LCSH: Mothers and sons—Fiction. | Mothers—Death—Fiction. |
    Tree of life—Fiction. | Psychological fiction. | GSAFD: Christian fiction.
Classification: LCC PS3619.M83 D38 2017 | DDC 813/.6—dc23
LC record available at https://lccn.loc.gov/2017012124

Unless otherwise indicated, Scripture quotations are from the Holy Bible, New
International Version®. NIV®. Copyright © 1973, 1978, 1984 by Biblica,
Inc.™ Used by permission of Zondervan. All rights reserved worldwide. www
.zondervan.com

Scripture quotations marked NLT are from the *Holy Bible*, New Living Trans-
lation, copyright © 1996, 2004, 2015 by Tyndale House Foundation. Used by
permission of Tyndale House Publishers, Inc., Carol Stream, Illinois 60188.
All rights reserved.

17   18   19   20   21   22   23   7   6   5   4   3   2   1

To
Cade, Lucy, Abra,
Sam, Leo, and Poppy,
for being the main characters
in my favorite story.

And most of all,
to Maile.
Along with everything else,
this is for you.

You have been given questions

to which you cannot be given answers.

You will have to live them out—

perhaps a little at a time.

WENDELL BERRY, *JAYBER CROW*

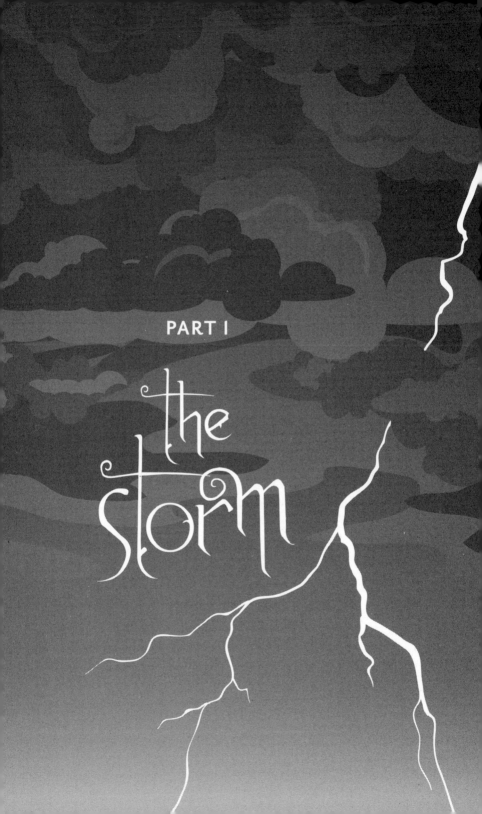

PART I

the
storm

Think of him still as the same. I say,

He is not dead—he is just away.

JAMES WHITCOMB RILEY

I AM OLD NOW. I still live on the same farm where I grew up, the same farm where my mother's accident took place, the same farm that burned for days after the angels fell. My father rebuilt the farm after the fire, and it was foreign to me then, a new house trying to fill an old space. The trees he planted were all fragile and small, and the inside of the barns smelled like new wood and fresh paint. I think he was glad to start over, considering everything that summer had taken from us.

But that was many years ago, and now the farm feels old again. The floorboards creak when I walk to the kitchen in the middle of the night. The walls and the roof groan under the weight of summer storms. There is a large oak tree in the front yard again, and it reminds me of the lightning tree, the one that started it all. This house and I are two old friends sitting together in our latter days.

I untie my tangled necktie and try again. I've never been good at these knots. My last friend's funeral is this week and I thought I should wear a tie. It seemed the right thing to do, but now that I'm standing in front of a mirror I'm having second thoughts, not only about the necktie but about even going. She was my best friend, but I'm not sure I have the strength for one more funeral.

Someone knocks on the front door, so I untangle myself from the tie and ease my way down the stairs, leaning heavily on the handrail. Another knock, and by now I'm crossing to the door.

"Coming, coming," I say. People are in such a hurry these days. Everyone wants everything to happen now, or yesterday. But when you're my age, you get used to waiting, mostly because you're always waiting on yourself.

"Hi there, Jerry," I say through the screen, not making any move to open it.

"I won't come in, Samuel. Just wanted to apologize for my boy again."

Jerry is a huge bear of a man with arms and hands and fingers so thick I sometimes wonder how he can use them for anything small like tying shoes or stirring his coffee. He's always apologizing for his boy. I don't know why—seems to me his boy simply acts like a boy. And because Jerry is always calling him "boy," I can't remember the child's name.

"I heard he was throwing smoke bombs up on your porch this morning."

"Oh, that. Well . . ." I begin.

"I won't hear of it," Jerry says. "In fact, as soon as I find him he'll be coming here in person to apologize."

"That's really not necessary," I say.

"No. That boy will apologize."

I sigh. "Anything else, Jerry? How are the fields this summer?"

"Green. It's been a good one so far."

"All right," I mumble, then turn and walk away because I'm

too old to waste my time having conversations that don't interest me. "All right."

"Oh, and I'm sorry about your friend," Jerry calls to me as I begin the slow ascent up the stairs. His words hit me like a physical object, make me stop on the third step and lean against the wall. They bring a fresh wave of grief to the surface, and I'm glad he can't see my face.

"Thank you," I say, hoping he will leave now.

"The missus says she was a good, close friend of yours for many years. I'm very sorry."

"Thank you," I say again, then start climbing the stairs. One foot after the other, that's the only way to do it. I wish people would mind their own business. I have no interest at my age in collecting the sympathy of strangers. Or near strangers. In fact, I can do without sympathy at all, no matter the source.

I still imagine myself to be self-sufficient, and in order to maintain that illusion I keep a small garden at the end of the lane. Sometimes, while I'm weeding, I'll stop and look across the street at where the old church used to be. After the fire they left the lot vacant and rebuilt the small brick building on a lot in town, but the old foundation is still there somewhere, under the dirt and the plants and the trees that came up over the years. Time covers things, but that doesn't mean they're gone.

If I'm honest, though, I have to admit that during some gradual phase in my life I became too old to work the farm myself. There was a time not long ago when my farm fell into disrepair, and I thought it would be the end of me as well, because I couldn't bear to watch so many memories collapse in on themselves. Then the family that moved into Abra's old farm, Jerry and "the missus" and his "boy," asked if they could rent my fields and barns. I said yes because I had no good reason to say no. Now they take care of everything and I live quietly in the old farmhouse, puttering in my garden or sitting on the large front porch, trying to remember all the things that happened the summer my mother died.

Jerry's son looks to be about eleven or twelve, my age when it happened. I wonder what he would do if his mother died.

I think he's scared of me, and I don't blame him. I don't shave very often and my hair is usually unruly. My clothes are old and worn. I know I smell of old age—I remember that scent from when my father started walking with a cane.

Sometimes Jerry's son will hide among the fruit trees that line the long lane and spy on me, but I don't mind. I pretend not to see him, and he seems to have fun with it, climbing up to the highest branch and peering through an old tube as if it's a telescope. Sometimes, though, when he gets to the top, I find myself holding my breath, waiting for him to fall. Everything falls in the end, you know.

I stare at the mirror again after climbing the steps and wonder where all the time has gone. I pick up the necktie and try again, but my old fingers can't quite get it right. I remember when I was a very young boy my mother would sometimes put a tie on me, her delicate hands weaving the smooth fabric in a magical way.

"There," she would say, patting the knot of the tie and looking rather pleased with herself. "Now you look like a young man."

The boy reminds me of myself when I was his age. He runs around the farm with sticks and pretends they are swords and magic staffs. Those days seem so long ago. Now I move slowly, carrying only a cane that is nothing more than a cane. I don't know if I have the power anymore to turn this cane into anything exciting, anything like a sword pulled from a stone or a gun that could kill an Amarok. Sometimes I feel like I have forgotten how to pretend.

I give up on the tie and sit with relief at the desk by the window that looks out over the front yard and the garden. It's rather eerie how the farm has returned to almost the same condition it was in the summer my mother died, the summer of the fire. Sometimes when I look down the lane I expect to see her walking back up from the mailbox, or my dad to wander in from the barns, dirty and ready for dinner.

After many years of wondering if I could get the story of that summer exactly right, I have decided to simply write it as I remember it. There's no one else left who was there when it happened, no one to compare stories with, no one to agree or disagree with my own version. As I think through the story, I wonder if it's even possible that everything happened as my memory tells me it did. It all seems rather incredible.

But one thing I'm sure of: after everything that happened that summer, life seemed fragile, like an egg rolling toward the edge of the table. It seemed like anyone I knew could die at any moment. But now that I'm old and all my friends have died or moved away, my own life feels almost unbreakable, like it will never give up.

Which reminds me of something that Mr. Tennin told me in his thin, wispy voice, right at the end.

"Samuel," he whispered. "Always remember this."

I leaned in closer as the fire roared on the far side of the river.

"Death," he said, then paused. "Is a gift."

I stare at the obituary sitting at the corner of my desk, the one I cut out of the paper yesterday—such a small amount of writing meant to tell the story of someone's entire life. I lift it up

15

and it's light, almost see-through, and for a moment life seems fragile again, and temporary.

Death, a gift? I would have shouted at someone had they said that to me at my mother's funeral. But I've been on this earth for many years now, and I've seen many things, and I finally believe that Mr. Tennin was right.

Death, like life, is a gift.

This is how I remember that summer.

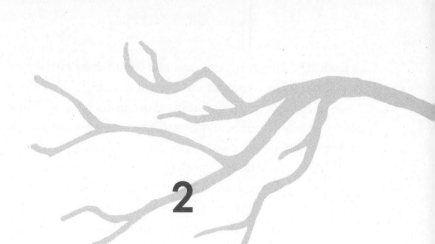

2

I WAS TWELVE YEARS OLD, and because I was crouched down in left field, picking at random blades of grass and not paying attention, I didn't notice the darkness gathering in the west. My father signed me up for baseball every year, even though I wasn't very interested in a game that seemed to be made up mostly of standing around and waiting, and on that particular day I was feeling happy the season was almost over. I stared at a small ant pile and poked at it, spreading panic. The ants dashed here and there, trying to rebuild what I had brushed away in an instant.

I heard the faint sound of distant thunder.

It would be remembered as the summer of storms. Nearly every week, massive dark clouds rumbled down over the western mountain range and drenched the valley. The fields outside of town were green from all the rain, and the creeks were muddy and full, bulging at the seams.

While I heard the distant thunder, it wasn't enough to get my attention, and I continued tormenting the ants. I glanced up at the parking lot and noticed that my mother wasn't there yet, which was unusual because she almost always came to pick me up well before practice was over. She normally parked up from third base and sat on the hood of the car, her feet on the bumper, until I saw her and waved. Then she'd get out a book and read until practice was over.

I had never had to wait for her before.

I heard a loud *ping* come from home plate, and I looked at the batter, maybe 150 feet away. It was Stony DeWitt, the biggest kid on the team, and he slammed a screamer that was rising, sailing over my head. I left the ants to recover what they had lost and started running back, back, back. The rest of the kids shouted at me to hurry. We grew tired of Stony hitting home runs every time he was up to bat, and we roared with delight whenever we could get him out.

The ball traced an arc over my head, bounced, and rolled to the short outfield fence. Beyond the fence was the town of Deen, Pennsylvania, which was nothing more than the intersection of two roads.

I reached for the ball, and the instant I touched it—the very instant, I tell you—lightning struck, and it was so close that the thunder clapped at the same time. It scared me and I dropped the ball. There are times in those kinds of storms when you begin to feel that there is no safe place, that the lightning will strike anywhere, that you have a target on your back and it's just a matter of time.

My breath caught in my throat and I scrambled after the ball, my insides jumping every which way. I turned to run toward the safety of the infield, but I realized the baseball diamond was empty. The lightning had scattered the kids to their parents' cars. Even Mr. Pelle, my baseball coach, who smoked the delicious-smelling pipe full of cherry tobacco, was running up the small hill to the parking lot, one hand holding a rubber home plate over his head, the other dragging a large red canvas equipment bag behind him. He stopped long enough to drop everything and cup his hands around his mouth.

"Go into the store!" he shouted, waving me off. "Get inside!"

My eyes scanned the parking lot again, the one that ran along the baseball field, but my mom still wasn't there. I turned and ran back to the chain-link fence, climbed over it, and raced toward the edge of town, only a few hundred yards away. Heavy drops hit the ground all around me. There were large amounts of time between the drops, and I could hear each individual one collide with the ground. When they hit my baseball cap or my arms they seemed far larger than normal, the size of marbles that exploded into patches of water wherever they landed.

I ran for Mr. Pelle's antique store, which was right at the inter-section. I had made it into the parking lot by the time the next lightning missile struck, and this time I not only heard the crash but felt the sizzle in the air, the electric pulse spreading outward. The air woke up, like a viper sensing a small mouse dropped into its cage.

The rain turned into a constant sheet of water, and I felt like I was trying to breathe underwater. The air was lost, taken over by the downpour. There was no space between drops anymore. Everything, including me, was soaked in seconds. Water dripped from the brim of my ball cap, and my shirt clung to me, suddenly heavy, like a second skin.

On one side of Pelle's Antiques was Uncle Sal's pizza, and the smell of delicious cheese and pepperoni came at me through the rain. I ran into the small alley between Uncle Sal's and Pelle's, through the small waterfall tumbling out from the gutters where the rain already overflowed. I pushed open the heavy brown steel door and vanished into the stockroom of Pelle's Antiques.

The door slammed behind me, and I went from a white-gray day full of the sound of pounding rain and splitting thunder to shadows and quiet and the smells of old cedarwood, dust, and paint. I stopped inside the door as my eyes adjusted to the darkness. Outside, when the rain was coming down through that July day, the falling water had felt almost warm, but in the air-conditioned back room of the antique store, the water spread a chill over my body, and I crossed my arms, clutching my baseball glove as if it might bring me some warmth.

The rain made a distant rushing sound on the roof, and as I meandered through the irregular rows of furniture, I wondered again why my mother had been late, and where she was, and who would take me home. I passed high-backed armchairs standing upside down on barn-door tables, and under them were old windows without any glass panes. There were desks and side tables and large hutches. Wardrobes stood closed and ominous, daring me to open them. Lamps of every shape and size filled in the gaps: tall, skinny ones and short, fat ones, lamps with shades and lamps without shades, some with small white bulbs perched at the top like crystal balls, others with empty sockets.

I stopped in front of an old mirror framed in black, twisting metal, and I stared at my reflection in the peeling surface. I was a skinny kid and, being soaked through, looked even thinner than usual. I'm sure I didn't look as old as I wanted to look. My brown eyes were still the eyes of a child. I spent most of my childhood wanting to be bigger, stronger, older.

I heard voices in the prep room. It was the space between the large storage room and the sales floor, where Mr. Pelle stained and repaired and prepared one piece of furniture at a time before taking it to the store out front with the big glass windows that looked out onto Route 126. It was unusual for anyone besides Mr. Pelle or his family to be in that middle room.

I moved to the door. I could hear my own heart thumping in my ears, and my breath seemed suddenly loud. My sneakers, waterlogged, squeaked with each step.

But as I got to the swinging door, it was already leaning open a few inches. Outside, another lightning strike sent thunder through Deen. The sound of the rain was a constant hum, but the voices were loud. I peered through the crack in the door.

Three old women sat on one side of a large, square table. They were dressed like gypsies, with long, flowing robes that draped down from their shoulders. Scarves were wrapped around their heads, with gray and white hair peeking out from under the colorful fabric. Large golden earrings dragged their flabby earlobes toward their shoulders, and their arms were lined with bracelets that clinked when they moved. They sat so close together that their robes folded into each other, so close that they almost looked like one wide, colorful body with three heads.

They looked intently across the table, but I couldn't see that side of the room through the crack in the door. Someone was there, though. Their shadow, short and wide, draped itself across the table and toward the women. When the person spoke, it was a man's voice. At first he muttered and grunted to himself, the words all jumbled together. But I could only see the three old women, and they stared at him as if trying to decide if they should stay or go.

Out of nowhere, the three old women interrupted him, quietly at first and then louder. They chanted words, but not English words, not old, dead words that can barely stand on their own two feet. No, the words they chanted were alive, words I couldn't understand, words that had a fluttering, startling life of their own. Their words terrified me, but they also intrigued me. I was like a confused magnet, repelled and attracted all at once.

Part of me wanted to turn and run back out into the storm I had escaped from, back into the hair-trigger lightning and the thunder and the rain that had drenched me, but their words pulled me forward until I was braced against the frame, fighting to stay outside the room.

The lights in the building flickered, then went out.

3

THE STORM RAGED OUTSIDE. The women's faces held a grayish tint from the stormy light dripping in through the one small window in the prep room. Sometimes, when the lightning flashed, their skin went white, almost transparent, and the man's shadow appeared solid black on the table. I kept expecting one of the women to look at me in those flashes of lightning, those moments of clarity, but their eyes focused on the table, where their fingers had joined together in one big pile. They swayed with the words, and their six hands writhed in an uneven rhythm.

I wondered if those women were traveling with the fair that had recently arrived in town. My dad called them "carnies," that rough group of travelers who brought wonder to our small community every summer, leaving behind deep tire tracks in the park outside of town and puddles filled with unredeemed ride tickets. These women could have been anything—funnel cake vendors or ticket takers outside the mirror maze or fortune-tellers. They might have been the ones who try to guess your age or spin the prize wheel. They could have been anything.

Their chanting stopped as quickly as it had started, and the world fell back into its natural order. I could hear the rain softening on the roof and the wind tapering down to random gusts through the alleyway, but the front of the storm had passed and the thunder had moved off into the distance. The woman in the middle straightened the large scarf tied around her head and pushed all those jingling bracelets and rings and necklaces back into place. She didn't seem to realize she had been saying anything out of the ordinary. She looked up as if expecting the person in the shadows to tell them what to do next.

"Is that it?" the man's voice rumbled. It growled with thick phlegm and the beginnings of an earthquake.

"Is what it?" the woman in the middle asked, leaning forward. She raised her stenciled eyebrows toward the ceiling. Some of her teeth were so sideways that they looked backward. There was nothing straight about her.

"I paid you good money for my fortune, the future, whatever you want to call it. Chanted words, spooky humming . . . is that it? Is that all I get?"

She looked back and forth at the women on either side of her and whispered over one shoulder as if consulting with someone. Someone who wasn't there.

"But you didn't tell us who you were," she said in a polite voice that I realized carried hints of a foreign accent. "The fortunes of your kind are dark. Men are easily read, but you?"

She stared at him with a face completely at peace. His threatening tone of voice did not seem to affect her in the least. The room was quiet for a moment, and then she spoke again.

"You didn't tell us what you were."

The man cleared his throat.

"But you saw something?" He sounded unsettled, even a bit distracted, by her knowledge of "what" he was.

"Something to write with?" she asked.

The man grunted and threw a pen onto the table. It slid toward the women. The one in the middle grabbed the pen before it stopped moving and began scribbling on the table. I cringed— Mr. Pelle would not be happy if he saw them doing that. But she kept writing. She'd cross out what she wrote and write again. And again. She spent a solid five minutes defacing that table with more ink than I thought any pen could hold, and it looked like she crossed out and scribbled over every single word she wrote.

Finally, with the sound of fluid clothes and wind-chiming jewelry, the three women stood up.

"This is for you," the one in the middle said, pushing the point of the pen into the table, where it stuck for a moment before falling over. "You may read it after we leave."

The man grunted again.

"The rest of the money?" the woman asked.

At first nothing happened, and I thought they might keep arguing. But three green bills floated down onto the scribbled surface. The woman picked them up and stuffed them into the recesses of her long, flowing skirt. She was clearly impatient to leave, and when she stood up her movements seemed anxious. The other two women were a half second behind her, as if they were three marionettes all controlled by the same puppet master.

Then something strange happened.

She glanced at me.

Or at least she glanced at the crack in the door. But I thought it was more than that. I thought I felt her eyes locking onto mine, and I was sure that if the man wasn't in the room, she would have come over and told me something. Something very important. But her sudden look scared me, and I spun around, stood with my back to the wall. I held my breath and listened, hoping no one would come that way.

The women must have left through the other door, the one that led into the front area of the antique store. Moments later I heard, far away at the front of the building, the bell ring over the entrance. They were gone.

There was a loud sound from outside the window—the last strong rumble of thunder, or a downspout leaning under so much weight—and the man left without getting a chance to spend much time looking at the table.

"Nothing," he mumbled. "Nothing, nothing, and more nothing."

He walked quickly toward the same door the women had gone through. I didn't get a look at his face, but I did see him from behind. He was short and wide. There was something very powerful about his neck and shoulders. He turned sideways so that he could fit through the narrow door.

The room was empty now. I pushed the swinging door aside and approached the table. The storm seemed to have passed. Sunlight lit up the room, and for the first time I noticed the window was open. The floor had a large puddle on it that reflected the light. I could hear water still running through the gutters and downspouts, splashing into the alley.

The woman with the pen had made a complete mess of the table. Ink was everywhere, filling deep gouges in the wood. She had written many things. Many things. But everything had been scratched out so effectively that it was all impossible to read.

Everything, that is, except for one small sentence I almost missed in the middle of that black cloud of dead, crossed-out words.

Find the Tree of Life.

Voices. The sound of someone coming back from the front of the antique store. If it was Mr. Pelle, I didn't want him to find me there with the window open, the water on the floor, and the ruined table, so I raced through the swinging door, through the storeroom, and out the side door into the alley. There wasn't a sidewalk back there, only a six-foot strip of dirt and loose rocks separating Mr. Pelle's store from Uncle Sal's.

I wasn't sure what I had just seen, but I knew I had never seen anything like it, not in my small town. I turned to walk back the way I had come, away from the main street, back toward the baseball field. I hoped my mother would be waiting there for me. But I stopped. I heard someone walking, their feet crunching slow steps over the loose gravel.

Drip. Drip. Drip. Water fell from a clogged gutter at the top of the building. I turned around. Coming toward me was the woman I had seen sitting at the table inside, the one in the middle who had written everything. She was alone, the other two women nowhere to be found. She walked unsteadily, in the trembling way of someone very old, and I froze. I stood there, staring. She was sort of hunched over, and her robe flapped every once in a while as leftover gusts of wind dashed through the alley, chasing the storm that had left them behind. The air felt cool for July, that kind of after-storm coolness that reminds you summer will not last forever.

She smiled as she walked, and her mouth opened as if she was about to say something, but then she closed it again. She stopped a few feet away, and I saw the stick she carried. It was a gnarled, barkless thing that bent this way and that. She grasped it with both hands, plunged it into the ground, and limped around me, muttering a small stream of those living words. The stick made a harsh, scratching noise in the dirt and the rocks. Her strength amazed me—the line she made was deep. A small trickle of rainwater welled up and filled it.

At that point I almost started to feel bad for her. She was obviously losing her mind. I held my breath, waiting for her to finish, trying to think of something nice to say. She made a circle in the dirt all the way around me with that stick, and I got another glimpse of those sideways teeth crowding for space in her mouth. Her eyes were kind and knowing.

I nodded at her, and she walked away. I sighed with relief and watched her turn the corner.

But I couldn't leave the circle she had made.

4

THERE WASN'T ANYTHING IN THE AIR, nothing that I could see that might be keeping me in that spot. I could hear everything going on around me. And I could move, but there was some kind of force keeping me inside the circle she had drawn.

"Sam!" I heard a voice shout. It was my friend Abra coming down the alley.

I tried to lift my arm to wave her over, but the circle kept my arms tight to my sides.

"Come on," she called out. "Your mom's been looking for you. She's going to take us home."

At that point I realized I couldn't talk. I could breathe, but that was it. My voice was gone. Nothing.

"Why are you standing there?" she said. "Your mom is waiting. C'mon!"

When she got closer she slowed down. I stared at her, and she looked confused. She reached out and pushed me playfully. Her foot scuffed mud and stones over the circle the old lady had drawn, and suddenly I could move. I jumped away from the circle.

What had just happened?

"What's your problem?" she asked. "Let's go. The Ferris wheel is going up and the livestock tents are out. I'm pretty sure I saw Steve and Bo sneaking onto the fairgrounds over by the break in the fence, where the cotton candy always is . . ."

She chattered on and on about the fair, and I followed her through the alley, expecting the old woman to jump out at us or that huge man to sweep down and question me. But nothing happened. We wandered out onto the sidewalk that ran in front of the antique store and walked toward my mother waiting in her car.

I climbed into the passenger seat and didn't say a word. I couldn't get the image of that woman out of my mind, the way she scraped that circle, the way it held me frozen.

"Hey," my mom said, disapproval on her face, "where were you? And where's your glove?"

I realized I had left my glove in Mr. Pelle's back room.

"Where was I?" I said. "Where were you?"

She could tell I had been upset when she didn't show up, so she let me get away with talking back to her.

"I'm sorry, Sam," she said, tilting her head and frowning. "I know I'm never late, but I got caught up talking to Abra's mom, and she asked if I could pick Abra up at the school, so by the time I got to practice you were gone. What a storm!"

Abra sat in the backseat and put her bag beside her. She kept glancing at me with a strange look on her face, but I tried to ignore her.

Yeah, what a storm, I thought, once again picturing the dark cloud of scribbles on the table around those words.

Find the Tree of Life.

We drove north onto Kincade Road. That's where the fair was setting up, in a park on the outskirts of town. The workers swarmed the area, building rides and putting up food tents, pulling trailers and backing up trucks. I looked and looked for the three old ladies, but I didn't see them.

"Look, the Ferris wheel!" Abra said. "I can't wait."

There was a whimsical sound to her voice, and I knew exactly how she felt. The rides, the food, the lights—everything about the fair embodied summer and freedom and being young.

At the far end of the fair I saw the Ferris wheel going up, section by section. Three or four large men joined the massive, curving pieces of iron pulled from the back of a semi.

We left town. Abra and I both looked out the back window of my mom's car for as long as the fair was visible. It was the best part of the summer, and I couldn't wait.

Today's Friday, tomorrow's Saturday, then Sunday night the fair opens, I thought.

"Can we come on Sunday night?" I asked my mom.

"Of course we can," she said.

We always think we have one more day. We always think tomorrow can do nothing but come around. It's one of the great illusions we live with, that time will go on and on, that our lives will never end.

"Of course we can," she'd said, but my mom wouldn't make it to the fair that year.

Route 126 and Kincade Road were both lined with restaurants and gas stations and a small grid of houses in those days, population 1,931 (or so said the small sign as you drove into town, and so said that sign for many years). Route 126 traveled east to west. Kincade Road was my road, the road that went north into the farmland and the valley where the eastern and western mountain ranges started pinching together.

We had already dropped Abra off at her farmhouse and were driving the last stretch of Kincade Road before getting to our place. There was only one more farm north of us, and Kincade Road ended just past its lane, giving way first to woods and then to the two mountains that lined the opposite sides of our valley as they converged to a point. A river spilled out of their collision and drifted south through the valley, all the way to Deen.

When I was a kid, that valley was my entire world, and the mountains that lined it were the boundaries. Beyond them, there was nothing. I loved my life there at the edge of the world. I feel sorry for children who live in the midst and never have a chance to wander close to where everything ends.

A clean, delicious wind rushed into the car. We had driven mile after mile out of town until the houses dispersed and gradually gave way to cornfields. The cornstalks were about two feet tall, their narrow green tassels waving back and forth. In most places the fields went all the way from the edge of Kincade Road to the forests that lined the mountains. Everything smelled like cut grass and blue sky. The farming families in the valley tried to squeeze as much out of the land as we could, and as I had grown older I had begun to feel part of the earth, part of the struggle for life.

We approached a meaningless stop sign. The road that used to cross Kincade Road was no longer there, but my mom still insisted on stopping. I wondered if anyone would ever take that sign down. As I glanced over at the grassy bank that kept the cornfields at bay, I saw the cat.

"Wait! Pull over!"

It was pure white, really small, practically a kitten, and it walked like it was proud of itself, flicking its tail behind it like a tall, white snake.

"What, for a cat?" my mom asked, but she was already pulling over. That's the kind of mom she was.

"Yeah, for a cat." I opened my door. The cat turned and looked at me.

Now, decades later, I still wonder why that cat couldn't have simply run away from me, disappearing into the corn and saving everything. Why did it have to come so willingly?

"Look at that," I said. "He likes me."

"How do you know it's a he?" my mom asked.

"Can we take him home?" I asked, reaching out to the cat. It paused for a moment, moved away from me, then leaned back into my reach.

"I don't know if your father will like that," Mom said, but I had already brought the cat into the car and closed the door. I looked at my mom and made sad eyes, a great big pretend frown.

She laughed. I loved how my mom laughed.

Then she sighed and shook her head, but she couldn't stop smiling. "You are going to get me into trouble," she said. "What will you name him?"

"I think I'll name him Icarus."

"Icarus? Where's that from?"

I shrugged. "Remember the story Dad told us the other night after dinner? The story about the father who built wings for himself and his son out of wax and feathers so they could escape the island they were on?"

"I think I was washing the dishes," Mom said, looking at me out of the corner of her eye. "By myself."

"It was a good story," I said, rolling my eyes. "You missed out."

"Well, what happened?"

"The father warned his son about flying too low because the sea's spray would clog his wings. But he couldn't fly too high or the sun would melt them."

"And?"

"He flew too high, the wings melted, and he drowned in the sea."

"That's depressing."

I shrugged again. "I like the name. Icarus."

"You'll have to buy food," she warned me. "Where will you get money for that?"

"Oh, I've got tons of money," I said, and we both laughed.

I wasn't exactly rich, but I made five dollars a week mowing Mr. Jinn's grass. Mr. Jinn owned the farm to the north of us, but I had never seen him in my life. Not ever. He was an old hermit and never left his house. His farm was all grown over with weeds, and the barns were falling in on themselves. He had a small yard that he kept mowed, though sometimes he called my mom and, in as few words as possible, asked if I could mow it for him. When I did, he left a five-dollar bill in an empty birdbath close to his house. Whenever I took the money from the birdbath, I could feel his eyes staring at me through one of the dark windows.

"Well, I guess you can name him whatever you want to name him if you're footing the bill," she said. The car turned in to the stone driveway that led to our house. "Just remember," she said as she turned off the car, "names are powerful things. Sometimes they can even form us into who we become."

But I wasn't thinking about who I was becoming, or who the cat would become, because that's how it is when you're young and feel like you have all the time in the world.

I tried to tuck Icarus under my arm when we got out of the car so that my dad wouldn't see, but at that moment he came walking in from the barn. He strolled over to my mom and kissed her on the cheek.

I murmured, "Gross."

They both laughed. My dad stopped laughing when he saw what I had under my arm.

"What's that?"

"What, that cute little cat?" my mom said, moving over to stand beside me.

Dad sighed. "As if we need another animal around here to feed." He looked at me and raised his eyebrows as if to ask, *And what do you have to say for yourself, young man?*

I pulled the cat in tighter against my side and stroked his head. "I'll take care of him, Dad, don't worry. I'll pay for the food. You won't have to do a thing."

He looked back over at my mom.

"He named the cat Icarus," she said, as if that was her only argument on my behalf.

"What am I going to do with you two?" he said, trying not to smile. He turned and walked away. When he was far off, he shouted without turning around, "I'm fine with the cat. But not in the house!"

I looked at Mom and she smiled, and we walked to the house together. I put the cat down and waited to see what he would do. Without hesitating, he ran up beside my mom and walked with her, trying to move between and around her feet.

"He likes you, Mom!" I shouted.

"How do you know it's a he?" she asked again.

"Because his name is Icarus."

"Is that your cat?" a voice shouted to me from down the

lane. Abra rode her bike up beside me. She had a goofy grin on her face.

"I got a cat! Can you believe it? Meet Icarus!" I laughed.

"Cats are for sissies," she said, but I could tell she was jealous.

"Abra, would you like to stay for supper?" my mom called from the house, and we grinned at each other.

———

At about six o'clock I ran out to the barn to find my dad and tell him supper was ready. Abra stayed inside to help my mom set the table.

"Dad?" I shouted into the dark barn, where he usually finished up before supper. "Are you in here?"

My voice sounded thin and vanished quickly in the aisles between the pens and the holes in the ceiling that went up to the musty haymow. Sometimes we'd throw a few bales of hay down and then jump through the hole, landing on them. It was a good ten feet from the ceiling to the floor, and the rush took my breath away. Inside that old barn, when the sun was going down but we hadn't turned on the lights yet, it was a dark place with a lot of deep shadows. It was the kind of place where you could believe in just about anything.

I thought back to the old lady who had drawn a circle in the ground around me. Who was the man in the shadows? Why were they all in the back room? What did *Find the Tree of Life* mean? I kept expecting one of the three women to walk out of a corner of the barn, holding that stick, looking at me with those eyes.

"Dad?" I shouted again.

"Over here, Son," he said. I walked through the half-light to the back corner of the barn, where he kept one of the lambs that had been rejected by its mother. "Hold this bottle for me."

It was warm in the barn, and flies buzzed everywhere. They dodged my steps and buzzed around me in a cloud. I grabbed the oversized bottle and stuck it between the bars of the gate, holding it with two hands. The little white lamb latched on and sucked, bucking its head and wagging its stumpy little tail a million times a minute. I reached out and petted the curly wool on its head.

"Thanks, boy," my dad said, ruffling my hair and smiling. "I'm going to go hook up the tractor. You finish up that bottle for me and I'll meet you inside."

When he left, the barn felt dark and still. I jumped at every shadow. As I helped the lamb gulp down the last of the bottle, I stared into a corner where a beam of sunshine fell through one of the dusty barn windows. The light illuminated a spiderweb, and as I watched, a fly collided with the sticky strands. It fought and churned and spun until it was hopelessly entangled. A small black spider darted out from the shadows, hovered over the fly, and began wrapping it in a sticky cocoon.

A strange sense of fear burned inside me, and I backed away from the lamb. But there was something else, some feeling I couldn't identify. I don't know what it was. Maybe it was nothing. Or maybe I could somehow sense the coming storm, the fact that things were about to change.

We ate supper together that night, our last supper together, though I didn't know it at the time. New potatoes and green beans from our garden, and a roast my mom had cooked in the oven all day.

We never spoke much at supper, the three of us. Sometimes Mom would try to get us going with simple questions: "What's the best thing that happened to you today? What's the worst thing?" And my dad and I cooperated, more or less.

There was definitely more talking when Abra was there. My mom was always asking about her family—how they were going to spend their summer and how her baby brother was doing. My dad always tried to get information out of her about what crops her father was planting, how the animals were faring, that sort of thing. Her family's farm was just to the south of ours, and we saw them a lot.

Every once in a great while my dad would tell a story during suppertime, and when he did I would listen with wide eyes. They were normally stories from his childhood injected with fictional characters or fantastic events. It was usually difficult to strain the truth from the fantasy, but they were always wonderful stories.

That night he cleared his plate and took a long drink of ice water. The outside of the glass was sweating because it was warm in the house, and it left a small, glistening ring on the table. He crossed his arms and leaned his chair back on two legs. When he sat like that he looked huge and old and wise, and I was reminded of how different a boy is from a man, how different I was from him.

"When I was a boy," he said, "there was a great big tree in the front yard of this farm."

"Like the oak?" I asked, looking over at Abra. But she didn't even notice me—she just stared at my dad. We both loved when he told his stories.

"Just like the oak," he said. "Only larger. And taller. Some of the boys in my neighborhood said that if you climbed all the way to the top, you'd be up in the clouds, maybe even in heaven. But that's a different story. In this story, I had a dog, a wonderful dog named Ike. Ike was a German shepherd my grandfather gave me for my tenth birthday. Ike was eight weeks old when he came to live at the house. He was a beautiful dog."

38

My mom stood up and took a few plates over to the sink, then came and sat down. She put her elbow on the table and leaned her face into the palm of her hand. She was a good listener.

"Ike didn't always know what was best for him, and one day he chased a rabbit around the barn as my dad was backing out the tractor. Well, my dad backed over Ike, and he died. I was very sad. I cried for hours. Finally, as it started to get dark, my dad and my grandpa came in and asked if I'd like to help them bury Ike under the old oak tree. I said I would, and we took turns with the shovel, digging the hole and burying good old Ike.

"The next day it started to rain, and it hadn't rained all summer. We'd been in a drought, and the farmers were happy to see the rain. Well, someone heard that we had buried Ike the night before out under that oak tree, and there were some superstitious people in the town. They started to think that old oak tree had the power to bring rain, and all you had to do was sacrifice an animal and bury it close to the roots."

"That's weird," Abra said, wrinkling her nose.

"Me and my grandpa and my dad, we all knew this was hogwash, but someone kept coming out at night and burying animals under our tree. It got to be pretty bad, and the rain came down harder and harder until it looked like it might flood. So one night my grandpa went out there with a can of kerosene and doused the tree and burned it down. You should have seen the flames."

For a moment he stared at the ceiling as if he were watching a massive tree burn.

"Everything went back to normal after that. But I was sad to see that tree go."

It was very quiet around the table as we sat there thinking about Ike and the tree and the generations of farmers that had come before us. I wished I knew how much of that story was true. You never knew with my dad.

After dinner, Abra helped Mom with the dishes while Dad and I went back out for a few more hours of farm work. By the time I got back to the house, Abra had already ridden her bike home. We did that a lot, biked to each other's houses, because there wasn't anyone else who lived on Kincade Road once you got outside of town, and the ride wasn't that far, maybe a mile or two. Well, there was Mr. Jinn, but no one ever saw him.

I made a house for Icarus by cutting apart a cardboard box, and Mom donated one of her old sweaters for the bedding. I put the box under the huge, green front porch of our farmhouse. I sat there on the steps and looked out over the massive garden, and the cat weaved a circle around my legs, purring.

The sun had gone, but there was still a bit of light in the western sky. The smell of cut hay filtered through the sunset. A few lightning bugs turned on and off and on and off, their yellow-green lights sharp like stars.

I saw the storm rolling in from the east, the clouds heavy and flashing with lightning. It sounded like some kind of war in heaven, a vicious battle that would end only after one side had completely destroyed the other. I had always thought of thunder coming after the lightning, a natural cause and effect, but that night I saw it in a new way. It felt like Thunder and Lightning were two beings battling each other, Lightning always striking first, Thunder coming later with the counter-punch.

The lightning and thunder grew close, and I thought again about what I had seen at the back of the antique store through the crack in the door. I remembered how the thunder had sounded, how the lightning had lit up the three women's faces, pale and clear, and how the scratched-out words on the table had looked like an angry cloud.

But that storm, the one coming in through the dusk, wouldn't be like scratches on a table. That storm would bring death and set everything else in motion.

5

I SAT OUT THERE WITH THE CAT, and the storm drifted in. All the limbs started to dance and the bright green undersides of the leaves turned up, silver in the near darkness. Some of the tips of the branches blew off when the wind came gusting in, and because the storm arrived from the east and the sun was setting in the west, there was an eerie, low-lying light that stretched all the shadows in the direction of the storm. It looked like the storm was sucking the darkness out of everything, or maybe chasing away all the light.

The lightning arrived in the valley, bright flashes followed by a moment of silence. Then, *KABOOM!* The thunder rumbled over the fields. It was right at that first peal of thunder that my little cat ran to the oak tree in our front yard, about forty yards from the porch. That crazy cat clawed its way up to where the first thick branches formed, about ten feet off the ground.

I always thought that particular part of the tree looked kind of like the palm of a giant hand with five fingers branching out, as if the hand was going to pick a piece of fruit or catch something falling from the sky. There was a little hollowed-out place up there—I knew because sometimes I used a ladder to climb up and sit in that spot.

I ran to the shed, and as I stepped inside to look for the ladder, the rain started to fall, tapping loudly on the roof and the walls and the small glass windows. I had to turn the light on inside the shed. I found the extension ladder buried under cobwebs and a thick layer of dust and dragged it through the rain to the tree. It banged on the ground and hit me in the knee a bunch of times—it was so long I could barely carry it. Eventually I propped the ladder up and leaned it against the rough bark.

That oak tree was like an old friend. It was way older than I was. We had picnics under that tree. I had played with my toys all among its gnarled roots. I had helped Mom and Dad rake up all of its leaves every autumn and put them in a big pile so I could jump in them. Its bark was an old man's skin, rough and peeling. That oak tree was practically a grandparent.

I scrambled up the ladder, now slick with rain, and peeked into the small area where all the largest branches forked out from the trunk. There was that silly white cat. Its eyes glowed.

"Here, kitty, kitty," I said gently as the rain came down harder, soaking me for the second time that day. My hair clung to my forehead while huge drops fell into my eyes. I climbed up a few more steps into the darkness, into the shadowy heart of the tree. I knew you aren't supposed to climb up onto the top step of a ladder, but I couldn't reach the cat without going up as high as possible. I stretched again, now up on my tiptoes. The ladder shook underneath me as another bolt of lightning fell to the earth.

KABOOM!

"Here, kitty, kitty!"

Still it wouldn't come to me. It huddled under a tiny branch. If I wanted to rescue that cat, I was going to have to climb over and get it.

I pulled myself up into the tree and stood in that area where all the branches started. I leaned over to grab the cat, but it jumped away and scampered out on one of the branches.

"Icarus, you stupid cat!" I shouted. "Come back here!"

Just then I heard my mom shouting from the porch. Her voice sounded worried and mad.

"Sam, what are you doing up there? You'll get struck by lightning! Come down this instant!"

"It's my cat," I shouted through the rain. "He climbed out onto one of the branches."

"He'll come down when it stops raining. Now listen to me and get down here!"

As if to emphasize Mom's words, the storm threw down a lightning strike that was followed quickly by an explosion of thunder.

When the lightning flashed it was like everything became midday, just for a moment. I could see the yard and the grass and the house and the church across the road. But after the lightning, everything seemed darker than usual.

I had second thoughts about the rescue mission. Maybe I should go back in the house. I stood there for a moment, trying to make up my mind about what to do. I decided to go inside, but then I saw my mom's hands at the edge of the tree's palm. She pulled herself up and scrambled into the nest of branches where I stood. Now we were both standing there in that hand, wet to the bone.

"Where is Icarus?" she asked. I could tell she wasn't happy.

I pointed out the largest branch.

My mom sighed and shook her head. "I am not doing this until you are safe inside. Do you hear me? Now go. I'll take care of this."

She held on to me and eased me down until my feet found the top of the ladder. I looked up into her face. She had a sad, resigned look, as if she knew what was about to happen and had resolved to let it happen. But that's impossible. Right? She couldn't have known, and if she had known, why would she have stayed there?

I scrambled down four rungs and jumped the rest of the way. I ran into the house, up the steps to the second floor, and around the corner to a window where I could see the tree. At first I could hardly see anything. But as I stared into the darkness, the lightning flashed, and I saw my mom walking out that large branch and holding on to overhead limbs. I had never seen her do anything like that before.

I couldn't always see her, what with the rain coming down in sheets and the wind blowing the branches all around and the night having fallen. But once, when the wind held and the lightning struck, I saw her edging farther out on the branch, farther out. She bent over a little and put her hand out for the cat. Her fingers curled up as she sort of waved it to come over to her. Her wet hair hung heavy around her face, and her clothes stuck to her body. I imagined her saying the same words over and over again. "Here, kitty, kitty, kitty. Here, kitty, kitty, kitty."

That's when the lightning bolt struck.

KABOOM!

It lit up the window so bright and close I could have reached out and touched it. The sound of the thunder shook me where I stood—the floor rumbled. In the moments that followed, I heard loud thuds as pieces of the oak tree rained down on the house and all over the farm. In the following days, as neighbors came to help us clean up, someone found a six-foot-long piece of that tree on the other side of the cattle barn, a few hundred yards away.

I regained my senses and looked out the window. Darkness. I peered through the night and wondered if Mom was okay. I thought about my dad, what he was doing, why he hadn't come running. A flash of lightning gave me another glimpse— the branch my mom had been standing on was shredded and hanging.

My mom was gone.

The ambulance arrived along with one police car, and they parked in our lane, their lights spinning and making me dizzy. I watched, never having moved from the window. I didn't want to go down, because as long as I didn't no one could tell me what I already knew.

Eventually I drifted to my bedroom, numb, and my dad came up and said words, but he could barely talk and the words he said didn't make a whole lot of sense. Sometimes there are no words that fit into the space provided. But I didn't need to hear any words, because when that lightning bolt had struck the tree, in that instant it was like a piece of me had vanished. I felt it flutter around inside my chest, a tiny, frantic moth, and then it was gone.

I knew that fluttering sensation was my mom leaving.

After my dad talked to me, he went back downstairs because neighbors had started to arrive and he had to call the funeral home and there was a lot to do in the face of such devastation. I walked quietly down the stairs, through the kitchen, and out the back door without saying hello to anyone. I felt eyes on me, the eyes of people who didn't know what to say, who had also come to the realization that words can at times be powerless. I wandered into the cornfield, the stalks whispering around my knees, and cut out to the road. I didn't want to go out the lane because I'd probably have to talk to someone.

I walked north, past Mr. Jinn's lane, as far as you could go on Kincade Road. Where it ended in the trees, the ground was flat and graded for a longer road, but the work had never been completed. Abra and I called it the Road to Nowhere. Before I walked into the shadows, I looked over my shoulder toward the town. I remembered that the fair was being set up, and I searched for the towering Ferris wheel. Maybe they hadn't put it together yet, or maybe the swells of the fields were too high. In any case, I couldn't see anything. Only the darkness of a storm giving way to the dark of night, and the flashing lights of the ambulance that for some reason no one had turned off.

At the northern edge of the Road to Nowhere there was a path that led even deeper into the woods, all the way to the river. At one point, where the eastern and western mountains began to converge, the river rammed right up against a stone wall. The rock climbed thirty feet into the air, a kind of cliff. And at the base of that cliff, at the very end of the path, was a small cave, barely big enough for me to sit in.

Not far from the small cave was an old graveyard. The stones were mostly ancient and covered in green moss, and quite a few of them were broken off or leaning to one side. The lettering was worn and nearly impossible to read, and some of the graves were actually old crypts, tombs large enough to walk into if the doors still would have opened. The church had its own cemetery, and that's where most of the folks in Deen were buried. This graveyard, the one out in the woods, was from a different era, and a lot of people talked about it being haunted, but it never really frightened me. There were even trees growing up among the headstones, so to me it felt like just another part of the forest.

From that spot in the small cave I looked out over the river beyond the graveyard, maybe fifty yards wide at that point and rushing fast with all of the day's rain. In the winter you could see the eastern mountain from there, up through the leafless branches, but in the summer everything was close and thick and stifling.

I sat in there for a long time and watched the water and wished I had never seen Icarus, wished I had never chased after him into the rain. The storm had stopped and the moon was out and a silvery light fell down all around me through the trees, sparkling on the river.

When I thought that maybe everyone had left my house, I walked back through the darkness. But some of that darkness stayed inside me. I barely recognized it at the time, but it would grow into a heavy shadow, something that would cause me to do many things I never would have done otherwise. Darkness can do that if you let it. It can move you.

By the time I got home it was much later, at a time of night when I was usually fast asleep, but I could still hear people milling around. I crept in through the mudroom, kept my head down while walking through the small crowd in the kitchen, and went up into my room. Silence followed me through the room, and I could feel their eyes again. I could feel the powerless words no one was saying.

From my room upstairs I heard the coffeemaker in the kitchen sputter out another pot of coffee and muffled voices offering condolences. Someone knocked on my bedroom door. I didn't want to answer because I didn't want to talk to anyone. Earlier, when my dad had come to my room, he had said a few quiet words about doing whatever I wanted to do. I could stay upstairs or I could come down. Whatever I wanted. I had hoped that meant I didn't have to talk to anyone.

But out of curiosity, I walked over and opened the door.

It was Abra. As soon as she saw me, she burst into tears and hugged me and put her face against my shoulder. She wept, sobbing like I myself hadn't yet sobbed, and it made me feel good to know that she missed my mom as much as I did. But it also made me feel jealous, or guilty, because I hadn't been able to cry very much, and it felt wrong, the not crying, so eventually I kind of pushed her away. The two of us walked over to sit on my bed, leaving the door open.

"It's just . . . it's just . . . awful," she said. "Are you okay?"

I nodded. Outside the storm had started up again. Rain pelted the glass, but there was no more thunder, no more lightning. That had been reserved for my mother's death, and once she was gone the storm had no more use for it.

"Did you see it happen?" she asked with a very serious face.

"Kind of," I said.

"Was it horrible?"

"Yeah, I guess."

"What will you do?"

"What do you mean?"

"Do you think you'll stay here, on the farm? Or do you think you'll . . . move?"

I shrugged, but the thought of moving hurt. That felt like something I could cry over. I had never lived anywhere else.

Besides, the farm's roots went deep in our family. My grand-father had bought that farm when he first got married. He and my grandmother were both gone, but the farm was a part of me. It felt like blood and bone.

"I don't think my dad will want to leave," I said, but my voice betrayed my uncertainty.

She nodded, and I must have convinced her with those few words, because she seemed happier after that, as if not all had been lost.

"Abra!" her father's voice called from downstairs. "Time to go."

She stood, and I knew she wanted to hug me again, but I was done with hugs. I was done with everything.

"How's your little brother?" I mumbled.

"He's good. Really good. Just starting to roll over and get into my stuff."

"That's pretty neat," I said, but my voice was hollow and the words didn't come out all the way.

"Yeah," she said, nodding. She acted like she was going to give me a hug, but that started to feel strange, so she didn't. She just walked out.

I followed her into the hall, but when she went downstairs I drifted into the neighboring bedroom, the empty spare room where I had watched everything happen, since it had a better view of the driveway. The attic door was in that room, and I never completely turned my back on it, because who knows what will come through an attic door when you're not paying attention?

From there I watched Abra and her father walk through the rain, dimly lit by the light pouring from our windows. Abra turned once, looked up to where I was, and waved. I waved back, a small wave with only my hand, not moving anything else. She and her father walked through the night, and soon they were gone.

I had strange dreams that night.

I'm flying over a dark ocean, my wings sturdy and strong. The sky stretches out ahead of me, and there is no reason to go back. But the sun is hot and feathers strip from my wings, one at a time. I glance back and see them all dropping like a trail of bread crumbs or falling stars. I start going down, drifting toward the waves.

Then I see land! I crash onto a flat island that is nothing but a grassy plain. I hike for miles, the blades of grass soft and long, and when I look back I see the dark green trail of crushed grass I leave behind me. When I arrive at the very center of the island there is an oak tree, the tree my father told me about in the story, the one that brought the rain. I know this not because someone told me but only in the way you know certain things in dreams.

I look up and my mom is in the tree, high up and calling for my help. She wears a white dress that billows around her like a sail. I start climbing, climbing, climbing, but the tree grows taller and my mother lifts farther and farther away. When I look down there is no island anymore, just the tree I'm in, growing in the middle of a vast ocean, and the water is rising.

Then I woke up.

It was still the middle of the night, but suddenly I wasn't sad anymore. I knew what I would do—it was as clear as anything I had ever known.

I would bring back my mother.

Somehow, somewhere, there would be a way to do it. Maybe it would be through the magic of a tree like the one my father had told me about. Maybe it would happen after I built myself a set of wings and flew to wherever it was she had gone. If I found her, I could convince her to come back with me. Maybe I'd have to travel to a faraway land and find the secret to bringing someone back from the dead.

It didn't matter. My father had told me many stories of warriors and heroes who had managed to travel to that place people go when they die, and I thought there must be some truth behind all those stories. I would find the way. I felt an immense sense of purpose and peace in knowing I had a mission, and that mission was to bring her back.

I remembered the three women. If anyone knew what I had to do to bring back my mother or where I could go to find her, it seemed to me that they would know. There was something about them that felt like the answer to every unknown thing. It was easy to believe that hidden somewhere in the folds of those great gowns was the truth I needed. I would go to the fair and I would find them and they would tell me how.

I fell asleep and slept peacefully the rest of the night. But the darkness I had taken with me from the cemetery grew just a little bit inside me.

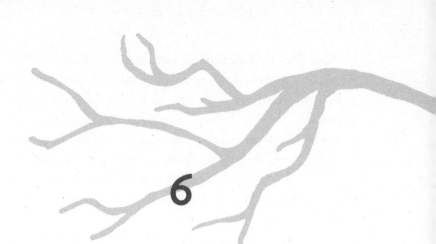

6

"WHY DON'T YOU TWO meet me back here in one hour?" Abra's mom suggested. She was a plump woman with curly brown hair. She smiled a lot, but worry clung to her like a subtle perfume, and it took all of Abra's cunning to get her mom to approve of anything that might be even slightly dangerous. I have no idea how Abra talked her mom into dropping us off at the fair on opening night, but somehow she had. I can only believe that my memories of those days are true, that they were simpler times when children were safe walking the streets alone, at least in Deen.

"Mom!" Abra complained. "That's not any time at all!"

Mrs. Miller sighed and looked down at her watch. Cars coasted past us along Kincade Road, dropping people off at the sidewalk before turning off into one of the large grassy areas to park. The lights from the fair reflected off Mrs. Miller's face, blinking and changing color.

"Okay, two hours, but that's it."

Abra squealed. "Thanks, Mom! Thank you thank you thank you thank you—"

"Fine, fine," she said, smiling, but her face grew serious. "Listen to me right now, both of you. You are allowed in the food area and the front part of the ride area, but no going back into all of that . . ."

She couldn't seem to come up with a word for the part of the fair that was the farthest from the road, the area down the hill beyond the rides. She waved her hand at us, knowing that we knew what she meant.

"That darkness," she muttered.

Our fair had five parts. Not that they were divided into specific categories or marked with boundaries, but you could tell as you went from one part into the next. As you left the road and went down the hill, you descended deeper and deeper into the various sections.

The first part of the fair was made up of the place where everyone parked, plus the road, plus a large chunk of food tents. It was always packed full of people of all ages, and it smelled the best too. Cotton candy, funnel cakes, fried anything-you-wanted-to-eat, candy apples—my teeth began to ache as soon as I so much as walked into that area. The lights there were bright as vendors tried to outdo each other with flashing bulbs and gaudy signs. Here everyone was in a happy and smiling stupor brought on by sugar and grease.

Down the hill a short distance—the tents and pavilions were all laid out roughly in rows—you got to the animal pens. Here you could find various award-winning beasts on display: sheep, cows, horses, chickens, rabbits, that sort of thing. The lights in this area were bright and glaring and uniform. Plain white. You always knew when you had wandered out of the food area because the animal area smelled like horse poop, the people had serious looks on their faces as they waited for the judges' scores, and they all wore overalls.

Past the food, past the animals, were the kiddie rides. Tiny Tilt-A-Whirls and miniature roller coasters roared around slides and the crown jewel of that area, the carousel. Loud, happy carnival music pierced your ears. This far down the hill, the smell of the food was a distant memory. The carnies who ran the kiddie rides had abnormally large smiles and probably doubled as Santa's creepy elves in the winter. Parents surrounded the rides, pointing and waving and laughing.

Farther down, farther in was the fourth area of the fair. These were the serious rides. The ones that threatened to steal the food you had just eaten at the top of the hill. This area was marked by teenagers hanging on to each other, screaming voices, and large chunks of shadows. Sometimes, if you didn't pay attention to the general flow of traffic, you would end up behind a ride in some kind of dark dead end.

This area housed the Ferris wheel, the House of Horrors, and anything that spun you wrong-side up or tried to turn you inside out. There the carnies were indifferent, even mean. They sneered when they took your tickets and took pleasure in stopping the rides at the most awkward moments, like when you were upside down. I think they kept track of how many kids they could make throw up, as if it was a contest they held among themselves.

At the very bottom of the hill, past the serious rides, was the "darkness" Mrs. Miller had mentioned. There the trees came up close to the small tents and dark trailers. There, for only one dollar, you could see a woman with two heads or a man with the body of a snake. Old, blind hags would tell you your fortune for fifty cents, or put a curse on your enemy.

When I was in kindergarten, one of my friends was accidentally stabbed with scissors in the art room when he tripped and fell. His blood spilled all over the floor like paint, more blood than I had ever seen. One of the girls passed out, and the art teacher's skin turned clammy and white as she called for help through the intercom. Later we found out that he had been to the dark part of the fair—who knows what someone his age had been doing there, or if it was even true. The kids all said he had mouthed off to one of the old carnies, who had in turn cursed him, calling down his death, and that the curse had almost worked.

There, among the trees, you could also see the remnants of campfires and tattered tents strung up with the help of low-lying branches. That's where the carnies lived during the weeklong fair, down at the bottom of it all—the darkest place—where the air smelled of wood smoke and porta potties, and a constant fog drifted like a lazy river.

But when Mrs. Miller dropped off Abra and me, we were still on the sidewalk surrounded by the light and the laughter of happy people eating fair food. She put a five-dollar bill in each of our hands, and we turned to face the fair, our eyes transfixed by the glory and freedom spreading down the hill in front of us.

"Two hours!" she called again with that same old worry in her voice as she drove away.

"Ready?" Abra said. I nodded and followed her.

It had been only forty-eight hours since my mother had died, but I couldn't wait to get to the fair. I knew the old women were there—I could feel it.

My mind raced. Abra would never disobey her mother and join me if I had to go into the Darkness. How could I get away from her? The words the woman had etched into the table had somehow found their way into me, and nothing could erase them.

Find the Tree of Life.

"What do you want to do first?" Abra asked.

"Bumper cars?"

She laughed and nodded and led the way through the crowd. We would buy food at the end if we had any money left. She reached back and grabbed my sleeve and pulled me along. That first hour passed quickly: bumper cars, the large Tilt-A-Whirl, and finally running into some friends from school who convinced us to join them on rides I was too scared to go on when it was only Abra and me. They ran back up to the street to meet the parent who was picking them up, and Abra and I still had some time left before her mother was going to meet us.

The best part about that night was that I forgot about real life for entire patches of time. Later I would feel guilty about it, but while we were on the rides and screaming and laughing with our friends, for brief moments I forgot that my mom had died. I forgot about the lightning tree. I forgot that my dad waited at home for me, silent and lost. So we ran from here to there and the lights flashed and the sadness inside me receded, like the slipping of the waves as they approach low tide.

"What next?" she asked.

"I could use a break," I said.

"Me too. How about the Ferris wheel?"

So we wandered all the way down to the bottom of the area where the rides were located, just on the edge of the Darkness. It was getting late, so the line for the Ferris wheel wasn't very long—it was mostly made up of teenagers hoping to get some time alone with their boyfriends or girlfriends. Eventually Abra and I were in and riding to the top, stopping every few seconds as more people got on.

The Ferris wheel stopped for longer than usual when we got to the top. It always sort of took my breath away, being up that high. I could see Kincade Road, and I followed it with my eyes to the main intersection in town. I could even see the antique store and the baseball field behind it, although the field was mostly dark. Cars were lined up on the street because of the fair, trying to get out of town, and their headlights and brake lights formed a perfect T where Kincade Road ran into Route 126.

I looked the other way, north on Kincade Road into the darkness of the countryside.

"Hey, Abra, there's your farm," I said.

"And there's yours," she replied.

They looked like lonely outposts, those individual pinpoints of light surrounded by so much night.

I looked closer, down toward the bottom of the fairgrounds, and a strange sense of foreboding filled me. Mrs. Miller had been right to call it the Darkness because it was empty and black. There was something alive about that Darkness, something moving and throbbing. It felt like something barely contained, as if it might break out at any time and take over. My eyes scanned the dim light around the low-burning embers of dying fires, searching for the three women I had seen on Friday.

I saw a few dogs tied to stakes, the kinds of dogs that looked like they would rip your head off first and bark later. There was a group of six tents at the back, under the trees. They caught my attention because their stakes barely held them to the earth. The tents' canvases flapped wildly in even the lightest of breezes. They billowed like robes.

Then I saw them. Three old ladies, hunched over, worked among those tents. They gathered things off the ground, then threw them into the fire. This sent up writhing flames at each offering. I couldn't be sure the ladies were the same three from the antique store, not from that distance, but they looked old and fragile, and one of them had a thick stick in her hand that she leaned on.

I tried to memorize the quickest way back to where they were, but the tents and trailers and trucks in that part of the fair made up a kind of scattered maze. If I was going to find that spot, it would be based simply on my sense of direction.

"What do you see?" Abra asked.

"See those ladies?" I said.

She nodded.

"They were in the back of the antique store on Friday, when you and my mom came looking for me."

"Huh." She shrugged, and I could tell she wasn't impressed.

I couldn't keep it in any longer. I had to tell someone. So I told her what I had seen inside Mr. Pelle's prep room. I told her what I had read on the table.

Abra's eyes squinted in thought, her mouth in a straight line. I could tell she understood why it was such a big deal to me. But I didn't tell her about the one old woman who had drawn a circle around me, the way the stick grated against the stones, the way I couldn't move when it was completed. I was having enough difficulty believing that one myself. So much had happened since that moment.

The Ferris wheel crept back toward the earth.

"C'mon," Abra said with resolve. "We need to talk to those old ladies."

"Really?" I asked. It was something I desperately wanted to do, but when she said it out loud it kind of scared me.

"Hey!" she shouted at the carnie operating the ride. "We're getting off here."

He didn't stop the Ferris wheel, but that didn't stop Abra.

She pulled the bolt that locked the door, opened it, and hopped out of the slow-moving car. I was right behind her.

"Hey!" the man called out. He had a patch over one eye and an unlit cigarette propped in his mouth. It stuck to his top lip when he talked. "You can't get out when the ride is moving."

"So kick us off!" Abra shouted back at him.

We ran around the side of the Ferris wheel. That bottom-most part of the fair was unofficially portioned off by a line of 18-wheelers parked on a stone lane. We peered between the trucks. It seemed especially dark back there. Somewhere off in the distance I heard voices and laughter from the food section at the top of the hill, but there, as we faced the Darkness on the other side of the trucks, those sounds seemed to be a million miles away.

"Well, what are we waiting for?" Abra asked, and even though she was trying to sound brave, fear left little edges in her voice, edges that caught in the air. I stood there, frozen in space, but she took a few quick steps and vanished on the other side of the trailers, melting into the shadows.

I followed her.

7

THE FIRST THING I NOTICED when we entered that lowermost part of the fairgrounds was the lack of sound. The fair we had left behind on the other side of the huge trucks suddenly sounded muffled, like a thick curtain had been drawn between two worlds. The air around us felt ancient and full. Almost all the carnies were working the fair, so the Darkness was empty too, like a ghost town.

But there was a sound, the kind of sound that grows on you in the silence, the kind of sound that's always been there but you haven't noticed before. As we snuck farther in, I realized it was the sound of classical music playing on an old record player. After about a minute, the record got stuck, always at the same exact sequence of notes, and those notes would scratch and repeat and scratch and repeat for as long as it took the listener to walk over and put the needle back at the edge of the record. The music started up again, loud and moving, headed inevitably for the scratch that would knock the needle into repeat.

"Shh," Abra said, raising her finger to her mouth, listening. "Which way?"

I pointed down the hill to the right. Abra nodded and walked ahead. I followed her. Because grass covered the ground in that part, it was possible to walk without making any sound. It was possible to creep around corners and stand quietly in shadows while strangers walked by, muttering or crunching up beer cans in their hands and throwing them under the trailers. The air seemed to grow warmer and heavier as we descended. High up above us, the moon shone through that hazy July night.

I wasn't even sure why we were there. What did those three old women have that I wanted so badly? Why did those words that I read, etched into the table in the back room of the antique store, mean so much to me?

"Look . . . at . . . this," a shattered voice said, the three words coming slow and spaced apart and filled with wonder at some unexpected gift. We turned. The voice belonged to a man. He wore a white tank top, jeans, and unlaced, heavy work boots perfect for stomping on things. When he took another step closer, the boots flopped around, loose on his feet. Black hair covered his arms and the backs of his hands and sprouted out of the edges where his tank top ended. He had a beard that tangled its way down his chest, and his eyes were hidden in deep shadows. He held a leash in his hand that restrained a medium-size, powerful-looking dog that growled when he spoke.

Abra and I leaned closer to each other. I felt her grip on my arm.

"Now what on God's green earth are two pretty little children doing . . . back . . . here?" he asked, and his smile was all blackened teeth and cracking lips.

"We're looking for three old women," I mumbled.

"What's that?" he said, smiling bigger and letting his dog drag him one step closer. "I can't hear you, kid. You scared or something? Your voice is all shaker-y."

I don't know if he was just trying to scare us or if he would have done something terrible, maybe cut us up into little pieces and feed us to his dog. I had visions of my bones lining whatever hole he kept that animal in. I imagined his canine going back days later and gnawing on my femur.

"We're looking for three old women," I said louder.

"You don't want to find them," he said, still mean and aggressive, but the mention of the three old women had changed something in him.

"Why not?" Abra asked. She was always asking why. Always.

The man loosened his grip on the leash, and the dog jumped at us, only to be jerked backward when it reached its new limit.

"It doesn't matter," he said. "My dog's hungry. And little children shouldn't be wandering around back here behind the scenes."

Then he stopped and pulled the dog closer. The change that came over him was almost comical. He went from leering and confident to skittish and uncertain. The dog crept backward and hid behind the man's legs, the hair on its back standing up.

The three old women came out of the shadows. I hadn't even noticed them until Abra tightened her grip on my arm. I glanced at her, and her wide eyes stared off to the side, into the trees. At first I thought the women were floating. They walked with light steps, and the remaining parts of their fragile bodies stayed very still. Instead of those gypsy scarves they had worn in the antique store, they were donned in cloaks with hoods pulled up, casting shadows over their faces.

"Aw, no, that's not, it's not, you know . . ." His voice went on and on, making no sense, explaining himself even though no questions had been asked of him.

The three women got closer. The one in the front held a stick.

The second woman held a large bowl in her hands. The third woman hung back. She stopped and crossed her arms, her bony wrists vanishing in the thick folds of her cloak.

The man kept talking, but his voice was now a whisper. The woman with the bowl walked over and held it out to him. She didn't say a word, but somehow I knew that she wanted him to take it.

"You hexin' me?" he asked in a frightened, belligerent voice. "You know you ain't allowed to be hexin' us. You know that, not if you wanna keep traveling. They won't let you stay, you know that."

The woman sighed but didn't say a word, just pushed the bowl closer to him. He took it from her, and it must have been very heavy because he nearly dropped it, and when he walked away he had to keep balancing it on his legs or his hips to get another grip on it. Sometimes he set it down and stretched, as if his arm muscles were tired, but he always picked it back up again. He walked away into the shadows, finally crouching and disappearing inside a green tent that had a bright blue tarp as a door.

"Remember," she called after him, the single word carrying more meaning in it than an entire book of stories. Her voice surprised me. It sounded young and beautiful.

I was relieved. As far as my imagination was concerned, the dog's teeth had come all too close to ripping the flesh from my bones. I wanted to say thank you. I looked over at Abra and smiled, overjoyed at our unlikely salvation. I expected her to return my relieved glance, but the look on her face sent a jolt of uncertainty through me. She didn't look relieved at all. She looked horrified.

The three women walked toward us, but somehow they

looked completely different than before, when I had seen them in the antique store. All three of them had their mouths open, as if gasping for air that never came. Their eyes formed hollow, dark caves, and the whites were barely visible. Their cloaks weren't black or brown or gray but shadow colored—which didn't make sense to me at first, but I don't know how else to explain it—and around the edges of the hoods I thought I saw thin worms crawling all around their heads. I realized it must be hair, silver and wiry and somehow moving on its own.

They were in some kind of a trance, and the one with the stick nudged us apart and began drawing a circle around Abra.

"No!" I said, pulling Abra toward me.

The old woman looked at me, and I could tell she was annoyed. She tried again, pushing her stick between us and plunging it into the earth.

"No, I won't let you do it," I said, suddenly aware that the faraway recording of classical music was stuck and repeating itself.

The other two hovered over to us, and the three of them stood there for a long time, staring. They looked disgusting, like rotted corpses somehow moving, somehow alive. A kind of reluctance moved around them like a cloud, and they turned to go.

Off in the distance I heard the record scratch and start over again.

"Who were you talking to in the antique store?" I asked, my voice loud and out of place.

They stopped, and one of them answered, or all three of them answered, but we couldn't tell who was talking because they never faced us.

"Jinn," I thought I heard them say.

"Jinn?" I asked. "You mean my neighbor?"

But they didn't give an answer.

"What's he got to do with anything?"

"His story, not yours," one of them said in a weary voice.

"Well, what's it got to do with me?" I asked, feeling bolder with each question answered.

"There is a certain kind of death that leads to life," they said, and in that moment I remembered my mom, and it made me tired and sad and homesick. I didn't care so much anymore about this great mystery. I wanted to go home and find my dad and sit with him. But all the questions I had, all the things I wondered about, fought through my sadness.

"Why did you write 'Find the Tree of Life' on the table?"

"Because the Tree is here. Now."

Their answers frustrated me, but even more than that, my questions frustrated me. I'd had this idea that if I asked the women the right questions, they would tell me everything. But the right ones eluded me.

"The Tree of Life? What is it? Where is it?"

They took a few more steps away.

"Why'd you draw a circle around me?" I asked.

"For protection," they said, still drifting away.

"Protection? Protection from what?"

"Protection from what lives in the shadows," they said.

They were almost gone, off into the shadows.

"What if I need to find you again?" I blurted out.

They turned a corner, one after the other, still walking slowly, still hunched over. In the silence around us I could hear the gentle thud of the first woman's stick against the ground.

"What is coming?" I shouted after them. When they didn't say anything, I moved to chase after them, but Abra grabbed my arm.

"No. We're out of time. We have to go."

"I don't know what you were thinking, young lady," Mrs. Miller said from the front seat for at least the tenth time. Abra and I were both in the back. Her mom had been talking nonstop since we had found her walking up and down the sidewalk along the road. She had looked frantic, pacing and craning her head to look into the fairgrounds.

We knew the best defense in that case was not to say anything, so we sat quietly. Eventually Mrs. Miller's voice faded in my mind as I thought about everything I had seen and heard the previous few days. What had happened to the small town I knew and loved? Why were all of these strange things happening?

"Answer me, you two!"

I looked up. Abra looked at me. She must have stopped paying attention about the same time I had.

"Um . . . what's the question again?" she asked.

"What! You haven't even been listening! Young lady, you just wait until I speak with your father. The question was, 'What will you do next time?'"

"Come straight to the car."

"That's right. Straight to the car. No dillydallying."

We had to look away from each other so we wouldn't start laughing, but as I stared out into the night, a seriousness settled over me. Something very big was going on in Deen. Something important.

We cruised north into the valley, leaving the blinking fair lights behind us and drifting into the open space of farm country. But it was such a different darkness there than the Darkness at the bottom of the hill at the fair. The darkness in the country was warm, welcoming. It was punctuated by stars and fireflies, and when we stopped at the unnecessary stop sign I could hear the distant rushing of the river as it drifted south, nearly overflowing its banks. It was at that age that I learned there is darkness and there is Darkness, and the difference between the two is day and night.

Mrs. Miller turned left at the church, drove up my lane, and stopped, not turning off the car. Between the lane and the house was the yard, and in the yard was the tree. The lightning tree. I tried not to look at it.

"Thanks, Mrs. Miller," I said, feeling sheepish after the scolding she had given us.

"Good night, Samuel," she said, sounding stern, but when I glanced up at her there was a softness in her eyes. I guess she was remembering that I had just lost my mother, and as the sadness gathered and tugged at her face I wanted to reassure her, tell her not to worry. I was going to bring my mother back—she would see. The three old women would help me, and I would go wherever I had to go, do whatever I had to do.

But I didn't say anything. I only nodded at her.

"See ya, Abra."

"See ya, Sam."

I climbed out and walked through the darkness to the farmhouse. I went inside and the screen door slammed behind me. I left the main door open because it was warm inside, and outside the cool night air had started to settle. It felt more like the end of September than the beginning of July.

My dad was on the sofa watching a baseball game. There were no other lights on in the house, so the light from the television flashed and swam all around him. His face was blank, and when I got close to him I could see the white square of light from the television reflecting in his eyes. For a moment

I realized what he had lost, or came as close to understanding as a child can come.

"Hey, Dad," I said.

No response.

"Had a good time at the fair tonight," I said, shuffling my feet, kicking at the worn carpet. "Crazy stuff going on over there."

He still didn't move, just sat there staring at the game, unblinking. I backed away slowly, wishing I had gone straight up to my room without speaking. At least then I wouldn't have had to endure him not saying anything.

"'Night, Dad." I walked up the steps, each stair creaking under the weight of my sadness.

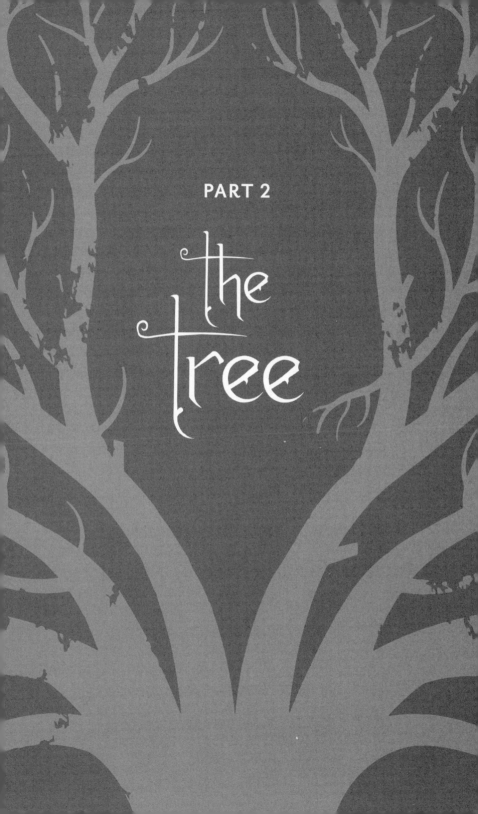

PART 2

the
tree

[He] stationed mighty cherubim to the east . . .
And he placed a flaming sword that flashed back
and forth to guard the way to the tree of life.

GENESIS 3:24 NLT

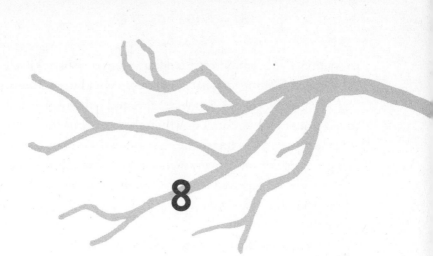

8

SO MANY YEARS HAVE PASSED. I sit out there with the oak tree not far away, my chair creaking on the old porch, and I light my pipe filled with cherry tobacco, the scent of which reminds me of Mr. Pelle and playing baseball and being a boy. Dusk is my favorite time of day, especially during the summer when it stretches long and lazy and the stars whisper to each other in the heat. Before coming outside, I opened all the windows on the main level, something that took me a bit of time to do, but the house needs to breathe at the end of a long summer day. I will spend the rest of the evening here on the porch, watching the fireflies blink and the day fade to black.

So many years have passed.

Tonight, as I walk through the screen door, I realize Boy is sitting on my porch roof, his legs dangling down. He surely hears me come outside but doesn't say anything. He doesn't pull his legs up, so he must not be hiding. I guess he's waiting for me to say the first word. Two can play at this little game, and I can guarantee you that an old man can outlast a boy when it comes to waiting. I've been waiting for decades longer than he's been in existence. Waiting for what? I'm not sure. But I'm good at it.

As I sit in the chair, I sigh with relief and pull my pipe and tobacco out of my pocket. I slowly go about packing the leaves into the pipe with my finger, the nail of which is stained brown along the edges from so many nights. I pull out a stainless steel lighter with the engraved letters *SC* on the front and spin the wheel. The flame dances into being. I hold it over the pipe and puff until it comes alive.

He makes me smile, this boy and his antics. I remember climbing up on that very roof when I was a boy, and I remember feeling bigger than everything, bigger than the world. There's something about climbing, something about the possibility of falling, that takes your breath away.

I become so engrossed in my nightly routine that I nearly forget about the boy, his feet dangling down from the sky.

"You know smoking is bad for you, right?" he says.

"Zat so," I say, inhaling, then sighing the smoke into the night. Sweet relief.

"Yep. Gives you cancer."

"Huh," I say. "So if I smoke, I might die of cancer before I can live a long, full life?"

He doesn't respond to that. He climbs down one of the decorative iron rails that prop up the front porch and sits on the step in front of me, keeping his face toward the night. Now that he's up close I notice for the first time that he's a rather small boy, not frail but wiry. When he talks it's like he's playing a chess match, not moving unless he can predict his opponent's next move. He doesn't say anything open-ended, anything that might lead the conversation in a way he cannot predict. It's a rather intriguing trait for such a young boy, this measured way of talking. His hair is curly and unruly, and his nose is round. When he looks at me over his shoulder, his green eyes flash in the light coming through the screen door.

"I guess you know why I'm here," he says in a glum voice. His eyes dart up and meet mine, then he turns again to face the darkness.

I lay the pipe down on the arm of the wooden rocking chair and shake my head. "No, I guess I don't."

He looks at me with surprise. "Thought my dad came by here today," he says. "Didn't he tell you?"

I shrug. "Let me ask you something before you get into all that."

"Okay."

"Do you like hot chocolate?"

"Hot chocolate?" His eyes light up, but he recovers his defenses and tamps down his happiness. "In the middle of the summer? Don't you have any ice cream?"

Kids these days. They don't know nothing about nothing.

"I guess I do," I say, trying not to grit my teeth. "But I've only got vanilla. I'm not much for all of these newfangled flavors with the fixin's already inside."

"I only ever eat vanilla," he said in a determined voice, as if it was a sore temptation to eat all the other delicious flavors and it was only by a supernatural feat of self-discipline that he managed to remain unswerving in his devotion to that plainest of ice cream.

"Well, then, vanilla ice cream it is."

I stand up and walk back inside, leaving my pipe on the arm of the rocking chair. A thin wraith of smoke rises out of it. At first I'm not sure if he will come inside with me, but I go into the kitchen anyway and take down two bowls. I open the freezer and find the ice cream, and by the time I'm closing the freezer door, Boy has come inside and made himself at home in the kitchen.

"Sure does smell funny in here," he says.

"It's because I'm old," I reply. These things don't bother me anymore. "You'll smell funny too when you're my age."

I bring two bowls of plain vanilla ice cream over to the table and set one down in front of Boy.

"I guess I have something to say before I eat your ice cream," he states in the same voice he used to proclaim his undying love for vanilla.

"I guess you'd better say it and get it over with before this melts."

He takes a deep breath, and when he speaks the words come out much quicker than usual. "I'm-sorry-for-the-smoke-bombs-even-though-I-saw-you-kick-the-cat-and-you-kind-of-deserved-it."

I try hard to keep from laughing. "Boy, did anyone ever tell you that you're incorrigible?"

He shakes his head.

"Well, you are. I kick cats sometimes because I hate cats, but it's a mean, nasty habit, and all it does is show that I've got some meanness stuck inside me. I'll try to do better."

He nods.

"That is," I say, glaring at him, "if you agree to stop hitting me with corncobs."

He nods again and takes a big bite of ice cream. Through the cold whiteness he murmurs, "I guess I have some meanness stuck in me too."

We eat quietly.

"I hear your friend is dead," he says. It's hard to get used to, the unrelenting nature of his words, the way they dart out of nowhere and stick you in the most sensitive places.

I take a deep breath, nod, and sigh. "Yes, indeed. My friend is dead."

It sounds rather bleak when I say it that way and not in the normal past tense: *My friend died.* It's much more polite to talk about death in the past tense, and it doesn't feel as bad.

But it's true all the same, I think. *She is dead.*

"Was she nice?" he asks.

I nod again. I feel the need to do something physical like nod or sigh before saying words to this boy. I feel the need to create space between the sentences.

"The nicest of all."

"When are they going to bury her?"

"The funeral is in a couple of days," I say, shrugging.

"Are you worried about it?" he asks, and I wish he would focus on his ice cream.

"I've been to many funerals in my life," I say. "I suppose one more won't hurt."

"But she's your last friend."

I look up at him and chuckle, because if I don't I might cry. "Where in the world did you hear that?"

"My mom told my dad."

I shake my head the way a boxer shakes his head after taking an uppercut to the jaw. "Yes, she was my last friend."

Outside, the crickets have begun to chirp and some other noisy bugs have started up alongside them. I'm hoping Boy leaves soon so I can return to my pipe. Conversations tend to exhaust me. I'm not used to them anymore. I'm not used to sharing the inside of my brain with someone else.

"What's your name, anyway?" I ask.

"Caleb," he says.

"Really? Caleb?"

This boy is full of surprises.

"Yeah, why?"

"Oh, I had a friend named Caleb when I was a boy."

"What happened to him?"

"What happened to Caleb?" I ask myself. "What happened to Caleb? That's the question, isn't it. What happened to Caleb."

I remember Caleb Tennin lying on the forest floor. I remember the way the rain sounded coming through the trees and the sound it made falling on the Amarok right there beside me. I remember how the Tree of Life shimmered behind me like a mirage.

Caleb, where did you go?

9

I'm not sure why I thought news about three strange dogs would make my dad finally speak to me. My mom had died in the lightning tree on Friday, and he'd barely said a word since. His voice seemed to have passed right along with her. Our paths crossed in the house and in the barn, and he made meals at the proper times, but his eyes were somewhere else.

When I saw the dogs in the front yard, walking around and nipping at each other, they gave me a strange feeling, like something out there was watching me, keeping an eye on me, and not in a good way. I hadn't seen them before, and it was unusual to see strange dogs in the valley. They foamed at the mouth and didn't behave like normal dogs, and even though they looked like black German shepherds, they were bigger, like wolves. But we didn't have any wolves in Deen. At least I didn't think so. I wondered if they had come down from the mountain.

I walked into our small living room. It was hot in there. The windows were open and a breeze smelling wet and green came through the screens, a summer day after a storm. In fact, it had rained, with thunder and lightning, off and on since Friday. Ever since my mom died. Every time lightning struck, I had this image of the tree, its largest branch shredded and broken, hanging down toward the ground. But on the day I saw the dogs, the storms had cleared and the July sun threatened to get hot.

"I saw three dogs," I told my dad quietly, not sure if he would even look at me. "I think they were sick."

My dad glanced up from his brown armchair. I missed being a little kid and sitting there with him, cheering on our favorite baseball team or pretending to watch world news in the evenings. I used to fall asleep there, and he'd carry me up to my bed. Sometimes I'd pretend to be asleep so he'd carry me.

It was strange, him sitting there. I couldn't remember anything like it ever happening in my entire life, not on a Monday morning—Monday was a day for work, a day to make up for not working on Sunday. What would happen to our farm if Dad didn't recover? I wondered if the world would fall in on us.

"Why?" he asked.

The sound of his voice sent a shock wave through me, a pulse of joy and sadness, and I didn't know if I could answer his one-word question without crying. I hadn't heard his voice since Friday night.

"Their eyes didn't seem right. They were foaming at the mouth. They didn't run away, not even when I shouted at them."

"Rabies," he mumbled. "Are they still out there?"

"Not last time I checked," I said.

"Let me know if you see 'em again. I'll have to shoot 'em."

I nodded. It was good to hear his voice again, but it was different. He sounded tired and sad and on the edge of giving up.

He leaned back in his brown armchair, sighed, and turned the television up even louder. The announcer's voice tried to drown out the emptiness in the house, but nothing could do that.

Just a bit outside for ball three. He's having some trouble controlling those pitches today. Not sure how much longer he'll be in the game. And now the bull pen is warming up.

I backed slowly out of the room. Ever since my mom died, Dad had kept the volume on the television louder than usual. It made my brain feel garbled and overwhelmed.

Suddenly there was a snarling outside, by the lightning tree.

I pushed open the screen door and it slammed behind me. Dad was always reminding me not to let the screen door slam. I stopped on the porch. Huge puddles sat everywhere in the yard—hidden in the grass and filling the potholes in the lane—and they were as blue as the sky they reflected. I heard a loud yelp and looked at the tree. Right there at the base, right there where the lightning scar met the grass, a crowd of animals was fighting.

"Dad!" I shouted. "Dad!"

There they were, the three large dogs. The other two animals were brown and furry and low to the ground, stocky and thick. When the animals drew apart for a moment, I realized the two small ones were groundhogs, and they seemed to be fighting the dogs. Then they were all back together, rolling and snarling and biting and clawing, a pile of chaos and teeth.

My dad charged through the door, raised his gun to his shoulder, and *BANG!*

The three dogs ran down the lane. My dad released the spent shell and moved the bolt back and then forward, pushing another bullet into the chamber of the gun.

BANG!

A small burst of dust flew up right beside the dogs. They ran faster over the road, dashed past the church across the street, and disappeared into the graveyard. Dad ran after them, his gun in hand. I walked toward the oak tree.

One of the groundhogs had disappeared into the garden, but the other one was still at the base of the lightning scar, and it wasn't moving. As I got closer, I could see it was still breathing, its furry chest rising and falling. Blood oozed from a bullet wound close to one of its front shoulders, matting its fur.

I picked up a small stick and nudged it. It shifted its weight a bit, but it couldn't seem to move. I got down on my knees beside it. I had never seen anything die, at least not until the Friday before, but even then I hadn't actually seen my mom pass away. Just a lightning bolt, darkness, and the space where she had been.

The groundhog's eyes were still open and shining. Its little tail twitched once, twice. Besides that, it didn't move much at all. Even its breathing came on either side of a long stillness. When I looked back at its eyes, I noticed that the groundhog was studying me, taking me in, as if he had heard a lot about me from someone else and was now seeing me for the first time.

The groundhog made a funny sound, so I moved even closer. But it went limp. It was dead.

My dad came walking slowly back up the lane. A strong breeze blew the lightning tree above me, and a thousand drops of rain from the previous storm fell on me and the dead groundhog— cold, wet drops that went down the back of my shirt and hit me hard on the top of the head. I knew my dad hadn't gotten any of the dogs because he walked slowly and came with only his gun in his hand.

I sat down on the wet ground with my back against the tree. My dad walked past me and into the house without saying a word. The farm seemed saturated with a great emptiness.

———

A few hours later I was back in bed. It felt strange lying in my bed during the day, sunlight streaming through my window, but nothing else felt right either. I heard my dad watch the end of the ball game, and he kept the volume loud—so loud, in fact, that I could follow the game pretty well from up there in my room.

My mother's funeral was scheduled for the next day, Tuesday, but all I could think about was the groundhog and everything that had happened in town that week—the man in the shadows at the antique store and the three old women. Mostly, though, I kept replaying the words I had seen written in the middle of the table.

Find the Tree of Life.

Had I really seen that? Or was my mind making stuff up? If I went back there, would that table still be there with the words scratched on it? I wondered if Mr. Pelle would let me go to the prep room or if I'd have to sneak in.

The sound of the television stopped. Dad must have turned it off. I heard his footsteps move across the creaky floor to the steps. He came up the stairs very slowly and stopped outside my room. I could see his shadow through the crack under the door. For a moment I wanted to run over, fling wide the door, and give him a huge hug. I didn't want to feel so alone anymore.

But I didn't. I was angry. Angry that he had killed the groundhog. Angry that he wouldn't talk to me now that Mom was dead. Angry that Mom was dead. Angry that life was changing. Angry that I had to figure out how to bring her back on my own.

The door started to open.

I fell back onto my pillow, held my breath, closed my eyes, and pretended to sleep. I could feel my dad looking at me from the doorway. Again I fought the urge to jump up and run to him. I heard the door creak shut. He was gone. I took a deep breath and let out a long, confused sigh.

I crept over to my window and put my chin down on the windowsill. I stared hard at the massive oak tree now marked by the lightning, the sunlight glinting off the leaves. I peered toward the church, searching for signs of the dogs. I didn't see any of them, or the remaining groundhog. They were gone.

Then I saw a man.

He walked up our lane, limping. He was a short, round person with a thick neck. He wore navy blue work pants and a button-up shirt. He wasn't walking fast, and he stopped every thirty seconds or so to take a comb out of his front shirt pocket and brush his hair straight back. And he was constantly frowning. Or scowling. Or muttering words to himself.

He stopped by the oak tree, in the spot where the animals had been fighting, and he got down on one knee and reached toward the ground. He touched the wet grass and raised his hand up close to his face, scowling the entire time. He ran his hand down the long, pale scar the lightning had left.

He turned and walked toward the house, and as he got closer, I thought I had seen him before. The way he hobbled from side to side, the shape of his shoulders and the roundness of his body—all of it reminded me of the man in the antique store. Granted, I hadn't seen the man's face, but I couldn't help but think this was him.

He kept walking slowly, always limping, sometimes stopping to comb his hair, and when he got close enough to the house I could no longer see him. I heard his footsteps go up onto the front porch and move toward the front door. All went silent.

And then I heard a loud knock.

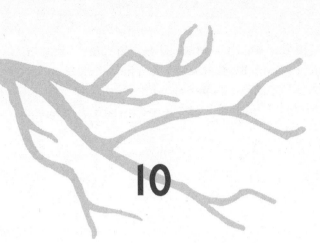

10

WHEN I HEARD THE KNOCK AT THE DOOR, I knew
I'd have to go answer it. There was no way I could stay up
in my room and pretend I wasn't there. I felt certain there
was some connection between this man and everything else
that had been going on. I wondered if he might be a piece of
the puzzle in bringing my mom back. He had connections
with the three old women. He might be able to help me.

So I left my room and walked down the stairs, trying not to
make a sound. I wasn't even breathing. I crept to the edge of
the door and stood there, my back against the wall, waiting for
who knows what. It's one thing to decide you should talk to
a complete stranger who you think might be a little bit crazy.
It's another thing entirely to open the door and let him into
your house.

I heard a knock again, really loud, so hard on the wooden
frame that it made the screen door rattle. I took a deep breath,
and as I was about to look through the door, I heard a voice I
didn't expect.

"Sam? Are you in there?"

I looked through the screen. It was Abra.

"What are you doing here?" I asked as I opened the door.

"I don't know. I'm just here."

"No, no," I said. "There was a guy out by the tree. He started walking up to the house. I heard a knock . . ."

"Which was obviously me," Abra said, then asked in a quieter voice, "Are you sure you're feeling okay?"

Her blue eyes got all sad, and I knew she was thinking about my mom, which made me feel sad.

"I'm fine," I muttered. I pushed past her and walked down the porch steps and out into the yard.

"What's wrong?" she blurted out. "I mean, I know what's wrong, but is there something else?"

We walked through the soft ground over to the tree, and I leaned against the trunk. I looked at the lightning scar that had split the bark, and there were definitely red marks on it from where the old guy had been touching it. He must have touched the blood on the ground where the groundhog died and used the same finger to examine the tree.

"There was an old man here not thirty seconds ago," I said, looking hard into her eyes. "These are his fingerprints. I don't care if you believe me or not."

"I believe you," she said, and I knew she was telling the truth. She gave me a hesitant smile and pushed some strands of her blonde hair back behind her ears. I went ahead and told her about the three dogs and how they fought with the ground-hogs, how one of the groundhogs had died, and how it gave me a strange feeling.

"It's all connected somehow," I said, wishing I could figure it out. My voice trailed off under the weight of that uncertainty. We sat there in silence for a long time. I noticed a shovel stuck

in the ground in the corner of the garden, so I walked over to
it. Abra followed me, her shoes squeaking in the wet grass.

"I'll bet my dad buried the groundhog here," I said, looking
over at Abra. But she was looking up at the sky, shielding her eyes.

I actually heard them before I saw them. *Whoosh, whoosh,
whoosh*, long and sinister, like someone saying "Sh!" over and
over again. I looked up.

There were at least thirty vultures. They glided through the
air like dark holes in the sky, following each other around and
around, looking for a place to land. The sound came from the
long flaps of their wings—*whoosh, whoosh, whoosh*, the sound
made when you swing a green branch through the air.

"Where did they come from?" Abra asked. Usually the vultures traveled the valley in groups of two or three, looping lower
and lower to clean up roadkill, but I'd never seen that many in
one group. The highest ones were nothing but black dots, but
I could see the feathers ruffling on the wings of the lower ones,
and their pink heads were bare and gaunt.

Suddenly they wheeled and flew in an almost straight line
for the northern end of our farm, the side that bordered our
neighbor Mr. Jinn's place.

"Jinn," I said.

"What?" Abra asked.

"Remember what the three old ladies at the fair said? They
had been talking to Jinn at the antique store. Mr. Jinn."

"So what?"

"So what?" I said. "I want to find out what they meant by
'Find the Tree of Life.' If that was Jinn in there on Friday, he
can tell me."

"Sam," Abra said, concern in her voice, "why do you care so
much about this Tree of Life?"

I couldn't explain it because I didn't think Abra would believe me if I told her I wanted to bring my mom back. Or at least I was pretty sure she'd think I had lost my mind. I think I was scared that I wouldn't believe myself if I heard the words out loud, outside of my own mind. So I didn't try to explain.

But I knew there was something there, some connection between all the strange happenings and Mr. Jinn, the neighbor I had never seen before. Everything felt like pieces to a larger puzzle, a puzzle I didn't even have the picture for.

I put my hand on the shovel in the corner of the garden and yanked it out of the ground. It was a little long for me to use, and kind of heavy. I carried it in two hands, and my walk turned into a run as I passed the house and entered the cornfield, the same direction the vultures flew. I looked over my shoulder, and Abra was right behind me.

It was deep in the afternoon, that time during a summer day when it feels like the sun will never set. By the time we approached the northern edge of my father's fields, the vultures were already circling again, this time over a spot close to Mr. Jinn's ramshackle farmhouse. A few of them had landed and were hopping through the almost-waist-high corn, pecking at something.

I slowed to a walk and Abra practically ran into me. When I looked back past her, I could see the farmhouse where I lived way off in the distance, tiny against the southern sky. I was startled at how far away I had gone, and how quickly my familiar surroundings had faded. On both sides of us, off in the distance, the mountains stood like walls covered in the deep green of summer trees.

I held my finger up to my lips, bent over as low as I could, and crept forward. My jeans were already wet from running through all that corn. The stalks still held a lot of rain from the previous storms. A strong breeze came down from the mountains and raced through the valley. The sky was cotton-candy blue with puffy white clouds drifting from west to east.

Most of the vultures had landed. A few stragglers glided in and skidded to a stop. They tore at whatever it was they were eating, and they fought among themselves for the strips of dead flesh. I thought it must be a huge animal if all of those vultures were trying to eat from it.

"On three, we'll stand up and scare them off," I said.

Abra nodded, her big blue eyes reflecting the sky. "Sure must be something big," she muttered.

"One . . ." I gripped the shovel tightly in my hands. "Two . . ." I turned away from her, toward the host of vultures.

"Three!" we said together, and we both stood up and started shouting, waving our arms.

I didn't expect what happened next.

They came at us.

As soon as we stood up, they looked at us, cocking their heads to the side. Most of them raised their wings up as if they were trying to frighten us away. But as we kept yelling and I kept waving the shovel, they came at us, half flying, half hopping through the corn that was just about as tall as they were.

Abra scooted behind me, and I started swinging the shovel at whatever black shapes I could find.

"Get some rocks or something!" I shouted. Soon baseball-sized rocks started humming over my shoulder toward the approaching birds. She had a good arm and managed to hit a few. The first wave of birds paused, but when more started coming, they joined back in.

I had never seen anything like it. Vultures always fly away. Always. They might fly a short distance away and perch in the upper branches of a tree. They might drift to the other side of the road and wait for you to pass by. But they never stayed. They never advanced. And they most certainly never attacked.

What was going on?

I brought the shovel down hard on the first one that approached us. It didn't get back up. I caught the second one with a glancing blow and it kept coming, so I had to hit it again. And again. Which made me feel kind of sick because I had never killed anything with my hands before. I'd shot small animals with a pellet gun, and more recently with my dad's .22 rifle, but I'd never felt the impact. I didn't like it.

But I kept swinging because now they were on us. I heard Abra scream and saw that they had circled around behind us. She was flailing, and I realized she had one on her hands. She threw it away from her, but it came back faster than before. They tangled their claws in our hair and our clothes, and I imagined that they leered at us, suddenly aware that we were nothing more than scared children.

Soon all I saw was flapping black feathers and their naked little heads. Their beady eyes. Their beaks pecked at our faces and their talons reached for us. They were all over us. Abra let out a few screams as the birds started to overwhelm us, but I was silent. I don't know why—maybe I couldn't catch my breath with all those beating wings. Maybe I was so focused on fighting that my mind didn't have room for calling out. Maybe I didn't think there was anyone in the whole world who could save us.

I had always heard that vultures aren't strong creatures, that they can only eat food that's already been torn apart for them. Maybe that's true, but in that moment, covered with flapping, scratching birds, I thought we were goners. I thought for one moment that I was about to die.

At least I'll be with Mom.

I heard the blast of a shotgun as loud as thunder. Then another. The birds rose and heaved their bodies into the sky. I lay on my back in the corn and heard another shot. One of the vultures plummeted from the blue, and the rest flew west as quickly as they could. Another shot, and another vulture fell.

I reached around and found Abra, and the two of us helped each other to our feet. She had scratches on her face and her shirt was torn at her shoulder. I reached up to wipe away a bead of sweat, only to realize I was bleeding from a few cuts on my forehead. Both of us were covered in mud from falling into the field.

What had just happened? What was going on?

But nothing about those vultures shocked me as much as when I turned and saw the person wielding the shotgun—or when I finally got a look at what the vultures had been eating.

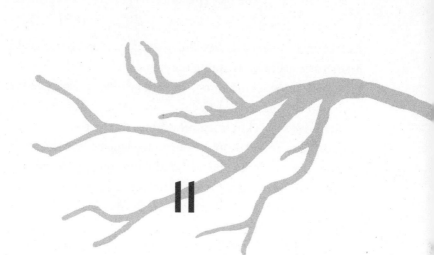

IN THE SILENCE I HEARD the whooshing sound of the
vultures' wings fading up into the mountains. Soon even
that sound stopped. The breeze died down and the corn
stopped rustling. Through the heavy silence I stared at the
man holding the shotgun, the very same man I had seen
snooping around the large oak tree in my front yard only
an hour or so before.

He had the same clothes on that I had seen him wearing at
my house, only this time everything was covered by a tattered
brown overcoat that looked way too hot for July. He had the
same squinting eyes and the same slicked-back hair. He held
the shotgun against his shoulder and looked very relaxed, as if
nothing exciting had just happened.

Halfway between him and me was a large white animal lying
among the corn, but I couldn't get a good look at it from where
we stood. It seemed that Abra and I both had the same question
at the same time, because we started walking through the corn,
one hesitant step after another, trying to see what it was that

had drawn so many vultures. But as we grew close to it, the old man's voice erupted, breaking the silence.

"Come along, come along," he said gruffly. "It isn't safe for you out here, not anymore."

He moved quickly, without a limp, and for a moment I doubted that he had been the one in my lane because his steps were so sure and quick. He grabbed Abra roughly by the arm and pushed me along in front. Whether it was intentional or not, he led us on a way that avoided the dead animal. Still, I got a look at it.

At first I thought it was a horse, or even something a little larger, but what in the valley would be larger than a horse? And there seemed to be a lot of feathers around, but not black feathers from the vultures—they were white feathers, and they were big. Then my attention shifted from wondering about that animal to wondering how it had died. It looked like something had taken a bite out of it. One large bite.

The old man kept looking up at the sky and ducking his head, as if at any time something might come swooping down and carry us all away. Once we were in Mr. Jinn's weed-infested yard, he let go of us and plowed ahead, muttering the entire time.

"Hurry now, almost there. No time for chitchat. Have to get inside."

Abra and I looked at each other.

"Why are we following him?" she whispered. "Shouldn't we run?"

I understood how she felt. It was one thing to go with that man when he was pushing us along. It was another thing entirely to follow him on our own. But I wanted to talk to him, now more than ever. I wanted to ask him about the women and what they had written on the table.

Find the Tree of Life.

"What about the vultures?" I asked. "Won't they attack us if we walk back through the field?"

She frowned. We kept walking.

"That's the man I saw at my house," I said. "The one who came up the lane before you."

"Are you sure?" she asked.

"I'm pretty sure," I said. "Same clothes, minus that ridiculous-looking overcoat. But I didn't think he could walk this fast. He limped when I saw him. And he must have been cruising to make it back here so fast."

"Hurry, hurry!" he shouted from the porch of Mr. Jinn's dilapidated house. "The spies are everywhere now. No safe place."

"Stay close," I whispered to Abra.

"We have to stay together," she said.

When we got to the porch, the old man had already gone inside. I saw the birdbath where Mr. Jinn usually left my lawnmowing money. The outside of the house needed paint—what was left of the siding had peeled and twisted away, exposing rotted wood. A few of the porch floorboards had fallen through. The windows weren't broken, but there was such a thick layer of pollen and dust on them that from the outside it was impossible to tell if there were any curtains. Not that he needed any. The grime would have blocked anyone from peering in.

We stopped for a moment, and I walked over and held open the door for Abra. "Ladies before gentlemen," I said.

She smirked and we walked inside.

"Close the door. Quickly!" the old man shouted from inside the house. I pulled the door up against the frame, but as I was about to close it the entire way, I stopped. Something inside me said, *Don't. Don't close the door.* So I left the door leaning up against the frame, but not latched.

What surprised me most about the inside of Mr. Jinn's house was that it was immaculate. While it was not brightly lit, I could still tell the carpets were vacuumed and the surfaces dusted. He didn't have much furniture, but the furniture he did have was well placed and relatively new. It was strange to think of that untidy man living here, in such a clean place.

We followed his voice back to the kitchen. A very clean kitchen. In the middle was a small green table with two chairs. The table had deep, random scratches going in all different directions, like a three-dimensional road map. As we entered the kitchen, he came bustling in from some back room bearing a third chair, which he slid up against a third side of the table. He sat down in that chair and motioned for us to sit at the other two, one on either side of him, but just as we moved toward our seats he stood again.

"Go ahead, sit down. I'll get you some water."

I sat down in his chair so that he would not be between us. It seemed a silly thing to do, but Abra's words from outside still stuck in my mind.

We have to stay together.

He didn't seem to notice that I had taken his seat. He placed two glasses of water on the table and handed each of us a wet washcloth to clean up with. He took a seat at the end. I say "the end" even though it was a very small table, and if we all would have leaned forward at once, it's likely we would have banged heads.

He stared at us. His eyes were dark, his pupils large so that very little white showed around the edges, and when I stared at them they felt like deep pools, a swirling mass of shadow from another universe. Time slowed. His eyes scared me.

"Well, go on," he said, the first non-gruff words I had heard him utter. "What do you want to know? Ask away."

Abra and I looked at each other out of the corner of our eyes. I might have been the curious one, but when it came to situations like this, Abra was the most straightforward.

"Who are you?" she asked.

"My name is Mr. Jinn. Yes," he said, as if reassuring himself of his identity, "Mr. Jinn."

"Why don't you ever come out of your house?" she asked.

"I don't like people very much."

"So why did you help us?"

"Because I like children. Children aren't people."

That stopped her in her tracks, but just for a moment. "Yes they are!" she said, sounding deeply offended.

"What ate the dead animal in the field?" I asked quietly.

"Mmm," he said, as if tasting a delicious food for the first time. "Finally a good question. But I don't know if you're ready for the answer."

He took a comb out of his shirt pocket and combed his hair straight back. I realized he still had his overcoat on, but he wasn't sweating.

"What do you mean?" I asked.

He stood up and walked over to one of the kitchen windows. A small fly buzzed up against the glass, colliding over and over again with the frame. It stopped and wandered up to the top of the window before buzzing and flying again, twitching in its flight. Mr. Jinn opened the window. I thought he was going to let the fly out, but instead he clapped his hands together. The dead fly stuck against his palm. He flicked it out through the window and slammed the window shut.

"Some people aren't always ready for the truth," he said.

"Some people are so blinded by what's real that they're not ready for what's true."

"I think we're ready," Abra said, still sounding indignant after being told children aren't people.

Mr. Jinn looked at me. "What was written on the table in the antique store?"

Abra turned to me, waiting for me to answer the question.

I stared at my water and took a sip. I looked at Mr. Jinn. Why would he ask me that? He had been there. He had looked at the scribbled table.

"I don't know," I said. "I don't know what you mean. I thought I saw something, but now I'm not so sure."

There was something inside me that felt hesitant about telling him. What if he hadn't been the man in the shadows? What if the writing was important information, information that Mr. Jinn shouldn't know about? He made me nervous, and I wanted to leave.

"Just as I suspected," he said with a hint of sadness in his voice. "I guess you're not ready."

Abra didn't say anything, but she stared hard at me, and her eyes asked the question, *Why won't you tell him?*

I shook my head. "Do you know what ate that animal in the field?" I asked Mr. Jinn.

He squinted those dark eyes, and when he nodded his entire body moved forward and back, forward and back, and the chair he sat on creaked under his enormity.

I sighed. I thought he might know a lot of things that I needed to know, and we wouldn't get anywhere if we stayed stuck at this part of the conversation. Reluctantly, I let the words escape in a whisper.

"I thought the words on the table said, 'Find the Tree of Life.'"

At this Mr. Jinn leaned forward and stared at me. "Is that right?" he asked. "Is that what you saw?"

There was something eager in his face, something hungry. I wondered how he had missed it, why I had seen it but he hadn't. I nodded slowly, feeling as though I had told him something I shouldn't have. It was a feeling I would always have around him, that I was letting things slip, that I was saying more than I should.

"'Find the Tree of Life,'" he said quietly to himself. "So it is finally here."

He stood up and paced back and forth in the kitchen. When he passed by me, his overcoat flapped, and it smelled like mud and summer. He snapped out of that short reflection and looked at me again, saying matter-of-factly, "It was an Amarok."

At first I didn't know what he was talking about.

"What?" Abra said in a sharp tone. She sounded almost angry, as if she believed Mr. Jinn was trying to make her look silly.

"You heard me."

"An Amarok?" I asked. I didn't even know what that was.

"Is that even a real animal?" Abra asked.

"What is real?" he asked. "What is true?"

Abra jumped to her feet, her chair shooting out behind her. "I want to go look at that dead animal," she said. "Let's go right now."

Mr. Jinn didn't look upset or bothered. "It won't be there any longer," he said, shaking his head and pulling his comb from his pocket. "They'll have taken it."

"The vultures?" I asked.

"The vultures may have come back," he said. "Or maybe the black dogs." He gave me a knowing look. "Maybe the Amarok came back for it. If it did, you probably won't make it home through the field. But that's not likely in the day. The Amarok prefers, shall we say, the shadows."

I remembered the combined voices of the three old women, and a chill swept through my body.

Protection from what lives in the shadows.

He raised his eyebrows and shook his head, and his mouth showed regret. His voice hardened. He stared first at me, then at Abra, who was still standing.

"Do you know what it means to 'Find the Tree of Life'? Do you want to know why the old women wrote those words on the table?"

He paused. Abra looked at me. I nodded.

"Your mother and that oak tree were killed at the exact same moment by that lightning strike."

"The tree's not dead," I interrupted. "It's still green."

"That tree won't survive the year," he snapped. "Your mother substituted her life for yours. Her sacrifice, combined with the death of the oak tree, brought something wonderful into the world."

I stared at him. All of his talk about my mother made me angry. Who was he to talk about her? What did he know, this man who never left his house, this man who wore overcoats in the summer? But he just kept talking.

"Now the Tree is here, somewhere." He waved his arms around. "The war is beginning. They are gathering and taking sides."

When he said "the Tree," he sounded like he was talking about something very holy or very dangerous or both. And he liked it. There was a lust for blood in his voice, a desire for destruction. He seemed excited at the idea of war.

"Who's taking sides?" I asked.

Abra backed away from the table. "Let's go, Sam," she said. "We need to go."

"What do you mean by sides?" I asked him again.

"You would do well to heed the words you read on the table," Mr. Jinn said, his eyes piercing me. "You would do well to find the Tree."

"You still haven't told us what an Amarok is, or what it was doing in the field, or what that animal is that it killed."

"The Amarok being here, it's a sign," he said, and in his voice was a pleading for us to understand, as if a greater understanding would lead to our being on his side. "A sign! Just one of many signs that prove what I told you about your mother is true, and that the Tree is close. The Amarok is drawn to the Tree. It is always drawn to the Tree. It's how we know the Tree is here."

His voice sounded more and more like a plea. We stared at him, and I wondered if he was sane.

Abra pulled at my shoulder and I stood up.

"She's right," Mr. Jinn said, looking at the window in the kitchen. "You should go. Before it gets too late in the day. You don't want to be walking by yourselves at night anymore."

We walked quickly out of the kitchen and across the porch. The sun was already dropping behind the western mountain. I saw small black specks against the darkening sky, some of them flying, some of them perched in the highest branches of faraway trees. Vultures? Or my overactive imagination?

We half walked, half jogged through the weeds to the cornfield. We stopped for a moment where the white animal had been, but Mr. Jinn was right. There was nothing, not even any blood. Only broken cornstalks and feathers, some black, some white.

Mr. Jinn shouted to us from his house, "Don't worry. I'll come

101

to your house tomorrow, after your mother's funeral. We have a lot to talk about and even more to do. Remember, find the Tree! Now run! Run! The darkness is coming!"

The sun was barely over the mountain as we ran through the corn, our shadows dashing along beside us.

12

I HAD A DREAM the night before my mother's funeral.

I'm standing at the window and the rain pours down, battering the glass. The sky is a greenish-gray and the clouds bubble like a pot of boiling water. I wonder if the barns will be okay, or if the wind will tear them into small pieces and drive them up against the house.

I see my mom. She's up in the oak tree, walking out on the branch. Her wet clothes whip around her and her hair dangles down in her face. I suddenly wonder if I might be able to warn her. If I run out to the tree and tell her to get down, will she be spared? Will the lightning miss her?

Before I know it, I am running through the warm summer rain. The dream is so real that I can feel the squishing of my shoes in the muddy ground. I get to the base of the tree, but I'm too late. The lightning strikes. The tree explodes. I see a bright light.

But something changes. The weather goes from stormy to sunny, with the bluest sky ever. I climb the old oak and it is perfect. No missing branches. No long, white scar from the lightning. And it's bearing fruit! It's not an oak anymore, or at least that's what I think. I climb higher and higher, and I look off in the distance and see my mother in a white dress, sleeping on the green grass.

Sleeping? Or dead?

I realize that the fruit of this new oak tree will bring her back. I grab a piece and it's soft in my hand. It's speckled, a mixture of red and orange and yellow, and oblong like a pear. But by the time I get to the ground, it is rotten in my hands, and it smells terrible. So I climb the tree again, grab a new piece, and race back down.

The bark is like sandpaper on my knees and my hands. My legs start to feel dream-heavy, nearly impossible to lift. And every time I climb down, the fruit rots. I look over at my mother lying in the grass, and I feel so sad that I cannot take her any fruit.

I hear a loud growl behind me. I turn. It's the largest wolf I've ever seen, much bigger than any of the three dogs. It's black with brown paws, and its teeth are like white daggers. Its nose wrinkles back in a snarl, and it speaks in an angry voice.

"That fruit does not belong to you."

The wolf springs at me, and just as its jaws are about to close around my face, I wake up.

My window was open and the early morning sun shone in, fresh and new. Personally, I had hoped for rain. It was the morning of my mother's funeral, and I didn't think sunshine was appropriate.

My dad knocked on the door, and even his knock sounded tired. I walked over, rubbing my eyes. The day didn't seem real. I thought that maybe if I rubbed my eyes and didn't open them, it wouldn't happen. None of it would happen. But as soon as I opened the door, I knew it was real. All of it.

"Time to get ready, boy," my dad said. He turned and walked back downstairs.

I liked hearing his voice. I turned around and pulled some clothes from my closet, though I didn't have very many dress clothes. Most of what I owned had been slightly ruined from working and playing and living on a farm my entire life. But I managed to find a nice shirt, a pair of slacks, and some black socks buried at the bottom of my drawer.

My dad made breakfast for both of us, and as I sat there waiting for the eggs to fry, I found myself running my index finger along a scratch on our dining room table. That reminded me of the table in the antique store, and of Mr. Jinn, and of all that he had said the day before.

Find the Tree.

And what was an Amarok?

"What's an Amarok?" I asked my dad as he put two plates of eggs and toast on the table and sat down beside me. I hadn't really thought about the question. The words escaped from my mouth before I had a chance to check them out, and if I could have, I would have chased them down and swallowed them again. I was too tired of not getting a response from him. I was weary of the one-sided nature of our new relationship, the one created in the wake of my mom's death.

But he surprised me.

"Where did you hear about that?" he asked.

I didn't know what to say. I didn't want him to know that I was sneaking all over the valley, visiting with Mr. Jinn and being attacked by vultures. And everything else. He'd think I was losing my mind. He'd never believe me.

I shrugged. "I don't know. I think we might have talked about it at school or something."

He nodded. "There are a lot of great stories out there. The Inuit people have legends about the Amarok. Do you know the Inuits?"

I shook my head and kept eating, trying not to scare him back into his silence with too much attention. It was like watching a snow leopard in the wild.

"The Inuits, I guess they're a type of Eskimo. They have legends that the old men pass down to the young," he said. His voice was musical again, if only for a few moments. Stories will do that for us, bring beauty back even in the midst of such overwhelming darkness. "They're wonderful legends. Terrifying stories. Some of them involve an Amarok."

He took a bite of breakfast, then continued with his mouth full. If my mother had been there, she would have given him a look that said, "Don't talk with your mouth full." But she wasn't there. So much was changing. I was running around the fair with only Abra. I had met the mysterious Mr. Jinn. Dad was talking with his mouth full.

The entire world felt upside down.

"The Amarok is a legendary wolf, as big as a horse and black, the color of a shadow. Unlike normal wolves, it hunts on its own. Not in a pack."

I shuddered. What if there was an Amarok prowling the valley right now? My dream swept back into my mind, and suddenly I wasn't hungry anymore. I remembered the black wolf that had stared at me in my dream and told me in a growling voice, "That fruit doesn't belong to you." Was that an Amarok?

"But there's one thing to remember about the Amarok—it only devours those who are foolish enough to hunt alone," Dad chanted in a voice that made it sound like he had memorized that phrase once, long ago.

He shrugged, and the music fell out of his voice, and it was just me and him again—no stories, no legends, eating breakfast a few hours before we buried the body of someone we loved more than anything else.

"Or at least that's how the legend goes."

I had been alone in my dream. I shuddered again, and Abra's words echoed in my mind, the words she had said before we had walked into Mr. Jinn's house.

We have to stay together.

"You don't have to worry," my dad said. He must have seen the fear in my eyes. "Amaroks aren't real."

And once again I heard a voice in my head, but this time it was Mr. Jinn's from the day before.

Some people are so blinded by what's real that they're not ready for what's true.

My dad and I walked down the lane. My fancy shoes rubbed around the bottom of my ankles, and the shirt tugged under my arms. The sun refused to go behind the clouds, and the sky was a beautiful blue. The recent rains had turned every plant and crop and tree a deep, lush green. The oak, however, didn't look quite right. The edges of the leaves looked black, and the branches drooped like a wilting plant. The lightning scar that went all the way down the tree and disappeared at the roots had gone from bright white to a sickly yellow, like someone's last, decaying tooth.

We crossed the street and walked into the church. The parking lot was full. My mother was well loved by many people in the neighborhood, and her passing was a great tragedy in Deen. The main auditorium of the small church held maybe two hundred people, and it was standing room only. Ushers walked my father and me to the front row, and we sat down. My mother's casket was there in front of us. I couldn't believe she was in there.

The pastor across the street had agreed to have the service there. He was a tall man, mostly thin but with a little round ball for a belly. His nose was sloped, and his eyes were sad and eager to show you that sadness. His voice had a wavering quality to it, the way it sounds when you're talking to someone underwater.

We sat there, listening to him drone on and on about my mom, someone he barely knew, and my attention began to fade. I wanted it to be over and done. I wanted this part to be in the past so I could focus all of my energy on the future and figuring out how to bring her back. This all seemed like an unwelcome distraction that I didn't have time for.

I heard the sniffles and quiet crying around me more than I heard the words the pastor said. But there was one verse he read from his black book that caught my attention.

"Our final reading today comes from Revelation." He paused and closed his eyes. When he opened them again, he read the passage with a somber, reverent voice that somehow swept me up and carried me to a far-off place.

"Then the angel showed me the river of the water of life, as clear as crystal, flowing from the throne of God and of the Lamb down the middle of the great street of the city. On each side of the river stood the tree of life, bearing twelve crops of fruit, yielding its fruit every month. And the leaves of the tree are for the healing of the nations."

The Tree of Life. Healing for the nations. Again, the phrase echoed over and over in my mind.

Find the Tree.

Find the Tree.

Find the Tree.

My father had petitioned the county to allow him to bury my mom in the graveyard in the forest at the end of the Road to Nowhere. It had taken some convincing, but eventually they gave in, not wanting to have a public fight with a grieving man. So the hearse drove away from the church and headed north on Kincade Road. It was one of the first cars to drive that way for a very, very long time.

I caught a glimpse of Abra as we walked from the church to the graveyard. I wondered if the pastor's words about the Tree had caught her attention too. She wore a long black dress and had a black ribbon in her hair. A thought entered my mind, something I had never considered before: Abra was pretty. Prior to that funeral, I had only ever seen her as a friend, someone to run around with, to have fun with. It seemed strange to me that I would notice her beauty at my mother's funeral, but I did, and I kept stealing glances at her, wondering if she thought I looked handsome in the clothes I had managed to rummage from the bottom of my drawer.

Because the road didn't go all the way to the cemetery but stopped beyond Mr. Jinn's driveway, a group of my father's friends and fellow farmers served as pallbearers. They bore the coffin from the hearse and over the crumbled-up pavement where the road ended. They forged through the weeds and wound in and out among the trees, trying not to stumble on the roots. Finally, they arrived at the ancient cemetery, the one close to the cave, my hiding place. The river was loud there, rushing as it did through the green forest.

The funeral director had managed to erect a small white canopy over the open grave. The men brought my mother's coffin through the forest, passed it over the low iron railing that surrounded the mossy headstones, and set the coffin on straps that lowered her slowly into the summer earth. I looked toward the river but could barely see it through the trees. It was still full to overflowing and muddy. It raced along even though I thought it should stop and pay its respects.

How could the world keep going? Why didn't everything stop, as my life had stopped, and watch as my mother vanished from the earth?

We stopped by the stone, and I stared at the letters. I knew by the phone conversations I had overheard that my father had paid a lot of money to have that stone ready for the day of the funeral.

Lucy Leigh Chambers
Wife and Mother
Meet Me at the Edge of the World

Below that was a picture of a tree. I thought it looked like the oak tree in our yard, and it filled me with a strange sense of awe. It seemed appropriate that my mother and that tree would be joined together forever, or at least as long as that gravestone could withstand the passing of time.

It's a tradition in our town to fill in the grave by hand, so people who knew my mother took turns using the shovels provided by the church and scooped in those dark brown shovelfuls. The clods made a thumping sound as they fell into the hole.

Eventually it was over. The hole was filled and, like the river, overflowing in the form of a small mound. People shook my father's hand and patted me on the head and walked slowly back through the woods to their cars, high stepping through the mud and the weeds, relieved to go back to their normal lives.

But I was left there with nothing. Nothing normal to go back to. I stared at the earth, and it reminded me of when we first tilled up our garden in the spring. It looked like earth that was ready to have something planted in it.

Abra came up beside me and grabbed my shirt sleeve down where it wrapped around my wrist. She wasn't holding my hand, but she was holding on to me.

We have to stay together.

I stared at that filled-in hole, and I felt her holding on to my sleeve, and I thought about the Tree of Life the pastor had read about. It seemed too good to be true, that the very Tree of Life might be here, somewhere in the valley, waiting for me to find it. But after all I had seen and heard in these few days, that's exactly what I believed, and the preacher's words confirmed it for me. I stared at my mother's freshly filled-in grave and thought, if there ever was a place to plant a Tree of Life, that would be the soil for it.

"C'mon, boy," my father said, and Abra and I followed him away from the cemetery. Everyone else had left. Everyone, that is, except for one man.

"Mr. Chambers?" the man said, walking up to my father.

"Adam," my dad said in a tired voice. "Call me Adam."

"My name's Caleb Tennin. I'm sorry for your loss."

The man was dressed in all black, with pointy black shoes

and creased black pants and a black shirt with a black tie, all covered by a jet-black suit coat. He had tan skin and long, thin eyes and a shaved, bald head.

"I know this might not be a good time," he said, looking away for a moment before looking back at my father. "But I hear you're looking for some help around the farm."

"You're right," my father said without any anger or emotion at all. "It is a bad time."

"And I apologize," Mr. Tennin said, bowing and backing away.

"Who'd you hear that from?" my dad asked, and I was shocked that he was continuing the conversation. I think he was too curious not to ask.

"Oh, you know, around," Mr. Tennin whispered. He stopped backing up, paused, waited.

"Well, I can't recall telling anyone I was looking for help." My father paused as he continued to stare at the man with interest. I wondered if he had the same doubts I had regarding this man's ability to put in a good day's work. The suit, the fancy shoes, the soft hands—everything about this man suggested he hadn't done a day of hard labor in his life.

"Any experience?"

"Enough," Mr. Tennin said with confidence. "I spent many years in a garden. And I have a way with animals."

My father shrugged, and he spoke every word reluctantly, as if he was running out of words, as if his daily allotment was nearly dry. "Well. When can you start?"

"Now, if you'll have me."

My dad clenched his jaw and nodded. "Okay. Join us for lunch?"

Mr. Tennin nodded back.

Abra and I followed them out of the woods and back to the

crumbling road, past Mr. Jinn's lane, and everything seemed to fall into step, fall into rhythm. But it only felt that way for a moment, because Abra nudged me in the side and pointed toward the northern fields that ran alongside the Road to Nowhere. Limping through the field, this time with a walking stick in his hand, was Mr. Jinn. High above him, so high that they were merely tiny black specks in a great blue sky, the vultures circled.

13

"SO THIS IS WHERE IT HAPPENED?" Mr. Tennin asked with deep concern in his voice, stopping under the oak tree.

My father nodded, not saying anything. Mr. Tennin moved closer to the tree. He reached up and put his hands on the scar, running his fingers along it. He closed his eyes and said something too quietly for me to hear before speaking louder to us.

"So sad," he said, shaking his head, and his words sounded genuine. "So sad."

A gruff voice called out from the other side of the yard, the side that grew up against the northern fields.

"That's the tree?" the voice asked, and I knew without looking that it was Mr. Jinn, though I couldn't figure out how he had gotten through the field that fast. I had thought we would have at least a few minutes to get my dad and Mr. Tennin inside before he arrived.

My father looked bothered by Mr. Jinn's intrusion. "I'm sorry," he said. "Who are you?"

"Condolences, condolences," Mr. Jinn said, pulling his comb from his shirt pocket. He wore the same gray mechanic shirt

114

with thin, barely visible red stripes and the same navy blue pants I had seen him in before. His dark brown boots were muddy from walking through the field. He ran his comb straight back through his hair, returned it to his pocket, then held out his hand. "I'm your neighbor, Jinn."

"Mr. Jinn," my father said, looking surprised. The reclusive nature of Mr. Jinn had been legendary in our area. My father gathered himself and began introducing everyone else. "This is Mr. Tennin. We're discussing terms to have him join on here as a hired hand."

"I could use one myself," Mr. Jinn said. "If you need more hours, I'm the farm straight back that way."

But Mr. Tennin didn't seem to pay any attention to him.

"This is my son, Sam," my dad continued. "And this is his friend Abra."

"How do you do?" Mr. Jinn said, not mentioning that we had met the day before. When he bent close to shake my hand, our eyes met. His gaze was heavy with one unspoken question.

Did you find the Tree?

I said nothing.

An awkward silence filled that warm July day as the five of us stood there, no one saying anything. Mr. Jinn didn't seem to mind. He just stared up into the branches of the tree. Mr. Tennin still hadn't taken his hand from the long, jagged lightning scar. Abra's eyes were wide open, and I knew how she felt, waiting to see what would happen next.

Finally my father sighed, and when he spoke there was a heaviness in his voice. I could tell he wanted to be alone. I couldn't figure out why he didn't send everyone away.

"Why don't you all come in for lunch," he said, a reluctant invitation. "We can make some sandwiches, and there's some fresh milk in the fridge. But I need to get back to work in about an hour."

He walked toward the house, not waiting to find out who would take him up on the offer. Mr. Tennin and Mr. Jinn followed him, walking side by side.

"This is strange," Abra said, shaking her head, and the two of us followed the three men into the house.

—

Mr. Jinn took a huge bite out of his sandwich, leaving a piece of ham and a sliver of bread crust hanging from his mouth for a moment. He attacked his food like a man who hadn't eaten for days.

"So tell me about that oak tree out there," Mr. Tennin said. "That's one of the oldest I've ever seen."

My father nodded, finished eating what was in his mouth, and took a drink of milk. "There used to be two oaks in the front yard. The other one was much older than this one and a little closer to the house, but we had some problems with it, so my grandfather took it down."

I thought about the story my father had told me, of how his dog had died and brought the rain and how people had started sacrificing animals to the tree. I wondered if all of that was true.

"Two trees," Mr. Jinn repeated, as if verifying an important fact.

"I believe my great-grandfather planted both of them," my father confirmed. "This one maybe seventy-five, eighty years ago?"

"I can only imagine the amazing stories that tree would have to tell us if it could talk." Mr. Tennin took a bite of his sandwich, and I could tell he was deep in thought.

"Tell them the story you told us," I said to my dad. "Tell them about how the tree brought the rain."

My father looked embarrassed. "Not now, boy."

"That sounds intriguing," Mr. Tennin said, looking at me.

"My dad loves stories." I looked over at him, but Dad was looking at me in a way that said, "You should stop talking," so I took another bite of my sandwich.

"I know a wonderful story about a tree, if you'd like to hear it." Mr. Tennin ate the last of his sandwich, drank the rest of his milk, set his cup down on the table, and smiled. "Delicious." His voice sounded both mysterious and hopeful, like wind through the leaves. "Delicious."

"We like stories too," Abra whispered, but she couldn't hide the eagerness in her voice.

"It's a story about the most important tree in the history of the world," Mr. Tennin said. "But it's rather long." He looked at my father and raised his eyebrows as if to ask for permission.

My father looked curious. "We need to get to work." He glanced at his watch. "But I think we have a little time."

Mr. Tennin cleared his throat. He looked at each of us around the table, including Mr. Jinn, who by now was combing his hair again and muttering things to himself. This is the story Mr. Tennin told us, in a lyrical voice that sounded like the wind and the river.

In the beginning of time, when all the world was young and the trees had only just begun to grow, there were two people. The first two people. Perhaps you've heard this story, or at least the beginning of it.

The first two people lived in a beautiful forest that contained everything they could ever want. There were trees with fruit, good for eating, and there were four rivers with clear water. These two people, one man and one woman, walked the paths and tended to the trees. And there was a lovely Voice that guided them, a beautiful Voice that lived among them.

But there was also evil in that garden forest, because there are always shadows, there is always darkness. There is the hidden side to what we can see. Lurking in the shadow was a Darkness that sang dark songs, one who wanted to destroy the beauty that the Voice had created.

When the Voice had first guided the two people to the forest, he encouraged them to take whatever fruit they wanted. There was nothing in the forest they could not have, except for one thing. They were not permitted to eat from one of the trees, because if they did their eyes would be opened. Not their physical eyes, mind you. The Voice was talking about their inner eyes.

"Eat of any other tree," the Voice said. "But do not eat of the tree that will open your eyes."

For a long time, peace reigned in the forest. But always there was the Darkness in the shadows, waiting.

Until one day the Darkness sang its song and convinced them to eat from the tree, and just as the Voice had said, their eyes were opened. They realized they were naked. They realized they were not perfect. They realized they had done a terrible thing, and they hid. But of course the Voice found them.

Now there was a problem, because there was a second Tree (and for a moment Mr. Tennin looked knowingly at my father) *in the middle of the forest. This was the Tree of Life. The Voice knew that if the two people ate from that Tree, they would live forever. They would be like gods, because they would live forever with open eyes. So the Voice cast them from the forest. They were not permitted to reenter. Ever again.*

And the Voice gave them a gift—it was called Death. It was a gift because it would be the path they would follow that would take them back to who they had been before their eyes had been opened, a path back to innocence and pure joy. Without Death, they would have been forced to wander the earth forever without any hope of returning to perfection, always decaying, always rotting, until they were nothing but scattered particles of dust trying to come back together, molecules lost from one another, forever separated.

This is what the gift of Death keeps from happening.

Just to make sure that those first two people didn't try to come back and eat from the Tree of Life, something that would steal the gift of Death from them forever, the Voice sent two cherubim, a type of angel, to guard the way into the forest. And there was a flaming sword to frighten anyone who might wander near.

That is the story that is well-known. But what most people do not know is what happened after that.

(Here Mr. Tennin paused and stared at the table for a short while, as if weighing the cost of revealing the rest of the story.)

The two cherubim remained there guarding the entrance to the forest, guarding the Tree of Life. Decades passed. Centuries. Eventually one of the cherubim allowed his mind to wander. He thought about how humans had spread throughout the earth, and how they lived a hard existence. More than anything else the humans feared Death. They didn't remember where Death would lead them, so they didn't realize it was a gift and not something to be feared. This cherub realized that if he could possess the Tree of Life, humans would worship him. They would do whatever he wanted them to do.

But even more important to that cherub was the knowledge that if humans ate of the Tree of Life, they could never escape earth, and they would be forced to live in his kingdom forever. He knew that humans are often weak, and they would do anything to avoid Death, something they knew so little of, and trade it for the endless stay on earth that the Tree of Life would give them. They could not possibly imagine the horrid existence that awaited them without Death.

That cherub's own inner eyes began to envision the throne upon which he would sit, the scepter with which he would rule. And lust for power grew in his heart. More than anything, he began to desire the Tree of Life so that he could give its fruit to humans and make them his servants forever, with no escape.

One day he moved toward the Tree to steal a piece of its fruit. He planned to run away with it, plant it, and nurture it. For many different reasons he could not possess the Tree itself, but with a piece of its fruit he hoped to fashion a tree of his own, a powerful tree. He could have his own Tree of Life. The Voice could never destroy him, and people desiring the Tree and its fruit would worship him and do whatever he told them to do, and once they ate from the Tree they would be trapped on earth.

But the second cherub saw him move for the Tree and tried to stop him, and the two of them fought. For forty days and forty nights they wrestled in the forest. Both of them grew weary, yet neither would give up. As they fought, their fury turned to fire, and as they rolled through the forest the trees caught and burned. Finally, their battle took them to the center of the forest, where the Darkness had deceived the first two people long, long before.

The tree from which the first two people had eaten—the tree that had opened their inner eyes—had become small and twisted, like an old cedar that cannot reach the sun. The fire from their fight lit this old tree and it went up in hot smoke.

But the Tree of Life had grown tall. Its leaves were broad and green, and its branches reached up nearly to heaven. Its fruit, untouched for thousands of years, hung heavy and ripe. When the fury of the cherubim lit the Tree of Life, it burned for another forty days and forty nights. Humans gathered in the surrounding mountains and plains and watched with terror, because at night the burning Tree looked like a comet ready to collide with the earth, and during the day it looked like the beginning of an eclipse that might drown the sun forever.

When the cherubim realized what had happened, they stopped fighting and sat quietly beside one another, spent and waiting. And the Voice came down to them.

To the first cherub, the Voice said, "You have desired the Tree of Life more than anything else, and so you are cursed. For eternity you will try to find the Tree. Your only desire shall be to possess it, and your fate will be tied to it."

With that, the first cherub vanished and began to roam the earth, always searching for the Tree of Life, because it is always reborn after it is destroyed.

In the peace that remained in that smoldering garden forest, the Voice said to the second cherub, "You have done well, good and faithful servant. Will you take on this purpose? Will you also roam the earth, but to keep the other cherub from possessing the Tree? The Tree of Life, because of its nature, can never be completely destroyed, and even now it is being remade and will reappear where someone who is faithful gives up their life for a friend. But when it is reborn, you must destroy it so that humankind does not lose the gift of Death."

The second cherub nodded, took flight, and roamed the earth, always looking for the Tree of Life in order to destroy it, keep the first cherub from possessing it, and preserve the gift of Death for humanity. This cherub, legend says, has destroyed the Tree many times—maybe a hundred times, maybe a thousand—but the Tree of Life must be destroyed many more times before the end.

Mr. Tennin leaned back in his chair.

I glanced at Mr. Jinn, and he was glaring at Mr. Tennin, his eyes thin slits. He sat unmoving, still as a cliff, and somehow, in that motionless stare, I sensed a kind of recognition, as if he had finally realized something, as if he had spotted the one missing piece to a puzzle he had been working on for years.

My father looked impressed. He always loved a good story. He even chuckled to himself and shook his head, smiling.

But me? I felt an urgency rising up. The Tree, the Tree, the Tree—everywhere I turned, people were talking about it. Telling stories about it. I thought it must be real. It must be close. And who were these two men, Tennin and Jinn, wrapped up as they were in the life of the Tree?

"Where did you hear that story?" my father asked. "I've never come across anything like it."

Mr. Tennin gave a tired smile. "Some stories, you don't know where they come from. Some stories, they just grow up inside you."

I wanted to stay silent, to not draw attention to myself, but my curiosity got the better of me. I had to ask.

"You said the Tree of Life could keep people alive," I said quietly. "Could fruit from the Tree of Life bring someone back from the dead?"

The man grew silent. I knew that everyone around the table realized what was on my mind: the fresh grave of naked dirt at the end of the Road to Nowhere.

Mr. Tennin had a sad look on his face. "Sam, the Tree of Life, as spoken about in this legend, was a powerful tree. That's certain. If anything could bring someone back from the dead, it would be fruit from this Tree. But even if it could, would that be the best thing to do?"

I stared at the table, embarrassed. "So you think it could?" I asked again, not looking up.

"Sam," my father said with the sound of warning in his voice.

Mr. Tennin held up his palm toward my father. "It's okay. It's an important question." He turned back to me. "It might be able to, Sam. But sometimes the correct question isn't, 'Can we?' Sometimes the correct question is, 'Should we?'"

I glanced over at Abra. She stared at Mr. Tennin, as if waiting for him to start telling us another story.

"Imagine this, Sam," Mr. Tennin continued. "What if death isn't as dark and scary as we think it is? What if death is simply the path from this world, full of hurt and pain, to a better place?"

He waited and let that sink in.

"Now imagine destroying that path, covering it up so that no one could follow it. Imagine eliminating the only way to escape from this broken world. Because the Tree of Life doesn't eliminate pain, at least not forever. It doesn't eliminate disease or old age or scars. So when you introduce the Tree of Life, you eliminate the only means of traveling away from all of those things. If people would eat from that Tree, they would be trapped here. Their bodies would eventually decay even as they lived, and their skin would grow thin and their eyesight would dim and eventually they would be nothing but bones, wearing away in the wind and the water, and still they would be here, alive. Do you know what this earth becomes when people are trapped here for thousands of years in their pain and their decaying bodies?"

I shuddered.

"Hell," he said. "That's what this earth would become if there was a Tree of Life and everyone ate from it."

"But it's not real, right?" Abra interrupted. "I mean, you're talking about this Tree as if it exists for real."

Mr. Tennin smiled at her, and it was kind of a sad smile, but he didn't say anything.

"What's real? What's true?" he asked, and my gaze darted over to Mr. Jinn.

"Yes, yes, a good story," Mr. Jinn said. When he had ambled into our yard, he had the look of a man staring down a day of leisure, but now he seemed nervous, anxious to leave. "Moving and all that. Now it appears lunch has come and gone."

He stood up and took his plate into the kitchen, and the rest of us followed. But I couldn't stop thinking about this Tree of Life. I thought about the words scribbled on the table and the words the preacher had read at my mother's funeral. I thought about Mr. Tennin's story. And my mind became obsessed with one thing: finding the Tree of Life and bringing my mother back from the dead. I wanted her there with me. I wanted to hug her and hear her voice in the kitchen. I wanted to see her waving from the third base line at the ball field. If we both ate from the Tree of Life, we could figure out the future together.

I felt a certain kinship with that first cherub. I would do many things in order to possess that Tree. In fact, I couldn't think of anything I wouldn't do, if it meant plucking one piece of fruit from that Tree, if it meant bringing my mother back from her dark grave.

My father and Mr. Tennin walked out toward the barns. Mr. Tennin didn't look ready for work, still dressed in his all-black fancy clothes, but he had taken off his suit coat and rolled his sleeves up, and my father had lent him a pair of knee-high boots. I figured they wanted to have a look around and talk about pay out of the hearing of nosy children. I watched them both disappear into the dark shadows of the barn, where only a few days before I had bottle-fed the lamb.

"We've no time to lose," Mr. Jinn said once they were out of sight. He put his comb back into his pocket. "That much is clear to me now. We'd best do what that old hag wrote on the table. We'd best find the Tree."

He stomped out onto the porch, hurried down the steps, and crossed the yard to the lightning tree. I looked at Abra, and we both followed him.

14

"So your mother was right up there in the tree when the lightning struck?" Mr. Jinn asked, his round head leaning back, his thick neck bulging.

I bristled at the casual way he talked about my mother's death, especially considering we had buried her body in the ground not three hours earlier. I didn't know what to say. Abra moved up beside me and grabbed my sleeve again. I thought I might start crying. In that moment I was thinking about how my mother had been such a good mother. And once again I thought, *I would do anything to bring her back.*

Mr. Jinn looked over at me and squinted, as if he was trying to figure out what was wrong.

"Oh my," he said, shaking his head. "Oh my. Come here, kid. Come here."

I went to him, Abra reluctantly letting go, and Mr. Jinn raised his arm and welcomed me against his side.

"There, there," he said. "There, there."

But it didn't comfort me. It didn't comfort me at all. He smelled like the stone road after a storm—heavy and dark. His

embrace felt more like he was luring me in than trying to make
me feel better. And once his arm came down around me, I felt
stifled, trapped. Still, I wasn't sure what to do. I had never had
to pull myself away from an adult before.

"Listen," he said, and then, as if on second thought, he shook
his head. "No, sit down. Both of you. You might as well know."

We sat down on either side of Mr. Jinn, but once he had settled
in, Abra stood up and came around to my other side, which put
me in between both of them. I looked up over my shoulder, and
the lightning scar in the tree crashed down right on top of Mr.
Jinn's head and continued down where his back rested against
the tree. The sky was very blue, and carefree clouds wandered
over the fields from one mountain to the other.

"What would you do to bring back your mother?" Mr. Jinn
asked me.

It shocked me, like he had been reading my mind. He didn't
wait for an answer.

"I know. You'd do anything. Anything. Just as I would. Or
you," he said, pointing over my head at Abra. "When someone
we love dies, we'd do anything to bring them back."

He was right. A sense of resignation washed over me, from the
tips of my brown hair to the soles of my nice shoes that I hadn't
taken off after the funeral. I would do anything, and I wasn't
the only one. I was justified in how I felt. It was an admission
that filled me with both relief and guilt.

"Here's another question. What would you say if I told you
I could help you bring her back?"

A wondrous hope surged through me like a jolt of electricity.
That thing I wanted—here was someone willing to talk about
it, someone willing to help. To feel her skin again, to hear her
laugh, to smell her hair as she bent over my bed and kissed me

good night—he could bring all of that into reality. Deep inside, I knew it was true.

But all of that hope, all of those good feelings, popped like a soap bubble at the sound of Abra's voice.

"You're crazy," she said. "No, you're not crazy. You're evil."

Panic rushed through me. I wanted her to keep quiet. I wanted Mr. Jinn to keep talking and feed the small flame of hope growing inside me. I didn't want to face life without my mother. I wanted to chase after her return, no matter how long it took, no matter what I had to do.

"Shut up!" I said. "Wait."

I had never told her to shut up. She was my best friend, and it didn't feel right. She looked at me as if I had slapped her.

"I can do it," Mr. Jinn said in the softest voice I had ever heard him use. He pulled out his comb and made long, sweeping motions as he slicked back his hair again and again. "I can do it. But I need your help."

Abra stood up. "If you don't stop it, I'm going to tell his father about your lies. If you don't stop saying these things, I'm telling everyone."

"You think they'll believe you?" Mr. Jinn said, still in his soft voice. "Will you tell them about being attacked by the vultures? Will you tell them about the Amarok?"

Abra's face went empty. No one would believe her. No one would believe any of it.

"So what if you bring her back?" she asked. "What if it works? Do you have to go dig her up out of the ground? Will she still have all that stuff in her from the funeral home? You can't bring someone back from the dead! It's impossible."

At the mention of digging her up, I stood to my feet and stared into her eyes. And in that moment I hated her, or at least I hated what she represented—the end of my hope and the finality of death.

"Don't you dare talk about my mother that way," I said. "It's disgusting."

Fury rose up in me, and I let it take over. It felt good to be out of control, to let that simmering anger boil over, and I could tell immediately that it rose up out of the darkness I had been nurturing inside me. I stared hard at Abra, and the words that came out surprised even me.

"Leave. Now."

And I pointed down the lane.

This time it was worse than slapping her. Her face pulled back, hurt and red. Her eyes filled with tears, like new puddles in a spring rain. She pushed past me, crying for real, sobbing and sniffing and trying to cover it all with a stubborn scowl. Once she was out from under the shade of the old oak tree, the lightning tree, her walk gradually turned to a jog, then a run. At the end of the lane she glanced back toward us, slowed to a walk, and slid out of sight down the long country lane. I watched her the whole time.

"I can do it," Mr. Jinn said, as if none of that had happened. As if Abra had never even been there. "But I need your help."

I looked away from him, up into the lightning tree. "I would do anything," I said, and it felt like a handshake. It felt like an agreement that I would not be able to back out of.

I waited for him to say something, to continue the conversation, but when I looked over at him he was staring at the church. I followed his gaze. Three large, black dogs came trotting up the lane. They looked like German shepherds except they were all black and their noses were shorter. Long, pink tongues hung out between their oversized white teeth. They were the same three dogs that had been in the fight with the groundhogs.

The darkness inside me seemed to swell with the approach of those animals. It felt like a living thing, that darkness, and my insides twisted, the way my mom had twisted a dishrag before she hung it to dry on the spigot. And like that rag, all the goodness was wrung out of me, and I was focused on finding the Tree. Bringing back my mom. That's all I cared about.

The dogs seemed to be headed right for us, and even though the darkness had grown inside me, I still felt fear as they got closer. They looked unpredictable. They looked angry. I glanced up into the tree but knew I could never make it to the first branches without a ladder, so I got ready to run. I looked at Mr. Jinn to see what he was going to do, and I saw him make these subtle shooing motions with his hands. He whispered something, and the dogs somehow seemed to hear him, even from that distance. They curled off to the side, cut through the small pasture back out to the road, and headed the same direction as Abra.

"What are you doing?" I asked.

"They're here to protect us," he said.

"Like the vultures?" I don't know if I meant it to, but it came out as an accusation.

"Now that the vultures know you and I are working together, they won't do you any harm either."

"They were protecting you?" My mouth dropped open.

He didn't reply.

"Did you send those dogs after Abra?" I could feel the edges of panic gathering inside me.

"They won't hurt her," he said. "They're here to protect us."

He emphasized the word *us* as if Abra was no longer *us*. As if Abra was on the other team, and the dogs would do what they needed to do to protect "us" from "her."

"This tree right here, the one where your mother died," he said, as if still trying to explain the presence of the dogs. "There will be more and more coming for it. The Tree of Life is close by. It must be."

I felt heavy inside, sad, and unsure of myself. It was hot and I was still in my nice clothes. The sun moved slowly toward the west, but we had four or five more hours of heat ahead, and even after the sun set the night would be warm. I wanted this to all be a dream. I wanted everything to be the way it had been before lightning struck the tree, before my mom stopped the car so that I could pick up Icarus, before I ran into the antique store and saw the words *Find the Tree of Life*.

"Why will the animals come looking for the tree?" I asked.

His words came out in the form of a spell, a monotone recital of a long-dead incantation. "It's the nature of everything to seek unending life. Nothing, no one, wants to die. And the Tree of Life will be somewhere close to this tree, the one that died."

The words fluttered around us, and they reminded me of the words of the three women in the darkened room, the words I hadn't been able to understand. The living words.

"What do I have to do?" I asked.

"The Tree is important, but we need more than the Tree. We need a suitable container to hold it in, something made of stone. We need the right kind of water. And we need the right kind of sunshine." When it was clear I was more confused than ever, he spat out a list. "Four items. Four seasons. Four rivers. Do you see?"

I nodded, but I didn't see. Not completely.

He shook his head and waved his hand at me. "No matter. All you need to know is this: we need to find the Tree. It will still be small, maybe six inches tall, maybe only an inch or two.

A tiny green thing is all. At first you might think it's a plant." His eyes came alive as he spoke of it, like an old man reciting tales from the glory days of his youth. "It will have two or three small white flowers on it by now. The flowers are important. We mustn't break the flowers."

"Only an inch or two?" I sighed. "It could be anywhere."

He didn't say anything, and I looked closer into every nook and bend of the tree.

"It has to be up there somewhere," he said. "It always forms around or inside the tree that died. Do you have a ladder?"

I hurried to the shed and dragged the extension ladder over, and it banged against the ground, banged against my legs. I couldn't carry it across that stretch of grass without thinking back to the night my mom died, the night I propped the ladder up against the tree and climbed up.

What happened to Icarus? I wondered for the first time. And it felt strange, because I had barely thought of the cat since the lightning had struck and I saw the branch was missing. I didn't think I could care for that cat anymore, not after what it had brought about.

I propped the ladder against the tree and climbed up, then pulled myself into that first nest of diverging branches. I looked for the small tree that Mr. Jinn had described, but I saw nothing.

"A bit higher!" he shouted up to me, so I climbed higher. "A bit higher!" he shouted again, and up I went.

I was so high I started to shake. I didn't enjoy heights. From there I saw Mr. Jinn's house out across the field. I turned and saw Abra's family's farm to the south. I saw the three large dogs sitting in the middle of the road and vast fields of corn waving at me, waving in great green ripples of movement like an ocean. The vultures flew across the valley in a straight line, wheeled in a circle, and continued over to the other mountain. But I didn't see any small tree or plant, either hidden in the branches or anywhere else.

"Nothing!" I shouted down. "I can't go any higher. I'm too big for the branches."

"Fine, fine. Come down," he muttered reluctantly.

I made my way back down the tree, and it was like moving backward in time, back past all of these different choices to the heart of the matter. The beginning point. The beginning of all things. I stood there on the bottommost branches, in that palm of the tree's hand, and I didn't want to go back down. I wanted to stay there, and I wanted Abra to come up to where I was and hang on to my sleeve as she had done at the graveside service.

"Hey," a voice called up to me, and it wasn't Mr. Jinn. "What are you doing up there?"

I looked down. It was Mr. Tennin.

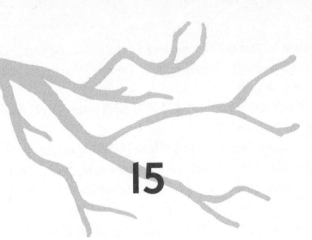

15

MR. TENNIN SHIELDED his eyes from the sun. Mr. Jinn looked annoyed.

"You climbed pretty high. Impressive. I bet you could see a lot of things from the top of that tree."

"Yeah," I said, feeling like a kid caught with his hand in the cookie jar. Mr. Tennin had a kind voice, the type of voice that was so kind it was almost unnerving. I thought back through our brief conversation after lunch about the Tree of Life, and it made me feel uncomfortable. I felt weak for the determination I had shown to bring someone back from the dead, and I felt more than a little foolish for putting all of this hope in someone like Mr. Jinn. He seemed convincing when it was just him and me, but when someone like Mr. Tennin came around, someone so full of kindness, Mr. Jinn seemed like a poor copy.

"I'm going to be moving into your house," Mr. Tennin said, spreading his arms wide the way people do when they make an announcement that surprises even them. "Your father said I could stay in the spare room, the one right next door to yours."

I nearly fell out of the tree. That room had been empty for as long as I could remember. I didn't like going in there because the door to the attic was in that room. I didn't say anything, but I sensed a movement and glanced quickly down at Mr. Jinn. He looked agitated at the news.

"Great," I finally said, but the word came out flat, devoid of meaning.

"I'm going to walk over to the church and drive my car back over here. It's got all of my things in it. I'll talk to you later," Mr. Tennin said.

I watched him walk down the lane in my dad's oversized rubber work boots. They jerked forward and backward as he walked, the way big boots tend to do if they're not tight. He looked all around, taking things in. His hands were halfway in his pants' pockets with his thumbs outside, and his bald head gave off a glare in the sunshine.

I looked to the north. "The vultures are circling again."

"They're helping us," Mr. Jinn said. "They're searching for the Tree." He paused. "You be careful about that Mr. Tennin."

"What do you mean?" I asked.

He waved his hand at me as he did whenever we discussed things he didn't think I would understand. "You be careful."

I looked all around the farm, and I noticed a lot of activity. I saw a groundhog in the far corner of the garden, standing up on its hind legs the way they sometimes do. Then I saw Icarus! He was walking along one of the rain gutters, high up on the second floor of the house. Icarus. My cat. He disappeared behind the house.

I saw the vultures too, still circling.

Up there in the tree, among the twigs and the leaves and the shattered branches, things moved all around me. Squirrels scampered from here to there. A trail of ants followed the scar up, up, up the tree. A large hawk perched in the uppermost branches, surveying the grounds.

So many animals. So much going on around me. I wondered which side was good and which side was evil, because that's how I thought of things—in pairs, with one thing on one side and the other thing on the other. I looked down at Mr. Jinn.

Which side was he on?

Then a small thought caught in my mind like a thorn. What if Mr. Jinn was the cursed angel, the one whose only desire was to possess the Tree? It wasn't the first time that thought had perched in my mind, but it was the first time I had looked directly at it, considered it seriously. Mr. Tennin's story might be real. The Tree might be here.

I took a deep breath, and as I turned around and reached my foot down for the ladder, another question came into my mind, a question I realized I couldn't answer.

Whose side would I join?

━━━

Mr. Jinn went back to his farm to, in his words, "Eat, take a nap, think, and call for more helpers." And when he said the word *helpers*, it sounded like the name of something specific, as if it should have been a proper name with its own capitalized letter: Helpers.

I went back into the farmhouse and thought about Abra, but I didn't let myself think about her too long because it made me wonder again whose side I was on. How could I have ended up on a side that didn't include her? It was lonely, facing an uncertain future without my best friend.

I turned on the television and found a baseball game, but on second thought I left it and walked up to my bedroom. My window was open and somehow that warm July day managed to send a cool breeze in through the screen. Flies buzzed around the window, trying to get in. I lay down on my bed and thought about Mr. Jinn and Mr. Tennin, and I wondered what my father was doing. It was unusual for him not to ask for my help, especially during the summer when I was home from school and bored. Perhaps he thought I should have the day off, the day of my mother's funeral. But I would rather be busy mucking out stalls or bottle-feeding the lamb.

I heard the screen door open downstairs, and then it slammed shut. I knew it wasn't my dad. He never let the door slam like that. He said it was lazy and worked the hinges loose. I heard someone walking up the steps, slow and heavy. Would Mr. Jinn come into our house without being asked?

I walked out into the upstairs hall and waited. Just as the person rounded the stairs I remembered: Mr. Tennin had been going to get his car. He would be collecting his things and bringing them upstairs. And there he was.

"Hi there, Sam," he said in a friendly voice.

"Hi," I said, and it felt awkward having a strange man in the house. I felt like I had to be more careful, but I wasn't sure why.

"Is this my room?" he asked, motioning toward the first door on the right at the top of the stairs. His voice was timid and his eyes were hesitant, as if he was trying to figure out what I was thinking, where I was settling in the whole scheme of things. His eyes gave me the same feeling I got when I first looked at the stars after learning the light that came from some of them was thousands of years old.

I nodded and pointed to the next door. "That's my room. Dad's room is there at the end. The bathroom is the door straight ahead."

"Thank you, Sam," he said in a smooth, quiet voice. He carried his two bags into his room, turned on the light, and closed the door behind him. I heard the lock turn, the smallest click.

I went back into my room and left the door open. Everything felt still, as if the house was holding its breath, but that's probably because I was listening more intently than I usually did. I lay down in my bed. What was Mr. Tennin doing over there? And as I wondered if he knew the door to the attic was in his room, I heard it open.

I knew it was the attic door because every so often my dad would go up there to look for something he couldn't find, and whenever he opened that door, it made a long whining sound followed by a loud snap. When you opened the door the whole way, it popped up right at the end and collided with the door frame.

Lying there on my bed, I heard the long, slow whine and the snap. Very far away, or what felt like it, I heard the slow thudding of footsteps as Mr. Tennin walked up the attic stairs. I didn't envy him that. You couldn't have paid me to go up there. All those spiders and boxes of mice-infested clothing and old keepsakes. My baby clothes were up there somewhere. And my old papers from kindergarten. My mom had kept a box up there with all of my old stuff in it. She could never throw anything away.

I heard him walking through the attic. Soon he was directly above me. The only thing I moved was my eyeballs as I looked straight up above me. I heard him slide a few cardboard boxes around, and they sounded like sandpaper moving slowly over rough wood. Then he slid the boxes right back to where they had been.

At first I didn't know what to think. *Is he going through our stuff? Is he here because he wants to rob us?*

But then I heard him walk back through the attic and down the stairs, and as I heard the door snap and whine all the way closed, I realized what was going on.

He's hidden something up there. He's hidden something very important, because he's worried that someone might snoop through his car or his room and he doesn't want anyone finding it.

He opened his door and walked out into the hall, then peeked his head around the corner of my doorway.

"Have a good afternoon, Sam," he said, nodding his head at me before turning and walking down the steps. I heard his footsteps again, and I was beginning to recognize the cadence to them, the particular rhythm of his movement. The screen door slammed shut.

I darted over to my window, and while I couldn't see him walking through the part of the yard hidden by the rest of the house, I saw his shadow stretching long and thin and moving toward the barns. I waited. I waited some more. I could hear the baseball game announcer still on the television, still talking about baseball in his slow, easygoing, summery voice. One thought took over my mind.

I have to go up there and find out what he's hiding.

So I moved away from the window, walked into the hallway, and stared at his closed door. I reached over, and the knob felt cold in my hand. I turned it, and the door swung open on well-oiled hinges, but the breeze coming in the open window threatened to slam the door shut again. I went into the room and let the door close behind me.

His small, single bed was against the wall that separated his room from my room. Directly in front of me was a window that looked out over the porch roof. Since his room was a corner room, there was also a window to the right. That was the window where I had watched my mom try to rescue Icarus. I had stood in that spot as Abra walked away from the house after my mother was gone. Now I stayed to the side of it and glanced out. No one was in the yard. No one was coming.

There it was—the lightning tree, looking more wilted than ever. I didn't know if a lightning strike could kill an entire tree, as Mr. Jinn claimed it could. Could lightning go all the way down and char the roots under the earth? I didn't know anything about lightning or the life cycle of an old oak tree.

I heard a small buzzing noise and looked up. A hummingbird hung in the air on the other side of the glass, no more than two feet from my face. It was a brownish gray, the size of my fist, and its whirring wings moved so fast that they were invisible. It cocked its head and seemed to be asking me a question, a simple question, one I could answer if I only spoke hummingbird.

Or maybe it wasn't asking me a question—maybe it was trying to read me, trying to figure me out, trying to find out what I was going to do next. I raised my finger up to my lips and said, "Shh." I don't know why, but I did. It flew away in fits and starts, darting here and there and disappearing in the distance. I had the strangest feeling that it had been sent there by someone, and that it would now report back.

Still, no one was coming. I took a deep breath. I didn't like going into the attic for normal reasons, much less to try to find an object hidden by a stranger who had just moved into our house. But I opened the attic door anyway. It whined slowly all the way to the end, where it gave that loud *snap!* I had terrible visions of the attic door closing on me and somehow getting stuck, trapping me in the attic until Mr. Tennin came back. So I pulled his suitcase over and used it to hold the door open.

The stairwell was dark, but I knew there was a light switch

at the top. The unpainted wood steps were worn smooth by many years of rough use, and they were steep and tall so that I had to reach my foot up with each step. A narrow handrail ran the length of the steps, but the screws that held it in place were loose, so if I pulled too hard on it for support, it wriggled in and out of the housings and felt like it would fall out.

Under my bare feet I felt the smoothness of the wood, the way it had been worn down in the middle by a hundred years of footsteps. I stopped at the top and waited for my eyes to adjust, realizing that it was much, much warmer in the attic than the rest of the house. I started sweating immediately. Once my eyes adjusted to the dim light, I found the light switch and flicked it on, but nothing happened.

The bulb was dead. The only other source of light was a small, round window at the end of the attic, and it was covered in a thick layer of dust, like Mr. Jinn's farmhouse windows, so the light that fell through was dim and filtered. I listened carefully, wondering if anyone had come into the house, but I heard nothing besides the normal summer sounds of the farm: some bugs buzzing and chirping, a bird singing, and a tractor engine lurching and working its way through a wet field. They all sounded far off, as if I were in the bottom of a well, listening to a world high above me.

One main clearing formed a path down the center of the attic, and it was flanked by boxes, black trash bags, and huge plastic containers. There were cedar chests and old trash cans full of photos and memories and Christmas decorations. Ghosts from the past. Every so often a narrower cleared aisle led off the main one, an empty alley that gave access to the far corners of the attic. I thought Mr. Tennin must have hidden whatever it was he had hidden at the end of one of those narrow walkways.

I tried to figure out where to walk so that I'd be directly above the corner of my room, where I had heard Mr. Tennin moving things around. I found a small path through boxes that led back into the eaves of the house, toward the corner of my room. I had to turn sideways at some places where the boxes jutted out or the dusty plastic bags reached out to grab me.

The farther back I went down the row, the lower the ceiling, so eventually I had to duck down to avoid the beams. It was very dark. At the end, I had to get down on my hands and knees. Everything was covered in a layer of dust, and cobwebs, real and imagined, clung to my hair. I reached around with my hands, trying to find a few small boxes that I might be able to slide away, small boxes that might have Mr. Tennin's secret stash hidden behind them.

About this time the heat started to overwhelm me. The air felt unbreathable. I thought I should go back down to my room and get a flashlight.

That's when I heard a sound that sent a surge of panic through me. It was a far-off sound, but close enough and familiar enough for me to know that it was inside the house.

It was the sound of the front screen door slamming shut.

PART 3

the Sword

Death is no more than passing from one room into another. But there's a difference for me, you know. Because in that other room I shall be able to see.

HELEN KELLER

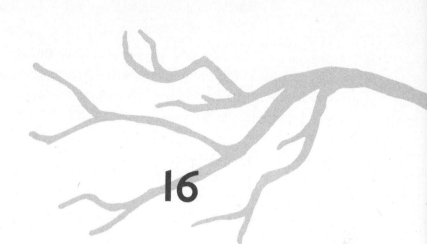

16

THIS IS THE LIFE of an old man whose friends are gone, who lives alone on the farm his father rebuilt, miles north of town. I stare at the large calendar on my desk, the one with an empty block for each and every day of the year. Most of the blocks are empty, except a few with things written in them in pencil, phrases like, "Plant the last of the corn" and "Give zucchini to Jerry." Most blocks, though, are empty white spaces, blank days that repeat again and again.

The block that is tomorrow is filled with one word that I, for some reason, wrote in all capital letters.

FUNERAL.

I look up from the calendar and find my eyes drifting back and forth between two things. One is the beautiful day outside my open window, unseasonably cool for a summer day. I can see the oak tree and the lane and, if I lean to the right, the space where the church used to be. On some afternoons the beauty of this farm overwhelms me, and I can sit and stare at it for hours. Of course, this might also be because I am getting older, and because of all the blank-space days in my life.

My eyes leave the window and focus on the box in front of me, the box I brought down from the attic just this morning, the box I haven't opened for decades. It's covered in years and cobwebs. I wipe some of the dust off the top and it sticks to my fingers, a fine layer.

Ashes to ashes, dust to dust.

I hear a knock at the screen door. I sigh. It's probably Jerry, and it's no good pretending I'm not home because he knows I never go anywhere. I rise slowly and walk to the stairs. He knocks again.

"Coming, coming," I say, and I wonder again why everyone is in such a hurry these days, such a hurry. What are they hurrying toward? What is there out in front of every single one of them that they can't wait to get to? What happened to this present moment?

"Mr. Chambers?" he says again while I'm walking down the stairs. "Samuel? Are you there?"

"For goodness' sake, man." I can't hide the irritation in my voice any longer. "It takes me a while to get to the door. At least allow me that."

I get to the bottom of the steps and walk over to the door, and there I find Jerry standing up rather straight. His son Caleb is beside him, reluctantly. I stare at the boy, and his glance, which at first looked defiant and aggressive, darts away into some corner to hide.

"Hello," I say through the screen without opening the door. I'm not in the mood for people today. Caleb interrupting my pipe smoking the night before took me to the end of my rope. I needed a few days of solitude to gather my strength. Maybe a few weeks. Of course, the funeral is tomorrow, so there is no clear end in sight, and that makes me tired.

Jerry moves his hand to open the door, but it doesn't budge when he pulls on the handle. It's locked. He looks first at Caleb, then at me, and finally back at Caleb.

"I think you have something to say to Mr. Chambers," he says.

I roll my eyes. "Goodness, boy, what now?"

But the boy stares down at the porch floor. His father nudges him with his elbow, but he refuses to look up.

"Is that all?" I ask, moving from the door. "I have other things to do."

"Caleb!" his father says in a sharp voice. I've never heard either of his parents call him by his first name before. I don't think the boy hears it much either, because he springs into full confession mode.

"I climbed up on your roof," he blurts.

I look at his father. "Is that all?"

His father nudges him again.

"To spy on you," he continues.

I roll my eyes again and send out an exasperated breath. "Am I going to have to put an electric fence around my house?"

"And I broke the downspout when I was climbing down," he says, and I can tell he is finished talking because a wave of relief washes over his face.

"Well, I'm sure your father will take care of that." I back away again, trying to pry myself out of a conversation that is going nowhere.

"No, no, Samuel," Jerry says in a determined voice. "Caleb will make it up to you. Of course I'll fix the downspout. But he needs to make it up to you."

Oh, these people and their endless quest to make it right. What scale do they measure by that must always be brought back to level? But an idea comes into my mind. I didn't call for it. I'm not sure where it came from, unless perhaps I've been thinking about it without knowing.

"Fine," I say. "He can come with me to the funeral tomorrow. That can be his penance."

Jerry looks rather shocked. The boy looks terrified.

"Well," Jerry begins, "I'm not sure how that—"

"I see," I interrupt. "I need someone to help me with something at the funeral. But if your offer isn't real, if it is, in fact, a false offer, I'll be going back upstairs, thank you very much." I say the last four words on their own, like a hammer striking a nail, and I turn to go.

"Of course he'll go with you," Jerry blurts out. "Won't you, boy?"

I don't even stop long enough to look at Caleb's face. I'm afraid I may start laughing.

"Eight a.m. sharp," I say, and I leave the two of them standing at the door. But when I get to the bottom of the stairs, I change my mind. I turn around and go back to the door. They are already down the steps and walking through the yard.

"Caleb!" I shout.

The boy turns.

"Come here."

He looks up at his father, Jerry nods his head, and the boy walks back to the door. I bend down as low as these knees will let me.

"Now listen here," I say, and he stares at me, his eyes unblinking. "I need someone at the funeral who can do something very brave for me. Very brave."

"Is it illegal?" he asks, looking mildly interested.

I think for a moment. "I don't think it's illegal. But some people wouldn't like it. Which is why I'm going to need your help."

He looks at me, but he doesn't say anything.

"Do you think you can help me?"

He nods. "Yeah, I can help."

"Bring some of your smoke bombs."

His eyes light up.

⁓

Upstairs, I sit back down at my desk and pull the lid from the box. Inside I find what I expected to find: a pack of articles and an atlas, its margins full of notes and dates and questions, but when I look at the writing I can't tell if it's my own from childhood or someone else's. The small sword is gone. I hoped it would be there. I thought the heat from it would convince me that everything I remember is true. Could it all have been an adventure I made up in my mind? Could it be nothing more than the way Jerry's Boy wanders the farm carrying a sword that is really a stick?

But I have a faint memory of giving it to her long ago. It's like the memory of a dream, but it feels familiar. In any case, the blade isn't there. I put the lid back on the box and slide it to the side of the desk. I pick up the necktie and walk over to the mirror. And I try again to weave that elusive knot.

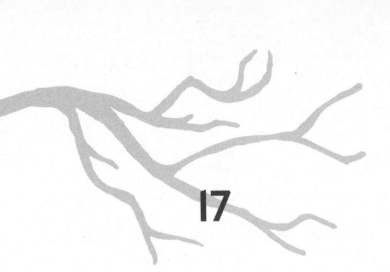

17

AT THE MOST CRUCIAL POINTS in your life, either you move without thinking and accomplish what needs to be done in the nick of time, or you hesitate, the moment passes, and you're left facing an entirely new set of problems. When I heard the screen door slam, I should have raced out of the attic without waiting one moment, pushed the attic door closed behind me, and dashed into the upstairs hallway. Even if Mr. Tennin found me there, breathless and looking very suspicious, he couldn't have proven a thing.

But I hesitated. I tried to think my way out of the situation. Which meant I acted too late.

By the time I got to the bottom of the attic steps I could hear him coming up from downstairs. I pushed his suitcase down so that it wasn't propping the door open, let the attic door close (*whine, snap!*), and retreated back up into the dark, dusty attic, moving as quickly and quietly as possible. I went down the main aisle and slipped back through one of the side paths across from where I thought he had hidden whatever he had hidden. I pulled myself under a fake Christmas tree we kept in a black garbage bag.

And I waited.

I heard him open the door to his room and close it behind him. I hoped Mr. Tennin was just in there to grab something and then head back out to work. But he wasn't. In fact, it sounded like he was going through the entire contents of his two bags. I heard him muttering to himself, and I heard things dropping onto the floor.

The sound of his footsteps moved over the creaking floorboards in his room and toward the attic door. The long whine and the loud snap at the end, and the door was open. The attic ceiling lit up with daylight from Mr. Tennin's room. His heavy, plodding footsteps climbed the steep, tall steps, all the way to the top. Through an empty space between boxes I could see him.

And it wasn't Mr. Tennin.

It was Mr. Jinn.

What was he doing up there? Part of me wanted to jump up and tell him to get out of my house. Who goes into someone else's house without asking? Who sneaks into someone else's attic for no reason?

But maybe he had a reason.

So I stayed quiet, and I watched, and I waited.

Mr. Jinn flicked the light switch and muttered under his breath when the light didn't turn on. He walked down the middle of the attic, opened a few boxes here, moved a few boxes there, but he didn't look very dedicated. To be fair, it was a large attic, and it was dark, and he had no idea where to begin, not like I had. But he did stop when he got close to my row, and I was sure he turned his head and looked right at the bag I was hiding under. But if he saw me, or if he knew I was there, he didn't say anything. He turned around and walked back to the stairs. And he descended.

I heard it again.

The front screen door slammed, but not because Mr. Jinn had left. No, someone else was coming into the house.

I heard Mr. Jinn hurry the rest of the way down the attic stairs, moving way faster than I thought he ever could have moved. He closed the attic door without a sound, which was strange.

Another set of footsteps came up the stairs from the main level to the second level. Meanwhile, I was getting hot. Sweat dripped into the corners of my eyes and off the tip of my nose. The dust stuck to my arms and my fingers and turned to a thin layer of grime. But I didn't move.

The bedroom door opened, then slammed shut, and I heard the lock turn fast. Footsteps dashed across the room and the attic door popped open. The person raced up the stairway, and as he came into the light I could see the bald head of Mr. Tennin.

"Oh my," he said quietly. He sounded worried.

He got to the space in the main aisle just in front of the row where I was hiding. He stopped and looked around. He stared in my direction. I could just see the one side of his face, the side facing the small attic window, and he looked suspicious. But he didn't stop for long. Instead he raced down one of the smaller rows.

I realized I had been searching the wrong area. I watched as he went down that row, moved a few boxes, and stood on them. He reached up onto one of the crossbeams and pulled down a small box. The inside of the box glowed orange when he opened it, as if it had some kind of small, battery-powered light inside. So, that was where he hid it. On top of the beam.

He seemed to take a quick inventory of what was in the box.

He put it back up onto the beam, pushed the boxes into place, and ran back down the attic steps and into his room. I heard him slam the window closed. Mr. Jinn must have climbed out the window.

Mr. Tennin left his room, closed the door behind him, and walked down the stairs. The screen door slammed. I breathed a huge sigh of relief, climbed out from under the fake Christmas tree, and moved quickly down the correct row. I pulled a few boxes out and climbed on top of them, reached up onto the beam, and grabbed the box.

I wanted to open it right there, but I decided that would be best to do in the light of my own room, so I pushed the boxes back in place and walked down the stairs. The box wasn't that large, but I still needed two hands to carry it, and at two different spots I nearly lost my footing and tumbled down the steps. At the bottom, I opened the attic door, relieved to find that it wasn't stuck.

Mr. Tennin's room was a mess—clothes everywhere, papers scattered on the floor, the mattress pulled off the bed frame. Mr. Jinn must have searched the room. For what? Probably for what was in my hands.

I raced through the room, closed the door behind me, and hurried into my bedroom. I locked the door, which I never did, and then ran to my two windows. I closed them, locked them, and pulled the curtains shut. I didn't know how Mr. Jinn had managed to escape through Mr. Tennin's window, but I didn't want him climbing in through either of mine.

I walked to my bed, set the box down, then lifted my shirt and wiped the sweat and dust from my face. The July air in my room felt wonderful and cool compared to the stifling attic. I sat on the bed and pulled the lid off the box.

It was almost dinnertime, and when I had closed and locked the windows I had noticed the sky growing darker in the east, over the church, as though another summer thunderstorm might be rolling in. The upper branches of the oak tree waved back and forth in a menacing manner. But I didn't dwell for too long on the weather. I just wanted to open the box. So I did.

There were three things inside. I would spend the next few days poring over them all with great interest, but I was twelve, so the one that grabbed my attention immediately was a twelve-inch blade that lay diagonally across the top, tied in place with two small leather straps. The hilt and the blade of this small sword were the same dull gray color and appeared to be made of the same metal.

I reached down to unstrap the sword from the box, but when my fingers touched the metal they were immediately scorched. It was like touching the burner on the stove. My thumb, index finger, and middle finger turned red, and each welled up with a tiny blister, like a teardrop.

"Ouch!" I shouted, grabbing my hand. I looked at my bedroom door to make sure no one was coming in.

I grabbed a piece of paper from my small bookshelf and held it against the metal. Nothing. It didn't burst into flame or even smoke. Nothing that I held against that small sword appeared to be burned, or even heated up, in any way. Yet when I tapped the hilt again, this time with my left hand, it was roasting hot to the touch.

Even though it had burned me, something strange happened on my insides. The darkness that seemed to fill me when Mr. Jinn and I were together—that darkness receded. Its presence wasn't as stifling, as suffocating. There was something about the sword that made me feel almost brave. Memories of my mother came and went, but they had joy in them, not bitter sadness. The desperation to bring her back faded.

I turned my attention to the other two items. One was a small book about six inches long by four inches wide. The other was a stack of papers, note cards, and newspaper clippings, all held together in a small leather strap tied in a knot.

The book was thick, four or five hundred pages at least. I picked it up and placed it on my bed, waiting for it to explode or cause my blankets to burst into flames. But nothing happened. Nothing extraordinary.

So I opened it. As I moved through the book, gently turning its light, thin pages, I realized that it was an atlas of the world. There were the occasional footnotes and headnotes, and at the end of a section—each of which spoke about a particular continent—there were various things that each continent was well known for.

But what drew my eye the most were the handwritten notes in the margins. All around the edges of one map, which appeared to be Turkey, I read the following:

Entry 7. The Tree appears to have taken root in a small canyon. Have secured the perimeter. Waiting.

I went further into the book and found more handwritten notes in a very fine cursive script, looping around a map of Iran.

Entry 12. The building has reached forty-three levels. They will now attempt to plant the Tree on a terrace overlooking the city before building higher. The end is near.

The end is near?

Entry 21. Forced to destroy the entire city in order to destroy the Tree. One family escaped.

I felt like I could spend the rest of the day exploring that book of maps with its writing in the margins, but I wanted to see what the stack of papers contained. Once again I tapped the strap with my fingers to make sure the stack of small papers wouldn't burn me. It sounds funny, I know, but the blisters on the ends of my fingertips were painful reminders.

I placed the papers beside the atlas on my bed and looked at the top one for a moment. Some of the newspaper clippings were brown and old, but others looked like they could have come out of yesterday's paper.

"Mysterious Monster of Loch Ness" (October 18, 1933)

"Hitler's Sea Wall Is Breached; Invaders Fighting Way Inland; New Allied Landings Are Made" (June 6, 1944)

What did all of these world events have to do with Mr. Tennin or the contents of the box? What was the meaning of all the writing in the margins of the small atlas? How did that sword stay so hot without burning its way through the leather straps that held it in the box?

There was only one thing to do. I had to take this box to Abra's house—she would know what to do. I cringed as I thought about how I had treated her. The image of her walking down the lane toward her house, staring down at the dirt, was one I couldn't get out of my mind. I pulled a duffel bag out from under my bed and gently placed the box in it with the papers, the book, and the short sword. The zipper barely closed around the box, but it did, and I threw the strap over my shoulder and left my room.

I walked quietly down the stairs, listening for anyone who might be on the ground floor, but I didn't hear anything. Only the television, which was still on. I was so anxious to get to Abra's house that I burst through the front screen door without even thinking to check if anyone was out there.

"Hey there, Sam," Mr. Jinn said from where he sat on the porch steps. Icarus sat on his lap. The cat jumped up when I came through the door and fled under the porch.

"Find anything yet?" he asked.

18

"No, I, uh, I kind of fell asleep," I lied.

He nodded, and his mouth turned into a line of regret, as if he was very disappointed but not very surprised. He pulled his comb from his shirt pocket and brushed his hair straight back, as he always did. He put it back in his pocket. But then his calm demeanor snapped and he thrust his hand straight down. The muscles in his neck and shoulders bulged as his thick hand sent a crack through one of the boards he was sitting on, and the wood made a wrenching sound as it split.

"I am normally a very patient man. But this . . ." He stopped and shook his head back and forth. "This is very important. I thought you said you would do anything to bring her back. Anything."

I put my hands on my duffel bag and clutched it to my side. "I would," I said. "I mean, I will. I just—I have to go apologize to Abra. I think she could help us. She's super smart. I think with her help we'd find it a lot faster. Honest, I do."

Finally he turned and stared at me. He didn't speak for a few moments as he scratched one of his eyebrows with his thumb.

"She's not going to help," he said, as if trying to explain a confusing concept to a child. "She doesn't believe. And even if she did believe, she doesn't think you should do it. She thinks your mother should stay . . . there. Why would we want that girl on our side? Why would we be allies with that kind of thinking?"

He stood and, stepping over the broken step, came up onto the porch. He walked toward me, and suddenly I knew that the topic at hand was not Abra or my mom or even my willingness to help him find the Tree. We were talking about the box in my bag. He knew it. I knew it. And he was coming for it.

I put my hand on the screen door, prepared to run back into the house, but at that moment Mr. Tennin and my father came around the corner of the house.

"Hey there," my father said. "Mr. Jinn. What can I do for you?"

Mr. Tennin looked surprised, almost alarmed. Mr. Jinn cleared his throat and took a step back, away from me.

"Oh, nothing much. Just coming by to say hello to the boy here. See how he's doing after the funeral."

"Very kind of you," my father said, but he didn't sound convinced. He stared at the broken step but, oddly enough, didn't comment on it. Something looked different about him. His face appeared brighter, and the fog in his eyes had cleared. I looked over at Mr. Tennin and wondered if it was because of him. But he didn't meet my gaze—he was staring at Mr. Jinn.

"Actually, Dad," I said, "Mr. Jinn here wanted to hear the story of the old oak tree. The story you told Abra and me the other day? I told him you'd be back in a minute and that maybe you could tell him while you washed up for dinner. Please?"

It was a lame attempt, but I said "please?" with such desperation that my father stared at me for an extra moment and then nodded. I think he could tell something was wrong.

"Sure, boy. If that's what you want."

I nodded, my head moving up and down so fast it's a wonder it didn't fly right off.

"Well, now, that's okay," Mr. Jinn began, but Mr. Tennin interrupted him.

"Come on, Mr. Jinn. Join us! I'm making dinner to celebrate my first night here. We'll pull up an extra chair."

I ran past Mr. Jinn and stood on the other side of Mr. Tennin and my father.

"Actually, Mr. Jinn can have my seat," I said as I continued walking away. "I'm going to Abra's for dinner tonight."

"Okay, boy," my dad said. "But don't stay too late. I'd like you to start helping with chores again tomorrow. We've gotten into a bad habit."

Chores seemed so bland in the face of all that was happening. I was still determined to bring my mother back—I didn't have time for feeding baby lambs and collecting eggs. But there was also something about the fact that my father wanted me to help him that made me think he must be getting better, back to his old self.

"Okay, okay," I said. But as I turned to run, Mr. Jinn called out after me.

"You'd best watch your way on Kincade Road, Sam. People in town said they saw some nasty-looking dogs roaming between here and the fair. Probably the carnies' dogs."

I turned and walked backward for a few steps. Was he threatening me? He shrugged, not looking very worried, and walked into the house. I continued walking backward, away from the house, then turned and ran down the lane, each of my steps kicking up a cloud of dust, small clouds that disintegrated quickly in the stiff breeze coming down from the eastern mountains.

I tired out fast and my run turned into a walk. I had decided not to ride my bike because Mr. Tennin's box was heavy in the duffel bag and I wasn't sure of my ability to ride while balancing it. But walking was slow. Very slow.

The road south of our farm ran along Abra's father's fields, but they were barbed-wire-lined pastures filled with a few hundred dairy cows, their lazy tails swatting at flies, their jaws chewing, chewing, chewing. They never stopped working over their food, not even when they looked up at you through those deep black eyes.

Those cows knew me, and a few of them meandered over to the fence where it ran along the road. I walked over and stopped for a moment, holding my hand out over their heads as if I was blessing them. They tried to lick me, their massive tongues curling out toward my fingers. They made me laugh, those long tongues.

But laughing felt so foreign. I hadn't laughed for days. And I remembered why. My mother had died because of me. Because I had insisted we stop and pick up Icarus.

I sighed and turned away from the cows, feeling torn. Should I continue on to Abra's house, or should I go back and spend what was left of the day looking for the Tree? It felt like time was running out. It felt like, if I was going to bring my mom back, it had to happen soon, or some kind of doorway would close.

That's when I saw the three large, black dogs, the same ones that had been fighting with the groundhog. They sat there in the middle of the road, just south of me. They didn't look aggressive, but they didn't look like nice dogs either. It seemed like they were waiting for me to make a decision, and that decision would determine their course of action. I had to pass them if I wanted to go to Abra's house, and they didn't look like they were going to move.

"Out of the way!" I shouted, waving my hand at them.

I thought about going home. But then it hit me: Mr. Jinn had sent them after me. He didn't want me meeting up with Abra. For some reason he wanted the two of us to remain separate.

I took a step.

The one in the middle bristled, and I heard it growl, a sound that came at the same time as a far-off peal of thunder. The storm approached. Low gray clouds boiled with anger and rolled in overhead. It was getting darker, too, as the day wore on. Large drops of rain exploded on the dusty road. The other two dogs walked around either side of me as if they were distracted, but I knew what was going on. They were surrounding me.

"Get out of here!" I shouted, but they only smiled at me the way dogs can sometimes smile, with their lips pulled back, their teeth bared, their tongues lolling to one side.

The rain came down in stinging pellets, and I knew I was about to get drenched. I was also about to get eaten. One of the dogs snapped at my foot, and I kicked it in the nose. It yelped and growled even louder, coming back in to take a snap at my elbow.

While I kicked that one back, another grabbed the duffel bag and pulled it away from me. The contents of the box spilled onto the ground, and I ran to it in a panic, trying to keep the book and the articles from getting wet. Then I saw that the sword lay in the road.

It looked like it was on fire, and it seemed to be growing larger. The rain wasn't hissing or steaming when it hit the sword. In fact, the rain came down even harder, but the blade and the hilt were writhing in flame, and nothing could extinguish it.

At first the dogs drew around it, forgetting about me at least for a moment. I scrambled backward away from them, getting ready to run for Abra's house, though I hated to leave all that stuff behind.

Then the dogs started yelping and howling. They bit at their own fur as if trying to pull hot embers out of their skin with their teeth. These enormous black dogs were reduced to rolling on the road. It was like the heat from the sword had gone inside them.

They rolled over and over on the road.

Then they stopped moving.

I was both relieved and horrified. Were they dead? I wasn't going to get close enough to find out. But seeing those dogs lying there, I suddenly realized how serious this quest had become.

I stared at the sword. What should I do with it? I couldn't leave it in the middle of the road.

It no longer glowed. It was no longer in flames. I tried to touch it but it was still hot. I bunched up my duffel bag and used it to pull the sword from the earth, then dropped it into the box, nudging it into place. Even through the duffel bag I could feel the heat. I placed the book and the articles back in their spots. They were soaking wet, and I hoped they weren't ruined. I placed the lid on the box and managed to fit the box back inside the duffel bag.

I looked at the dogs. They were actually quite majestic creatures. There was something very old about them, something ancient and mythical. Their fur was a deep, deep black, the night sky around a new moon. I wondered if they had been that mean when they were puppies, if that's how their breed was born, or if they had been trained to attack. I thought I knew the answer. I couldn't bring myself to believe that anything was born evil.

It seemed that evil had to be constructed, usually in the empty places left by pain or rejection or manipulation.

It wasn't too much longer before I arrived at Abra's farmhouse, but I was soaked through. The rain stopped and the sky darkened as night fell. The clouds had spilled over the western mountains, and now hints of a long, slow sunset peeked out from the edges, pink and indigo.

I walked up Abra's long lane and there she was, sitting on the porch alone. She looked tired and sad, but when she spotted me coming up the lane, her face brightened and she hopped up, ran through the wet grass, and hugged me. The light in the sky looked strange, as if it had been strained through many filters and what was left was light without any of the normal impurities. It was like the first day.

"I'm glad you came," she said.

"Abra," I began, "I'm sorry about—"

"Don't worry," she said. "I don't want to talk about that. I have something to show you. You're not going to believe what I found."

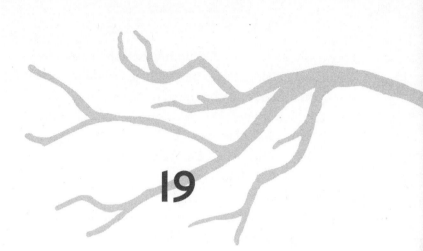

19

She grabbed my sleeve, then my hand, and jogged toward the house, dragging me along behind her. The duffel bag strap dug into my shoulder, and the bag itself banged against my leg as we ran.

"Wait, wait," I complained. "Not so fast. This bag is heavy."

She dropped my hand. "What do you have in there anyway?"

"I brought a surprise of my own. I've been busy too," I said, not wanting to be outdone by her.

"I think you're really going to like this," she said. "I think it's a sign."

Her house was similar to mine, with a large front porch attached to an expansive farmhouse. But their house was made up of two dwellings, and they often rented the other side out. That summer the other side was empty. We would often sneak into the empty half and pretend it was haunted. We would run from window to window, breathless with fear or excitement, until we'd hear her mother's voice calling out that supper was ready.

We walked quickly into the house. I heard Mrs. Miller putting the dishes away, the ceramic plates making loud sounds as they crash-landed into the appropriate cupboards. Her mom was always moving, always busy, and you could tell where she was in the house just by listening.

"Mom, Sam's here," Abra said as we passed the kitchen.

"Hi, Sam," she called out.

"Hi, Mrs. Miller," I said, but Abra pulled me in the opposite direction, into the dining room with its wood floor and echoing, high ceiling.

"I have ice cream if you want," her mom called after us.

"Okay, Mom, in a minute," Abra said.

At the far side of the dining room was the door that led to the empty side of the house. An old-fashioned key was in the lock, the huge kind with oversized teeth on the end. Abra turned the key and the lock clicked. She cringed, and I hoped her mother hadn't heard—her parents didn't really like when we played on that side of the house. We both froze in place, waiting for a voice telling us not to go over there. When none came, she turned the knob and pulled the door open, and we vanished into the other side of the house.

She closed the door behind us and picked up a flashlight. It always seemed so still in the empty side of the house. It felt like we had traveled to another time, another place, where we were the only two people alive. Who knew what kind of world we would find waiting for us if we dared to venture outside? Maybe everyone else had disappeared. Maybe everything was starting over again.

"I kept this here in case you came," she whispered. Light from the dusk outside drifted through the windows, but it wasn't much, and it left the rooms coated in a kind of blue darkness that was difficult to navigate. The flashlight pointed the way, a round circle of light with a dim inner core.

She led us up the stairs. My shoulder was weary from carrying the bag, so I changed it to the other side. We got to the top of the steps and doubled back to the landing to the front bedroom, the one that had a window that looked out over the lane.

"Here, hold this," Abra said.

I dropped my duffel bag and took the flashlight.

"Point it into the closet," she said, so I did.

She walked into the shadows and came out carrying a chunk of log that was almost too heavy for her, about a foot in diameter. She had to carry it with two hands and kind of leaned back as she bore its weight. She carried it tenderly, as if it might break, and placed it on the floor in front of me.

"What's that?" I asked.

She looked up at me, her blue eyes large and expectant. "It's a piece of log from your tree." Her voice came faster now. "The lightning must have blown that branch to bits, because this piece was all the way in our pasture. I saw it when I was walking back from your house."

"Wow," I said, but I wasn't that impressed. I'd seen similar chunks of wood littering our farm after the lightning strike. She treated the branch as if it was holy, as if it was some kind of a sign, but I just didn't get it.

"Look on this side," she said, pointing to the thick end of the log facing her.

I walked around, and then I understood.

First of all, I saw how she could carry such a thick piece of wood. It was hollow. Or at least part of it was hollow. I shone the light into the hollowed-out place of the thick branch, and that's where it was.

A small green thing, no more than three inches tall. It looked like a miniature tree in the winter, without any leaves, except even the trunk and branches were bright, shiny green. And while it didn't have any leaves, there were three white flowers, each the size of a pea, hanging on the tree, heavy and ripe. The branches those flowers hung on were weighed down and looked like they might break at any moment.

"That's . . . that's . . ." I said, unable to speak further.

"Isn't it amazing?" she said. "I've never seen anything like it. I think it's a sign, Sam. I think it's a sign that your mother, she's okay, right? I mean, this is a chunk of the tree where she died, and somehow there's this flower, this beautiful flower inside it, protected? I think it's just beautiful."

She was nearly in tears, and then I remembered. She hadn't heard Mr. Jinn's description of the Tree of Life—what it looked like or where I might find it or what it would need to survive and grow. She had already left before he told me those things. But this was it, for sure.

This was the Tree of Life.

"Amazing," I said, and with that one word I decided I couldn't tell her. I couldn't tell her what I knew, at least not right away. I couldn't show her what was in the duffel bag. I couldn't tell her about the three dogs or the flaming sword, because who knew how she would respond? She might laugh at me or try to convince me not to use the Tree to bring back my mother. She might even hide the Tree, or kill it.

I took in a sharp breath.

She might kill the Tree. I looked at it again. It was so fragile. It wouldn't take much to kill it. Just a deliberate movement of the hand. A swift kick. So much could be destroyed so quickly.

"What is it?" she asked. "What's wrong?"

I shook my head. "I don't know. I just don't know."

I felt evil again. I felt like she was good and I was keeping things from her, so surely that made me evil, right? Darkness spread in me, I could sense it, but I felt powerless to stop it. The only way I could stop it would be to give up on my mother, and I couldn't do that. I couldn't.

I would do anything to bring her back.

Right?

Anything?

"Thanks for showing this to me."

She put it back in the closet. "We can keep it here for now," she said. "Maybe your dad can come and get it in the car. It's kind of heavy."

"I can't believe you carried it all the way here," I said.

"I know! But I really wanted you to see it," she said, suddenly bashful. "So, what do you have in there?"

My mind darted here and there. "You know what? Nothing compared to that," I said, motioning toward the closet. "Nothing at all."

"But I'm curious now!" she protested, laughing. "You can't do that."

"Honest, it's nothing. Just a few old things I found in the barn."

"Whatever it is, it looks heavy," she said, and I was relieved that she seemed content to let it go, to move on. "You should leave it here. I could even lock the closet. When you and your dad come for that log, you can get your bag."

At first I panicked. I thought she was trying to steal it from me, to separate me from the blade and the atlas and the articles. But I calmed myself quickly. She didn't know. She was only trying to be nice.

"Do you think if we locked it in there tonight, I could take the key with me?"

She looked confused. "Sure, I guess. Why? Do you think I'm going to steal it?" She looked bothered, as if she had stubbed her toe on something in the dark, something strange, something she couldn't identify.

"'Course not." I forced a laugh, but it came out sounding hollow. "I just, you know, I really like it. I'd like the idea of knowing that little plant is mine. That the sign is mine and no one else can get to it."

"Okay . . . weirdo," she said, smiling.

We both laughed, and that time I laughed for real. It felt good. There is something about laughing that pushes back against the darkness, even if only for a moment.

"Thanks for coming," she said. "I was hoping you would."

I smiled, and it was genuine, because I had missed her too.

"What are friends for?" I asked, but those words made me feel worse, as if cementing my betrayal.

I clutched the closet door key tightly in my pocket as I got into the car with Mrs. Miller. She had agreed to give me a ride home since it was already dark and I didn't have my bike. They had one of those old station wagons with the fake wood panel that ran down the side. It always smelled like a pine forest in there, thanks to the little green tree hanging from the rearview mirror. It felt strange sitting in the passenger seat with only Mrs. Miller and me in the car.

"How is your father doing?" she asked.

"He's okay," I said.

"And how are you?"

"I'm okay, I guess."

"The funeral was beautiful this morning," she said, wiping

her eyes. She glanced over at me while she drove. "You know, it's okay to be sad. It's okay if you cry from time to time."

Silence. Only the sound of the tires spitting out muddy rocks and the clattering they made on the underside of the car.

I nodded and turned away, looking out the passenger-side window. It was strange how talking about crying made me want to cry. It sounded like something my own mother would have told me, if she hadn't died. But I didn't believe Mrs. Miller. Adults rarely cried. I hadn't once seen my father cry, not in my entire life, not even since the funeral, though sometimes when I came into a room unannounced or unexpected, his eyes were red-rimmed and tired.

No, what she said wasn't true. We weren't supposed to cry. I didn't know why she was trying to tell me any different.

That's when I saw it—a deeper shadow moving against the night. A blackness within a blackness. It stood on the eastern side of the road toward the river, in a clump of trees that led up into the mountain. At first I thought it was only a strange shadow, a trick of the early night. But after we passed it, and just before it went out of my view, it gathered itself, sprang out of the glade of trees, and ran alongside the car.

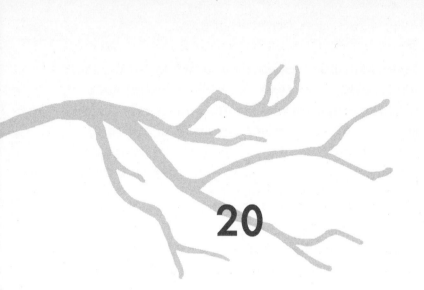

20

I COWERED IN MY SEAT, moving down farther until only my eyes and the top of my head were visible in the glass.

"That's okay, dear," Mrs. Miller said, reaching over and patting my leg. She must have thought I was bent over with emotion after her kind speech about the acceptability of mourning. But that wasn't it. I was scared. More scared than I'd ever been.

The thing that ran along beside us, off the side of the road, reminded me of the three dogs that had attacked me earlier on the road, except it was so much bigger. If it would have stood on its hind legs at the base of the oak tree, its forepaws and head would have easily reached into that small nest of branches where my cat had hidden, where I had stood in that terrible storm. And even though it was running alongside the car, it kept up with us easily. It didn't look tired or like it was trying very hard. It looked like it was loping, running for the fun of it.

Sometimes when I blinked I lost sight of it. It was a shadow within a shadow, a deeper blackness. It was a hole in reality. I couldn't see it. And then I could. And every time I caught sight

SHAWN SMUCKER

of it, every time its shape became recognizable, I ducked down again, fear gripping me.

We slowed to make the turn into my lane, and it stopped in the church parking lot. It bared its teeth at me as we drove away, a silent warning.

That fruit does not belong to you.

I remembered it. The fierce thing that had come to me in my dream, when the fruit kept rotting and I couldn't get a piece of it to my dying mother.

"An Amarok," I muttered to myself, and I realized what it had come for. It had come for the Tree.

I remembered my father's words.

It only devours those who are foolish enough to hunt alone.

"Sam?" Mrs. Miller asked in a kind voice. "Are you going to get out?"

We were parked in the lane, fifty yards from the house. I hadn't even realized she had stopped. I looked in the side-view mirror, backward down the lane, desperately searching for the Amarok. There were strange shadows in the church parking lot, sliding shadows cast by the single flickering streetlight mounted on the corner of the church. But I didn't see anything else.

"Sam?" Mrs. Miller asked again.

"Thank you, Mrs. Miller," I said, trying to contain the fear in my voice. "The ice cream was delicious."

I opened the door and cringed, expecting to feel the savage bite of an Amarok on my leg as it yanked me into the darkness, devouring me after I told it all of my secrets. But nothing happened. I only heard the rumble of the station wagon's engine more clearly, mixed with the summer sound of crickets chirping.

"Are you okay, Sam?" she asked.

I put my foot on the ground. I looked around the car. Every shadow was suspect. Every shadow was an Amarok waiting.

"Bye," I said, but at first I didn't move. I turned and looked at her with what was surely a desperate gaze. "Bye," I said again, dashing from the car and sprinting through the darkness, holding the key in my hand as if it were the one thing that could save me from the Amarok.

"Sam!" Mrs. Miller called out from the car, her words barely fast enough to catch me. "Sam! You forgot to close the door!"

My father's hand shook my shoulder, leading me away from the nightmares. Shadows. The Amarok running alongside our car before hiding in the blackness surrounding the church. The lightning tree exploding over and over again. And there was a key, always a key that I could never find or hide or fit into the lock. A key that slipped from my fingers and fell down, down through the cracks in the floor to a place I could never reach.

"Sam," my father said, shaking me again. "Sam, it's time for morning chores."

I was happy to escape those dreams, and I rolled over and climbed out of my bed without a single complaint. I was also happy to hear my father's voice again. He walked downstairs while I fumbled my way into my work clothes: jeans, holey socks, and an old T-shirt. My boots waited for me in the mudroom inside the back door. I put the key Abra had given me into my pocket, and while the dreams began to fade, that key felt very, very real. I rubbed my finger along the edges of the sharp teeth. I felt the ring at the top, smooth and cold.

I followed the smell of bacon downstairs.

"Breakfast is served," Mr. Tennin said, loading eggs and bacon onto the three plates on the table. He looked wide awake, re-freshed. Had he slept? Did he even need to sleep?

I didn't want to make eye contact with him. I couldn't tell whether or not he knew his box was missing. It didn't seem as though he did—nothing was said about it, and I hadn't heard him up in the attic after I got home the previous night. But he could have easily been up there while I was over at Abra's house. He even would have had time to search my room. On the other hand, he seemed happy enough. Still, it made me nervous even looking at him, so I kept my eyes down, focused on my food, and decided to answer any of his questions quickly, with as few words as possible. For some reason I was worried that he might find the truth somewhere in the sound of my voice.

Thankfully, we ate without talking, but breakfast was still a noisy business of tired breathing and silverware clanking on plates and the sound of chewing. It was a fast meal because there was always too much work to be done and not enough time, and soon our dishes were in the sink and we were walking out the front door into the mostly dark early morning. The eastern sky held a faint glow. The sun would rise in less than an hour.

Mr. Tennin and I followed my dad into the main level of the barn, and Dad turned on the lights. Five or six lightbulbs blinked on, reminding me of the attic, that the bulb up there needed to be replaced.

"Boy, why don't you go back and feed that lamb before I forget about it? Mr. Tennin and I will be up in the hayloft throwing down some hay."

He handed me the bottle and I walked back through the barn, past the cows waking up in their stalls, past the chicken run that connected to a small opening that allowed the chickens free access to the outside world. There in the back corner, where dusty light fell through a small window, I saw the lamb. As soon as it saw me it started bleating and shaking its little tail back and forth, back and forth, as fast as it could. Its face was tiny. Its whole body shook with excitement at the sight of breakfast.

I took the bottle my father had given me and stuck it between the bars. The lamb squatted down, stuck its butt up in the air, and reached up with its mouth, jerking on the bottle and wagging its tail. I laughed and patted it on the head. I thought about how my mom used to love to come out and feed the lambs. She wasn't much for the other farm work, the milking or the mucking out of the stalls. But she loved the lambs.

I thought, too, of Abra. She'd probably like to meet this little guy.

"Yeah, you'll have some more friends before this summer is out," I said quietly to the lamb.

I heard the sound of hay falling down through the large holes in the ceiling as my dad and Mr. Tennin used their pitchforks to shovel it from the upper level of the barn. It made a wispy, hushing sound, and hay dust swirled around in the light.

A shadow fell over the lamb, and at the same time the light coming through the dusty window was blocked out. I couldn't tell what was outside the barn that might be casting such a large shadow, but there was also something behind me. I looked over my shoulder.

Mr. Jinn stood there, his arms crossed, his eyes stern. His presence startled me and I jumped, banging my head on the bars. I looked around, but I had nowhere to run. When I finally caught his gaze, I could tell he wasn't happy.

"Hello, Sam."

"Mr. Jinn," I said.

The lamb jerked the bottle out of my hands. When it hit the

concrete on my side of the bars, the glass shattered, sending milk everywhere. I groaned.

Mr. Jinn looked at the ground and kicked lightly at the concrete, his foot sending up small clouds of dust and straw. He looked back at me, squinting. "I don't get the feeling that you're helping me very much."

"With what?" I asked, but I knew what he was talking about. When I first realized he could help me find the Tree, his presence had filled me with a kind of hope. Leery hope, perhaps, but still hope. Now? He made the pit of my stomach drop. I found it hard to breathe when he was around. I could feel my pulse beating solid and fast in my neck. But right alongside the fear he filled me with was the sense that I needed him. I needed his help.

He stared at me but didn't say anything, so I continued, stammering through whatever story I could come up with.

"Well, it's just that I had to show Abra something last night, and now this morning I've got to do my chores. I don't have much choice with that. But this afternoon—this afternoon I'll spend the whole rest of the day looking for the Tree. Honest. I'm sure we'll find it."

"Oh, I'll find it," Mr. Jinn said. "I always do. But we're running out of time. Your mother is running out of time." He paused and let those words sink in.

They sank in deep, resonating with me, and I had a moment of clarity.

Oh, I'll find it. I always do.

Mr. Jinn was the angel who wanted to possess the Tree. He was the one. A chill spread over my body, tingling in every hair on my head. He was the cursed angel. The realization should have shut down any other plans I had—knowing his true identity should have scared me off. But it didn't. It only entangled me with him even more. I needed his knowledge and I needed him, because he could help me with the Tree.

"This Tree doesn't hang around forever, Sam, and I've waited a long time for this. We've got about ten days from when your mom died until the Tree withers. If we don't find it before that"—he lifted clenched hands, then opened them suddenly—"pow. The small white flowers fall off and it will die, and that will be the end. The Tree will not show up here again. It might not even regrow in your lifetime."

I pictured those white flowers on the small tree Abra had shown me. They were heavy, all right, and weighing down their branches. I could imagine them snapping off at any minute.

"I'll help. Honest."

I tried to erase the images from my mind. I had a strange sense that he could go in there, inside my brain, and help himself to whatever it was I happened to be thinking about.

"I hoped you would," he said, "but I wasn't so sure. So I had to call in the big guns. I had to call in the helpers. Specifically, one helper."

I knew what he was talking about. The Amarok.

"I think you saw him last night on the way home from Abra's house, didn't you?"

I nodded.

"Sam," he said, suddenly very serious, "the Amarok will not . . ." His voice trailed off, and he sighed. I pictured the large shadow loping alongside Mrs. Miller's car, the long tongue, the eyes.

When he spoke again, his words came out with resignation, as if things had moved somehow beyond his power. "The Amarok is not easily appeased. It hunts for one thing: the Tree. It wants to feed on one thing: fruit from the Tree. But anything that stands in the way?"

He raised his eyebrows as if to ask me if I understood. I nodded again.

"It devours," he said with a shrug.

I looked over my shoulder through the dusty window, but that shadow was gone.

"Come to my house when you're finished here," he said. "We have a lot of work to do."

So that's how I found myself just after lunch, walking through the knee-high corn to Mr. Jinn's house. I had lied to my father, telling him that Mr. Jinn had some chores he'd like me to help with. I guess it wasn't a complete lie, but it felt like one. Anyway, my father said I could go but I had to be back in time for dinner and after-dinner chores. I agreed.

As I walked through the field, my own house growing smaller and smaller behind me, I noticed the vultures were circling. All of them wheeling and gliding, occasionally flapping their giant wings, their bare heads barely visible from the ground. They hovered over me as if they were protecting me, or perhaps pointing me out to someone or something.

I left our fields behind and entered the tall weeds, glad for the boots I still wore after morning chores. The small path used to have walking stones, but those were mostly buried by mud and time. I walked up the rickety steps to the porch and knocked softly on the door.

"Yeah," Mr. Jinn said from deep inside the house. "Come on in."

I pushed the door open, walked inside, and reluctantly pulled the door closed behind me. The latch made a loud click, and I stood there for a moment, wishing Abra was there with me.

We have to stay together.

I was so far from that.

"Hungry?" Mr. Jinn asked from the kitchen.

"No thanks. I just ate."

I walked in and sat down in the same chair I had sat in the first time I was there. Mr. Jinn's back remained turned toward me as he chopped something that smelled like onions with a large knife on the counter. The chopping made a solid sound, a kind of knocking that ran around the otherwise silent house.

"How's your friend?" he asked.

Chop-chop-chop-chop-chop.

I grew nervous. I couldn't think of her without picturing the Tree of Life, its small green shininess, its three white flowers. I tried to keep it out of my mind. I worried that if it was there, Mr. Jinn would see it and pluck it out of my head, bring it into reality.

Yet wasn't that exactly what I wanted? Didn't I want Mr. Jinn to have the Tree so that together we could bring my mother back? I thought that was what I wanted. I thought that was why I was there. But something in me hesitated.

"Fine," I said. "She's fine."

He threw a large slab of meat into a frying pan and added the onions on top. It fried and it spit and it hissed, and the rich smell of it filled the house. Still, Mr. Jinn didn't turn around.

Suddenly, I knew that he knew that I knew where it was. And he was angry. And he would get angrier and angrier until I told him. And if I didn't tell him, my mother would be gone forever.

Forever is a very long time, especially to a twelve-year-old boy.

"I know where the Tree is," I said quietly.

He flipped the large piece of meat in the skillet. I thought I recognized it as a slab of liver. I had never liked liver very much.

The texture reminded me too much of sawdust. I was glad I'd eaten before I came. But he didn't say a word. I wondered if he had heard me.

"I know where the Tree is," I said, louder and with more confidence.

"'Course you do," he said, turning to the side and emptying the meat and the onions onto a plate, which he carried to the table and put down with a loud thud. "'Course you do."

He started cutting and the meat was very bloody. Soon the bottom of his plate was nothing but a red pool of onions. He ate like a man who hadn't eaten in weeks, like a man who was eating for the very first time. He savored every massive bite.

"It's in Abra's house."

He stopped. He placed his knife and fork on the table quietly. He leaned back and stared at me, chewing and chewing that bite. When he swallowed, the whole thing went down. I could follow the lump in his throat as the food descended. It was like watching a snake consume a rat that was too big for it.

"That's not good."

"It isn't?"

"No," he said. "That's not good at all."

"What's wrong?" I asked.

"I can't go over there. You'll have to bring it here."

"Bring it here? Can't we go get it together?"

"Absolutely not," he said, shaking his head. "Absolutely not."

We sat in silence. I could tell he was thinking. It seemed he had completely forgotten about the liver and onions cooling on the plate in front of him.

"You'll have to go and get her. Bring the Tree here. Bring her here too. That's what we need."

"I don't know if she's going to—"

"Bring her!" he shouted.

A shadow darkened the dirty kitchen window. I looked through it, but I couldn't see anything.

"Bring her," he said in a calm voice, as if he regretted losing control. "Once she is here, once the Tree is here, we can find the rest of the things we need."

"The rock, the water, and . . ." I couldn't remember the final item.

"And the sunlight. That's right," he said. "But first, bring your friend here. And bring the Tree."

He seemed satisfied. He took another large bite, and the red juice ran down his chin.

I stood up. I knew that if I was going to do it, I would have to do it quickly. "Okay."

I walked out of Mr. Jinn's house and started the long walk to Abra's. It was a mild July day, and I realized the shadow I had seen in the window had not been from a storm cloud. The sun shone in a clear, blue sky. But I felt a darkness surround me, and the vultures came again, circling high above.

21

ONCE I WAS ON THE ROAD, everything seemed less mysterious. Without the thousands of rustling cornstalks all around me, the day took on an almost boring note. The July heat came up off the stones like a mirage. Even the cemetery and the church, both vacant, seemed drab and normal.

Soon I walked the stretch where the dogs had attacked me the day before. But again, the earth seemed to deny that anything supernatural had ever occurred. I wondered what had happened to the dogs' bodies. I thought about the tiny plant in the log, and it all seemed silly and impossible.

By the time I arrived at Abra's house, I fully expected us to find the closet empty. Maybe there was no Mr. Jinn. Maybe there was no Mr. Tennin.

Maybe my mother had never died.

Yet when I walked up Abra's driveway and slipped my hand into my pocket, there was the key. The skeleton key that would unlock the door. It was hard and metal and very, very real in my pocket. I knew that all of it had happened, every last strange thing, and in that moment I also knew that I would have to make a choice soon about what I was going to do with that Tree, a very real choice that would have very real consequences.

        —

Abra's baby brother was crying when I knocked on their front door. I walked in without anyone answering or inviting me in.

"Hello?" I called out to the house.

Mrs. Miller came into the room, carrying the baby. I could never remember his name. He cried a lot.

"Hi, Sam," she said with an apologetic smile. "Abra went out with her father to the milk barn. She'll be back in a minute. Can I get you a drink?"

"No thank you," I shouted over the loud cries of the baby.

"Oh my. Oh my," Mrs. Miller said to the baby. She placed him on one of the sofas, on his back, and looked over at me. "Would you watch Francis for just a minute? I have to run upstairs for something."

That's right. His name was Francis.

"I'm not so sure," I said.

"Just one minute. I promise. Here." She waved me over. "Sit here, like this, and make sure he doesn't roll off."

I walked to the sofa, but I didn't want to watch the baby. Babies were breakable, like fancy glasses with stems.

"Oh, stop it," she said, laughing at my hesitancy. "You'll be fine."

She was off and I was left sitting there on the edge of the sofa, my skinny, twelve-year-old legs the only things that separated the baby from a long fall and certain death. But he clearly didn't appreciate the crucial role I played in keeping him alive, and he kept crying.

"Francis," I said in a singsong voice. "Francis. Stop crying. Stop crying."

For a moment his cries grew even more shrill, making me even more nervous, but then his eyes caught mine, and he stared up at me. His mouth uncurled, smoothed out. His eyes went from that squinty crying position to wide open, though still filled with tears.

I looked down and understood what it was about babies that so fascinated people. Inside those bright blue eyes, eyes that reminded me of Abra, I saw the essence of life. A spark resided there that could not be explained biologically. It was life, and it was moving and beautiful and a little scary, like a flash of lightning or a fish showing its shiny self for a moment in a fast-moving river.

Francis looked up at me and, as if disappointed by what he found in my own eyes, started crying again. This time a louder, more persistent cry than before. Abra came running in the front door.

"Francis?" she called, dashing over to where I sat.

"He's crying," I said, shrugging.

"Is Sam being mean to you?" she asked the baby, picking him up.

Mrs. Miller came down and reached for Francis. "Aw, you poor thing. Thanks, Abra. Thanks, Sam."

Abra looked at me and raised her eyebrows, wondering why I was getting any praise.

"Hey," I said, "I was watching him."

"Is that what you call that?"

"I'm taking him up for his nap," Mrs. Miller said. "You two have fun. And be careful." She looked at Abra. "Your father found an enormous set of tracks by the river. He's still not sure what it might be. So stay close to the house."

She walked up the stairs, carrying little Francis, who by now had stopped crying and was sucking on his fist. He looked over at me with obvious contempt. Or at least that's what I thought I saw.

Once Mrs. Miller had disappeared upstairs, Abra looked over at me. "Want to go see it again?" she asked.

I nodded.

"Did you bring the key?" she asked.

I reached into my pocket and held it up like it was the answer to every question anyone had ever asked.

———

The feel of the correct key turning in a lock is a satisfying feeling. I pulled the skeleton key back out of the slot and looked at Abra before turning the knob and opening the closet door. Everything was where we had left it. The log was back in the shadow, the hole facing away from us just as I had placed it the night before. The duffel bag sat on the other side of the closet, the square edges of the box visible.

"There it is," I said, not knowing what else to say. I walked into the closet, picked up the log, and carried it out into the room. It was heavy. I wasn't sure how I would carry it all the way to Mr. Jinn's house.

"Oh no," Abra said in a sad voice, pointing to the hollow side of the log. "That little plant is gone."

I practically dropped the log and looked upside down into the end where the Tree of Life had been the night before. Nothing. I turned around, got down on my hands and knees, and peered deep inside the log, hoping that maybe it had fallen in further. But there was nothing there, nothing except the rich dirt and small patch of moss that I pulled out and held in my hands.

I thought I was going to cry. Every dream I had ever had about my mom returning evaporated into that hollow log.

"It was so pretty," Abra said. "But it was a sign. Your mom is watching over you."

No! I wanted to shout. *No! That was the thing that would make my life normal again. It would bring back everything I've lost!* That little plant was what I needed. I had to have it.

But it wasn't there. It wasn't dead, at least not in the log. Someone must have taken it.

Who?

I stared over at Abra. The darkness that had moved into my soul flared up.

"Did you take it?" I asked.

She looked hurt. "Take it? I gave it to you! I gave you the key to the closet. Why would I take it?"

The darkness subsided. She was right. If she had wanted it, she could have chosen never to show it to me. And she didn't even know what it was.

"What about your parents?" I asked. "Were they in here?"

"They never come over here," she said. "Why are you so paranoid? Why would anyone even want that thing? It was pretty, but that was it. It was just a flower."

I sat down under the weight of loss and shook my head, and before I could stop them, the words came pouring out.

"It wasn't. It was the Tree. The Tree of Life. Mr. Jinn told me to bring it to him so that we could bring my mom back. He said he could do that."

I wondered what she would say. I knew she had been skeptical from the beginning. But her response surprised me.

"So what's he going to do if we don't have it?"

"You believe me?"

187

"What's he going to do?"

"He won't be happy."

"Were you going to tell me, or were you just going to take it to him?" she asked.

"I don't know," I said. "I didn't know what to do."

She sat down on the floor beside me. We both stared into that empty log for a long time. And strangely enough, I felt a small seed of peace.

"So what's in the bag?" she asked.

I stared at it. The box seemed suddenly important again. Even without the Tree, I was left with something. Maybe something in there would lead me to it. Maybe something in that box would put the whole thing back on track.

"This has been one crazy summer," I said, looking over at Abra. She smiled, and it made me smile.

"What's in the bag?" she asked again, this time punching me in the shoulder, but not very hard.

"You're not going to believe it," I said, shaking my head. There was nothing believable about that summer. Not one single thing.

I pulled the bag over to where we were sitting. Everything seemed to grow serious, but the sun still shone in the window. The empty half of the house we were in felt even emptier. I felt like I always did on that side of the house, like we were the only two people in the entire world. But maybe that wasn't it—maybe we were the *first* two people in the whole world, and this was the first day.

"You're not going to believe it," I said again as I pulled the zipper back and lifted out the box.

"Try me," she said, staring as I drew the lid back.

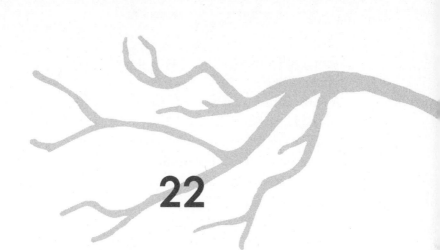

22

THE SWORD SEEMED LARGER SOMEHOW. I didn't know why. But there it was in the box on top of the atlas and the clump of news clippings and notes. More than anything, though, the sword felt significant. In my mind, it had replaced the missing Tree as the thing I must hang on to. I wasn't sure why.

Movement across the window caught my attention, but when I looked up I didn't see anything. I walked over and looked through the glass. The vultures circled high overhead. I must have seen one of them as its dark shape passed by. I was tired of seeing them. I wanted them to leave.

"The vultures are still out there," I said, turning back to Abra.

She was sitting there quietly, holding the sword and running her fingers over the blade.

"Abra!" I shouted, taking three quick steps toward her. She backed away from me, holding the sword by its small hilt. The blade was short, but for her, for both of us really, it was almost long enough to be a normal-sized sword.

"What?" she asked, inadvertently pointing it at my gut.

189

I stared at her hands. "Isn't that . . . doesn't that hurt?"

"Hurt? Why?"

"It's not burning your fingers?" I asked.

She laughed. "No. Why?"

I reached out for it. She stretched out her arm to give it to me. But as soon as it touched my fingers, it burned me again.

"Ouch!" I said, jerking my hand away.

"What?" she asked. "What's wrong?"

I shook my head. I didn't get it.

"That thing burns me if I touch it," I said. I showed her the red marks on my fingertips.

"Really?" she said, looking it over, staring down the sharp edge of the blade. "What else is in your box?"

I could tell she was excited, that she thought we were on the edge of something. The strange nature of the sword definitely got her attention.

Some of the things had gotten wet when I brought the bag over, and now they had that crinkly, dried-again look to them. But nothing had been permanently damaged, and all the papers I saw were still readable.

I showed her the atlas and we started scrolling through the pages. There were at least one hundred pages with notes on them. Some of them were places we knew or at least had heard of, like New York City or Jerusalem. But there were also strange places and names that felt ancient. Meshech. The land of Havilah. Miletus. The places that had smaller numbers beside them tended to be the ones we didn't recognize, while the pages that were numbered in the sixties and above were places we knew about.

"What do you think this is?" I asked her. "And why all of the numbers?"

"It looks like the kind of map someone would keep of their

journeys. Maybe they went to all of these places and numbered them?"

"All the places with numbers beside them?" I asked. "You'd have to be super old. Or super rich. Or both."

She nodded. "Yeah, but why else would you number different places?"

I skimmed through the atlas. "Maybe they're all places the person wants to go?"

She shook her head. "No. A lot of the notes are observations. Whoever took the notes had definitely been there. In person."

"If you were traveling to all of these places and you were going to number where you went, wouldn't you go to the closest place next? This person looks like they were skipping all over the world for no reason. Look here, in Turkey—#1 and #46. Why wouldn't you do those #1 and #2? Or #45 and #46?" I looked at her with my eyebrows raised, as if I expected her to have an answer.

"I don't know, Sam," she said, sounding frustrated. "I don't know. Why would *you* skip all around?"

I thought for a moment. "I guess if you didn't know where you were going next."

Her eyes lit up. "Or if you weren't in charge of where you were going next—"

"Or if someone else was telling you where to go!"

"Yes! That's it," she said. "Mr. Tennin works for someone else, some huge, rich, important company. Probably an oil company or something. And they send him all over the world to do his job!"

"With a short little sword," I said, unconvinced. "And a pack of old newspaper clippings."

Abra frowned at me. "I think we're onto something," she said. "It kind of makes sense."

"Maybe."

"Let me see those." She gestured to the papers.

I handed the entire wad to her—it was probably about an inch thick. She unwrapped the rubber bands and started spreading the articles on the floor in front of her. Some of them were stuck together from getting wet, and we had to gently peel them apart. Some weren't from newspapers but were old note cards with writing in foreign languages. Some were in English and some weren't. But all of them—the newspaper clippings, the note cards, the torn-off pieces of paper—had a number written in the top corner.

"Hey, careful," I said. "What if they're in some kind of order? Mr. Tennin's not going to be happy about us messing it up."

"That's it!" she said. "In order. Sam, look up this place." She handed me the atlas.

"What place?" I asked.

"Look, an article about a tree called L'Arbre du Ténéré."

She paused, and I saw her gaze flitting down the small newspaper clipping.

"It was the most isolated tree in the world, 250 miles from any other tree! A Libyan truck driver ran it over." She looked up at me. "Look, here's the number on the article—60. Can you find the Sahara Desert in the atlas?"

I looked in the back and found a page number for the Sahara. I scrolled through the book until I came to the page. There, in tiny script, right in the middle of the desert, was a number. #60.

"You figured it out," I said in a solemn voice.

"Let's try another one," she said with excitement. "How about this? It's another article with a number in the top corner." She skimmed over the note card. "Okay, this one is about a tree too. Its name was Prometheus and it was almost five thousand years old!" She looked up at me again, amazement on her face.

"Go on," I said. "Then what?"

"It was in the White Mountains of Nevada, and it was the oldest living thing on the planet. A graduate student was given the responsibility to count the rings." She paused, reading some more of the article. "But instead of taking a core sample, the student requested to have the tree cut down? And the park service agreed! That's ridiculous. Why would they give someone permission to cut down a five-thousand-year-old tree?"

"What's the number?" I asked.

"Sixty-two," she said.

I looked up the White Mountains in the atlas. Right there, along the mountain range, was another number.

#62.

She looked up at me, and I could tell she was connecting the dots. She spread out all the articles and note cards.

"Every single one of these is about a tree, either a really old tree or a tree that was vandalized or destroyed. At least the ones that are in English." She held up a note card written in some kind of strange slanting script that neither of us could read or understand. "So, what kind of a company would send Mr. Tennin to places with trees like that?"

"A tree company?" I asked.

She rolled her eyes. "I don't think so."

"How about one of those preservation societies—you know, the ones that try to save the environment?"

Abra didn't look convinced. "I don't think so," she said again.

What was the connection between the contents of Mr. Tennin's box and us? Where did he come from? Why was he here?

"What if he's here because of the lightning tree?" I asked quietly.

Abra looked at me. "What do you mean?"

"Well, what if my grandfather's oak tree is another tree that's been damaged, and that's why he's here?"

"That might be what brought him here, but we still don't know why he does this over and over again," Abra said. We were thinking on the same track. "Here's a question. If he's here for another company, why is he pretending to work for your dad? He doesn't need the work, not if he's working for this business that has enough money to send him all around the world."

"So he's lying," I said. I felt justified in stealing his box, and that gave me a certain sense of relief.

Abra nodded. "He's here for something else."

"The Tree of Life," I said without even thinking. Our eyes met. "He's here for the Tree of Life."

I thought about Mr. Jinn's words again, when he had said that he'd find the Tree. That he always found it.

"Mr. Jinn is the angel who tries to find the Tree. The one from Mr. Tennin's story."

Abra stared at me, curiosity mixed with excitement and a little bit of skepticism covering her face. "And?"

"Maybe Mr. Tennin is the other one. The angel whose job it is to find the Tree and destroy it before anyone eats from it and lives forever."

We knew this was serious.

"Maybe one of them already stole the Tree from the closet," Abra said.

"Could they have come in here?"

"I doubt it," she said. But neither of us felt safe anymore.

I looked out the window. "It's getting late. I promised Mr.

Jinn I'd bring you and the Tree to his house this afternoon. But I have to be home in time for dinner and to help with chores."

I couldn't decide what to do. If I didn't go back to Mr. Jinn's house, it would seem suspicious. But what would he do if I went back without the Tree? Without Abra?

"I don't think you should go back there," she said. "I don't think it's safe."

"Me neither."

We sat there quietly for a moment.

"We have a lot to figure out," I said. "But I have to go home. Can we leave everything here, locked in the closet?"

"Do you think it's okay here?" she asked. "The Tree was stolen from there."

"Do you have any other good hiding places?"

We went into a different room and found a different closet with a key in the lock. It didn't feel completely secure, but we didn't know where else to put the box, and I didn't feel right carrying it home with me, so close to the clutches of Mr. Tennin. He had seemed so nice, but now that I knew he was lying about why he was here and that he would do anything in his power to destroy the Tree, everything about him seemed dark and twisted.

I gave Abra the old key. There wasn't any reason for me to take it. She was in on this now. We were in this together. It felt comforting not having to bear everything on my own. But I still wondered, if it really came down to it, would she help me bring my mom back to life?

I told her about the three dogs that had attacked me on the road and the Amarok I had seen running alongside her mother's car.

"I'll come back tonight," I said, "after my chores are finished. Around eight?"

"Yes," she said, "but be careful."

"Don't worry, I'll get my dad to give me a ride. Don't walk onto our property unless it's an emergency," I said. "I think it's safe here, on your farm, but I'm not sure why. Mr. Jinn said he couldn't come here, or at least he didn't want to come here."

"Be careful," she said again.

She led me back to the side of the house where her family lived. I said good-bye to her mother. When her baby brother saw me, he started crying again. I rolled my eyes at him.

⁓

Mr. Tennin ate his dinner up in his room that night, so it was only Dad and me at the table. He had sunk back into a state of despair about my mom, so he wasn't saying much. Actually, he wasn't saying anything. We ate in silence, and he didn't ask me about Mr. Jinn or what the man had wanted me to help him with.

After dinner we went out to the barn and I did my chores. Mr. Tennin came out and worked mostly with my dad. He didn't say anything either. It felt strange. Why wasn't anyone talking? Why was everyone being so quiet?

Not only that, but I kept looking over my shoulder, waiting for Mr. Jinn or the Amarok to show up. I knew the Amarok would devour anything that came between it and the Tree. I wasn't necessarily between it and the Tree, but Mr. Jinn might think I was. What if he sent it here to devour me?

I stayed close to my dad all evening.

Finally, my part of the chores was nearly finished. All I had to do was get this bottle of milk into the lamb and I'd be free. My dad was in the cow stalls, shoveling out the manure. Mr. Tennin had vanished.

"Dad, could you drive me down to Abra's?" I asked.

"Drive you? Since when do you need a ride there?"

I shrugged. "I don't know. I thought it would be quicker."

"Sorry, boy, I don't have time to drive anyone anywhere tonight. Just ride your bike or walk."

Mr. Tennin spoke from the shadows. "I'll drive you down. I don't mind."

I shuddered. The lamb finished its bottle and I placed it up on the shelf.

"There you go, boy," my dad said. "There's your ride. Thanks, Mr. Tennin."

I didn't know what to say. For once I wished that Mr. Jinn would come walking in and interrupt us like he always did. I could go with him and he would probably—maybe—keep me safe from the Amarok. But I didn't have much choice. I didn't trust going in the dark all the way to Abra's house. I'd have to let Mr. Tennin give me a ride.

"Okay," I said.

"When do you want to go, Sam?" he asked.

"Whenever you're ready."

"Okay." He turned to me with a large smile. "Let's go now."

PART 4

the fire

Then Aslan said, "Now make an end."

C. S. LEWIS, *THE LAST BATTLE*

23

I FIGHT WITH MY TIE AS BEST I CAN, and it doesn't feel like a dress rehearsal anymore—this is the real deal. Somehow I manage not to strangle myself in the process, and it is crooked and a little lumpy, but no one will notice. That's what I tell myself. No one will notice the crooked tie of an old man, even if he is attending the funeral of his last friend. Perhaps they will simply see it as a sign of my profound grief. I make my way downstairs.

Dress shoes have always put me in a bad mood. Maybe that's why I stopped going to church some years back. I hated wearing those black shoes. I despised shining them, the smell of the shoe polish, and the way it got all over my hands. They pinched my heels and grated against my bony ankles, and they never felt quite right. I was always aware of them, which is perhaps the worst thing that can ever be said about a shoe. A good shoe isn't even there. You completely forget about it.

Anyway, I walk down the stairs in my pinching dress shoes and am surprised to hear a knock at the door. There's Caleb, dressed up and ready to go to the funeral. I hadn't actually expected him to show up. I look past him, out toward the barn, and his father is in the car, waiting to drive us. I nod at Caleb.

"Hello," I say.

"Hi," he says. That's it. His one-word response is almost as surprising as the fact that he showed up, on time.

"Did you bring your smoke bombs?" I ask.

He nods.

"And this. Can you carry this for me?" I hand him the old box. "It's very fragile. You'll have to be careful."

"Okay," he says, and I wonder who has possessed the body of this boy who used to wield his words like weapons.

"Okay," I say. "Well, let's go."

No one talks in the car. In my experience, no one ever talks in the car on the way to a funeral. What is there to say in the face of death? What is there to say when we are forced to remember that we have come from dust, and to dust we shall return?

"Careful," I say to the boy holding the box as we hit a bump on Kincade Road. It's paved now, the road to town, and Jerry drives faster than we ever drove down that straight stretch. The stones used to jump up and bite the bottom of the car, but now the only sound I hear as we fly down the road is that constant whirring. It reminds me of the river, or of eternity.

We get close to town and pass the park where they still set up the fair every year. The old dusty paths have been paved, and I don't think the carnies are allowed to camp out at the bottom of the hill anymore. The Darkness seems less, or at least it seemed less the last time I was at the fair, fifteen years ago or so. But it's still too early in the summer for the fair, and the park is abandoned.

The town comes up Kincade Road a little farther than it used to, but other than that not much has changed. A few of the restaurant names are different, and the houses look tired, but Pelle's Antiques is still there at the crossroads, run by his grandson, if you can believe that, who is not much younger than me. I wonder if that old back room is still there. I wonder what they ever did with that table the old woman scribbled on.

Find the Tree of Life.

Jerry says he will wait in the car.

"I'm not a fan of funerals," he says, looking away awkwardly because he realizes the obvious nature of his words. Who is a fan of funerals? Caleb and I walk toward the church, and there are a few dozen other people making their way through the parking lot. They wear black and carry a heavy burden on their shoulders, and it is strange for me to think that I could have perhaps stopped all of this from happening with the Tree of Life. All of this death. All of these heavy burdens.

What would these people say to me if they knew I could have stopped death in its tracks?

The boy carries the box, the dust leaving marks on his shirt and his clip-on tie and the lap area of his black dress pants. The contents rattle around inside as he walks, and I know he is desperate to look inside. I stop him before we get too close to other people.

"This is what I need you to do," I say, then whisper in his ear.

He shrugs. "No big deal. But where should I go after I do it?"

"Hide somewhere," I say. "Or go out and get in your father's car. But don't leave without me. I don't have any other way of getting home."

"Okay," he says.

I hold the dusty box on my lap and sit at the front right-hand side of the church. The preacher is a tall man with blond hair and kind green eyes. I have never seen him before, but that doesn't surprise me since I rarely leave the house—I just don't have much desire to get out. I go into town when I must. The only person I considered looking up was Abra, but after so many years of not being in touch, picking up the phone and calling her felt awkward, or somehow inappropriate. And now, well, that's gone.

The preacher seems to have been personally acquainted with the deceased, and emotion keeps leaking into his voice while he talks. The church is not as full as I thought it would be, but of course we are old now, and nearly everyone we knew growing up has left. She has a family, which accounts for most of the people there. I look around as the preacher's voice trips and skips, and I wonder who, if anyone, will come to my funeral. I can't think of a single person.

The casket is open at the front of the church, and some people walked by it before the service began, but I didn't have the heart. I didn't think I was ready to see her. Not yet. I grip the box tighter on my lap, and I shake it slightly to make sure the things are all still inside. The woman beside me gives me a nasty look for making so much noise. Some people.

The preacher keeps talking, and his voice fills in the empty spaces of the room. I look for her husband, and I see him sitting at the very front, to the right of the aisle. I can't remember his name for sure, but I think it might be John. Or Simon.

My heart starts to race, and I wonder if maybe the plan I came up with wasn't the best idea. Maybe I should have simply spoken with her husband, asked permission. Maybe he wouldn't have minded. But as I decide to walk out, find Caleb, and abort the plan, I hear the ear-piercing sound of the fire alarm going off. I sigh. Too late.

The people look around nervously at each other the way people always do when a fire alarm first goes off. Everyone wonders if it is just a drill, if it's a sound that can be overlooked. Lights flash brightly in the church, and the pastor looks around uncertainly. Just as he is about to reassure everyone that they can stay where they are for the time being, smoke pours in over the balcony and billows through the back doors.

Someone screams.

Everyone stands together, and the pastor tries to guide them with his voice, tries to calm them, but they are frantic, as most people are when facing death. Panic and pushing and shouting. Soon the smoke is thicker, but it is settling into an empty sanctuary. Everyone except for me has left.

I walk over to her coffin, and there she is.

Abra.

She is still as beautiful as I remember, though I haven't seen her for years. Her hair is white, the color of frost, and her skin, though old, still holds something of her youth. Her nose reminds me of how stubborn she could be, and I wish I could look into her eyes again, see those sparks fly during a disagreement or the way they softened in friendship.

Our last encounter is one I'd rather forget, one full of questions and doubt. I felt she had forgotten me, and perhaps she had, but it was no excuse for the things I said. She only stood there and took it, and we parted with a painful silence. Now there is only this: her closed eyes, her folded hands, and me, wishing there was a way to follow after her.

I pull back the blanket that lines the coffin and place the box inside with her. Where it belongs.

Outside the church, the crowd mills around. Their voices are full of chatter, and everyone wants to know what's going on, but as the minutes pass their curiosity dies down and they form small groups of people, friends and family. They make small talk—the weather, the town, the baseball season. They fill the morning with words because the silence is unbearable.

I decide suddenly that I have had enough. I got what I came for—a last view of Abra and one last gift from me to her. I weave my way through the crowd, trying not to push my cane down on anyone's toes.

I feel a hand on my shoulder. The pressure of fingertips. I turn around.

"Excuse me, are you Samuel Chambers?"

It's Abra's husband.

I nod, wordless, expecting to be charged (and rightly so) with disturbing her final peace. What right did I have to put things in her coffin, objects that would remain beside her body for decades to come? But he does not say what I expect. In fact, he hands me a small box of his own, and he gives me a sad smile.

"This is from Abra," he says. "She wanted you to have it."

I nod again, clear my throat to speak, but find there are no words waiting to come out. So I turn and walk away, wishing I would have asked him for his name.

I get to the car and climb in. "Thank you, Caleb."

"Sure," he says. "What's that?"

I look down at the box again. "I'm not sure," I say. "I haven't looked inside yet."

Jerry turns on the car and drives away.

24

I FOLLOWED MR. TENNIN out to his car, and something inside me was saying, "Run!" But I didn't listen. I crawled into the passenger seat of his old black car, and he started it up. The engine rolled over a bunch of times before catching, and it sputtered and spat before settling into a rhythm.

"There we go," Mr. Tennin said in his soft voice. He put the car in reverse, backed out of his space in the grass beside the barn, and drove down the lane toward the road.

I kept reminding myself that it would only take four or five minutes to get to Abra's house, and I resolved to say as little as possible. I didn't know how I'd answer if he asked me about the box with the blade and the atlas and the articles. Who else would have it? But then I remembered Mr. Jinn sneaking around Mr. Tennin's room and even going up into the attic. Maybe Mr. Tennin knew that Mr. Jinn was spying on him. If he did, he probably thought that Mr. Jinn stole the box, which put me in the clear.

I stared hard out my window and into the empty darkness of Abra's family's pastureland. I knew the cows would all be in the barn for the night, but still I peered into the shadows, thinking about the Amarok. I wondered if I would be safe walking from the driveway to the house. I imagined it jumping on top of the car and ripping through the roof, tearing Mr. Tennin and me to shreds.

As we got to Abra's long lane, Mr. Tennin pulled the car off to the side of the road so that two of the tires were in the grass. Then he turned off the car. It was so dark I could barely see his face. I felt for the door handle, getting ready to yank the door open and run for my life.

"I wouldn't do that," he said quietly. "You know as well as I do that it isn't safe out there tonight. Not for anyone."

He looked at me in the darkness, and I knew that he knew everything. He knew what was going on with the Tree. He knew the Amarok was on the loose. He knew about Mr. Jinn and probably even about the box stashed in an old closet in the empty side of Abra's house.

"What do you know?" I asked, trying to stay calm. I surprised myself with how steady my voice came out.

"I know much more than you do, so that's a start," he said. He continued with something like reluctance. "I know Mr. Jinn is searching for the Tree of Life. I know you would like to find it in order to bring your mother back from the dead. I know the Tree is on your property because of the sacrifice your mother made, and because of the presence of an honorable, dead tree. I found the remains of three large, dead dogs in the woods, so the time is almost here. Perhaps worst of all, I've seen the shadow of the Amarok." He paused. "There are many other things that I think I know but am unsure of. I'll spare you all my guesses."

His straightforward answer came out full of truth. He didn't seem worried at all by what I might do with the information.

For the first time in my life I realized the power of truth and of truth telling, how knowing and telling the truth will always give you the upper hand over someone who is being malicious or deceitful or even simply withholding information. But I was too afraid to tell the truth. It's always one fear or another that makes us lie.

"I have the Tree, but I don't want it only to bring my mother back," I lied. I felt that old darkness stir inside me.

"If you don't want it," he said in a kind voice, "give it to me."

Even though his words were kind, they also held power, a terrible power that I feared almost enough to rival my fear of the Amarok, and my hand moved to the door handle again. His words held the power of truth.

"I can't do that," I said. "I've promised it to someone else in exchange for . . . something. But I'll . . . I'll . . . Listen, I can make a trade with you if you'll help me."

"How can you offer it to me if you have already offered it to someone else?"

"I haven't offered it to anyone," I said, working hard to assemble these intricate layers of lies. "What I meant was that I need to have the Tree in order to fulfill my promise, but I don't have to give it to them. I can still give it to you and make good on my promise to them."

Where were all of these lies coming from? I couldn't figure it out. I wasn't a liar by nature, but there I was, scrambling to create some kind of reality in which Mr. Tennin would help me find the other three things I needed.

He didn't say anything, but I knew he was waiting to hear the terms.

"If you tell me about the stone, the water, and the sunlight, and help me find them, I'll give you the Tree."

He didn't seem surprised that I knew about those items required to grow the Tree, and that surprised me.

"Why would I give you what the Tree needs to grow? And why would you even want them unless you wanted to keep the Tree for yourself?"

I was done. I couldn't come up with anything. My lies had reached that natural end point where they collapse in on each other and begin to contradict every obvious bit of sense.

"I can't explain it to you now," I said. "But if you help me find those things, I'll give you the Tree. I promise."

I reasoned with myself that if he helped me do those things, I could somehow take a piece of the Tree, anything that would help me in bringing my mother back. I no longer even factored in that I didn't have the Tree to give, or that I told Mr. Jinn I'd give it to him first. In that moment the only important thing was for Mr. Tennin to tell me about the stone, the water, and the sunlight.

"I don't want you to misunderstand me," he said slowly in a kind voice. "I know you're not telling me the truth, or at least not all of it. I don't think you actually have the Tree. But I think you will lead me to it one way or another, willing or not. So I will help you. But I'm warning you with a reminder of your own words—you have promised the Tree to me. You might be surprised at how seriously your oaths are taken, if not by you, at least by others. Even by the Tree itself."

I sat there in his car, barely breathing.

"I'll tell you about each item one at a time. Once you find the item, come to me and I'll tell you about the next one. Understand?"

I nodded.

"First, the stone." He paused as if still considering whether or not he wanted to help me. But then he continued. "The stone is the first item. If the Tree represents life, the stone represents death. The stone is the foundation that all of the other objects build upon. Without it, the Tree will die quickly."

"What is it? Where can I find it?"

"The stone is not just a rock. It will be in the form of a vessel. Something that can hold the other items."

Immediately I thought of the bowl the old ladies had given to the man when we first saw them in the Darkness of the fairgrounds.

"Okay," I said.

"You know where it is?"

"I think so."

"Do not go by yourself."

I nodded. "Because of the Amarok?" I asked quietly. "Because of the Amarok controlled by Mr. Jinn?"

Mr. Tennin gave a grim smile. "Mr. Jinn does not control the Amarok," he said, and his voice was whimsical. It was his storytelling voice. "He may have called it here, but the Amarok is controlled by no one. By no thing. Enemies of Good are almost always enemies of each other, as allies of Good are almost always allies of each other. The Amarok is its own, and if the Amarok decides to devour Mr. Jinn, well, Mr. Jinn would have a fight on his hands."

He turned on the car, turned on the headlights, and drove up Abra's lane. I looked at him for a moment. He was nothing like what I expected an angel to look like. Could it be possible? Could he and Jinn be the cherubim who had been there for the creation of the world? Could they have seen when it all first fell?

"Thank you," I said, getting out of the car.

He nodded his bald head at me in the darkness. "Make sure you get a ride home," he said.

When Abra and I snuck into the empty side of the house and entered the upstairs bedroom where we had last hidden the duffel bag, I could tell she had spent a lot of time in there that afternoon. I stared around the room in astonishment, and she gave me a sheepish grin.

"I wanted to get things organized," she said. "Besides, some of the articles were still stuck together."

"This is incredible."

All the articles had been spread out in order by their number. There weren't as many as I had previously thought, maybe less than a hundred.

"Some of these earlier ones, I couldn't even read them," she said, pointing at some ancient-looking pieces of paper with scribbles and notes on them in foreign languages. "But the most recent half of the cards and articles are in English."

I glanced over them. One was about a five-hundred-year-old mesquite tree in Bahrain that the article called the Tree of Life. Another was about the Cotton Tree in Freetown, Sierra Leone. There was the Lone Cypress near Monterey, California, now held in place by cables.

"Tree after tree after tree." She poked a new article each time she said the word *tree*. "Ancient trees, and most of them burned down, cut down, or destroyed. Or trees that people are protecting or hiding. But every article is about a tree."

She waited and let me skim through some more of the articles.

"Mr. Tennin has a serious interest in these trees," she said. "Why else would he keep track of how each of them has been destroyed or hidden? Why would he have a matching map showing where each one was located? And why would he have taken special note of this?"

She pointed at the article at the very end, the most recent of all the newspaper clippings. It was one I had seen somewhere before.

"I think you were right," she said solemnly. "I think he is here to destroy the Tree."

Valley Woman Dies When Lightning Strikes Ancestral Tree

It was the story of my mother's death, with #68 in the top right corner of the article. I looked at Abra. She nodded, holding the atlas out to me. There was our small town in central Pennsylvania, flanked by the curving slopes of two mountains. Our valley.

"But our tree is already dead," I said, thinking out loud.

"You said it yourself earlier today. He's here for the Tree of Life."

I told her about the conversation I had just had with Mr. Tennin.

"How did he know it was here? It must have something to do with all these." I pointed to the articles spread out over the floor.

"I wonder," Abra said. "Do you remember the story he told us about the Tree of Life when he first arrived at your house?"

"Of course," I said. "But keep going."

"What if these are all times when the Tree of Life appeared?"

My eyes scanned the photographs that some of the articles contained, pictures of charred trees or lopped-off stumps, rings within rings. There was a picture of our old oak, dashed as it had been after the lightning struck and before the neighbors had come over to clean up.

I nodded. Not only was he the angel charged with destroying the Tree, but these were his notes on all the times he had already done it.

"You're brilliant," I said.

She blushed. "Well, if it's true, it's great that we know it," she said. "But that doesn't solve our biggest problem."

"What's that?" I asked.

"What do we do next?"

25

"WHAT WE DO NEXT kind of depends on who has the Tree. Who do you think has it?" I asked.

She paced back and forth from the window to where I sat among the newspaper articles. "It has to be Mr. Tennin or Mr. Jinn," she said. "Mr. Tennin doesn't have it, or he would simply destroy it. And if he had it, why would he be helping us find the other things?"

"So it's Mr. Jinn?" I said.

She nodded.

"Which would make sense, because he hasn't come looking for me or the Tree. But how did he get it? He told me he couldn't come here. He wasn't in your house, was he?"

"Who knows," she said. "Maybe he snuck in during the day when no one was paying attention or we were all out in the barns. Maybe he can just appear places."

"No, I don't think so," I said. "When he came into my house he definitely walked in like a normal person. I heard him come in through the screen door, and he crawled out the window."

She shrugged. "Does it matter how he got it? He controls

the vultures, right? Maybe he sent in little mice to steal it and take it out."

"I don't think he actually controls them," I mumbled, creeped out at the thought of Mr. Jinn sending rodents into my house to look for things.

"We'll have to deal with that later," Abra said. "I think our best bet is to start finding the other three things. Maybe we'll find it along the way. Maybe the three things will even lead us to it."

"We know the first thing to find is the stone bowl," I said. "It has to be the one the old ladies gave to that guy at the fair."

Abra sighed. I knew what she was thinking. The Darkness at the bottom of the fair was not a place we wanted to go back to, and the man with the bowl was not someone I wanted to look for, much less find.

"We'll have to do that tomorrow," she said. "I don't think my mom would take us to the fair tonight. It's too late."

Outside, the moon emerged from behind a small cloud and sent ivory light through the window.

"You should probably get home," she said. "It's getting late."

"Yeah, I don't want my dad worrying about me. He's been quiet again. Real quiet."

"I'm sorry," she said, staring hard at me as if I were a puzzle she was trying to put together.

Abra started gathering all the news articles into a pile to put back into the box. The next thing she said came out quiet and timid, not at all like the boisterous mystery solver who had been shouting out possible explanations not too long before.

"Sam, do you still want to find the Tree so you can bring your mom back to life?"

I didn't answer. I reached over and put the atlas in the box and stared at the sword.

THE DAY THE ANGELS FELL

"Because if you do, well, I still think it's wrong. But there's something inside me that keeps telling me I'm supposed to help you find the Tree. I don't think you're supposed to use it to bring your mom back, but I'm going to try to . . . to be part of this."

I nodded. I appreciated her honesty, but I didn't want to get into that conversation again, the one about bringing back my mother. If she was willing to help, that was good enough for me.

I pointed at the gray sword. "I think you should hang on to that. There must be some reason it doesn't burn you. I think you should keep it with you, in case . . ." My voice trailed off and the image of the Amarok rose in my mind. Abra hadn't seen it yet. I was glad she hadn't, but I wanted her to have some way of protecting herself if she ended up coming between it and the Tree.

She picked up the sword, and the drab grayness of the blade seemed to turn into something brighter, something closer to glass than metal. I could see it shimmering in the reflection in her eyes.

Mrs. Miller agreed to drive me home again, which was very kind of her, seeing as how Mr. Miller was out in the barn and Abra didn't want to stay at home alone with the baby.

"I don't understand why you insist on coming along," Mrs. Miller said as the four of us went out to the car. "It's seven minutes up the road, and Francis should be in bed."

She buckled the baby into his seat and gave Abra a quick glare. The truth was I was the one who didn't want Abra staying home alone. She was quite prepared to take the risk, but I didn't want her there by herself with the Amarok on the loose.

Fortunately, the baby kept sleeping, even through all of that movement. I sat beside the window and Abra sat in the middle, between me and the baby. This meant the front passenger seat was empty. Mrs. Miller started the car and pulled out of the long lane.

The bright moon cast dim shadows across the stone surface of Kincade Road. Every shadow seemed to move, to shift, and I kept looking up at the moon, hoping the night would stay bright until I made it through my own front door.

We got about halfway down the road to my house when the car sputtered.

"Uh-oh," Mrs. Miller said.

"What do you mean, 'uh-oh?'" Abra asked.

She groaned. "I forgot to get gas today when I went into town. I think we're going to run out."

"Mom!" Abra said. "Why do you always do this?"

As she said that the engine sputtered again, this time louder and more persistently. Before I even had a chance to hope that we'd at least make it to my driveway, the engine stalled out and Mrs. Miller guided the car to the side of the road.

Everything was very quiet. Abra's baby brother slept beside us, his face oblivious to the world. Mrs. Miller sat in the driver's seat, not yet accepting that we had run out of gas. She tried to start it again. Nothing. Abra and I looked at each other. I was more scared than I could ever remember—more scared than when I had been hiding in the attic, more scared than when I saw the lightning strike the tree, even more scared than when the three dogs attacked me. During all of that stuff I had been in the middle of the action, but there in the car, on that moonlit night, I was waiting. Waiting to see what would happen next. And the waiting filled me with fear.

"Well, who's walking to Sam's house?" Mrs. Miller asked with a wry smile.

I tried to think it through. I remembered my father's words about the Amarok.

It only devours those who are foolish enough to hunt alone.

"Why don't you two stay here with the baby and I'll go?" Mrs. Miller suggested. "It's not very far. The church's parking lot light is right up there."

"No," I said. "No. Abra and I will go."

"You just don't want to watch the baby again," Mrs. Miller teased. "Okay. Please ask your dad to bring me some gas, just enough to get me home. And tell him I'm so sorry."

Abra and I stared at each other across the dark backseat of the car, and I opened the door. The two of us got out. A cool breeze blew through the valley, much colder than you would expect to have on a July night. I slammed the door behind us. The sound of it closing felt sudden and irrevocable. There was no going back.

We walked quickly, our feet making far too much noise on the gravel road. Abra grabbed on to the side of my shirt exactly as she had held my sleeve at the funeral. But there was nothing affectionate about the way she latched on to me that night. She was scared, and I could sense it in her grip.

Halfway from the car to the lane, I stumbled, my feet kicking up loose stones.

"Shh!" Abra said quickly.

"I know, I know," I whispered.

We were getting closer and closer to my mailbox. The church light was getting brighter and brighter, and the nearer we got to that light, the better we felt. I looked over at Abra, and because of that light I could clearly see her face. She looked back at me and smiled. We would make it. We were almost there.

The church light blinked out.

I've always found it eerie when a streetlight blinks out, but usually where there's one streetlight there are many, and when one goes out it leaves a dim gap in the long line of those that stayed on. But this was different because there was only one light, and we were in the middle of the country, so when it blinked out everything went dark. We were left with the pale face of the moon and the faraway pinholes of light that came from my house.

We moved closer together and walked slower, quieter. We listened for any other sounds, and when we thought we heard something we stopped, my finger on my lips, Abra barely breathing. Then we took a few more slow steps, cringing at every crunch the gravel made under our feet.

Nighttime shadows can be tricky things, shifting and moving in ways that daytime shadows don't. The breeze rustled the weeds that lined the small space between the road and the fields, so the dim shadows on the road were always moving, waving back and forth. The trees, too, faded here and there, as if they weren't rooted to the ground, as if that cool wind had somehow freed them.

But from the depths of these nighttime shadows, a darker thing appeared. It moved toward us from the church, and the closer it got, the colder the wind became. The darkness I had felt in my heart during those days after my mother's death seemed drawn to it. All the lies and deceit and anger at my mother's passing gained lives of their own and rose inside me, as if they were given new life. As if they were rising from the dead.

Abra and I stopped walking.

"What's that?" she whispered.

I shook my head as if I didn't know, but I knew. I just didn't want to say the words.

It's the Amarok.

That dark shadow moved faster as it approached, and it raced past us along the side of the road. Everything in me screamed, *Run! Run into the woods and hide!* But Abra clung to my shirt and I knew I couldn't leave her. The darkness inside me shouted, *Leave! The Amarok isn't here for you. Run away, and it will take Abra but you will be safe. Better one of you is devoured than both of you.*

That voice, it was calm and convincing, and what it told me made sense. I grabbed Abra's hand, the one clinging to my shirt, as if I was going to hold it, but instead I dropped it down to my side.

"What are we going to do?" she hissed as the shadow blew past us again, back up the other side of the road.

Every time it passed us, the darkness inside me grew, and my desire to run became almost overwhelming.

"What about this?" Abra asked, pulling the sword out from behind her.

"You have it?" I asked.

There it was, the moonlight glinting off its surface.

"I tucked it in the back of my pants, under my shirt," she whispered.

She pushed it slowly out in front of her. The shadow paused, then approached. I could finally see its form—the wolflike shape, the massive size, the huge paws, agile and ready on the gravel. Its eyes glittered in the moonlight, and something else shone.

Its teeth.

Abra brandished the blade, but the Amarok only drew into itself before expanding larger, taller, fiercer. Before, it seemed ready to play with us, to bat at us with its paws and devour us happily—but once it saw the sword, it seemed full of rage. It took one step toward us. Another. Its eyes squinted, and I could hear the softest movement of gravel as it approached. Soon it was so close that even in the dim moonlight I could see its nose curling. I remembered what it had said to me in my dream.

That fruit does not belong to you.

I got ready to run.

Then I saw a bright light and heard a voice calling out to us through the darkness. The nighttime breeze got warmer and stronger, and I caught the smell of cut hay coming from a neighboring field, mingling with the far-off sound of the river. The Amarok melted away, like a shadow when the light comes on.

26

THE APPROACHING LIGHT got brighter and brighter, and for a moment I felt like we were rushing forward through a tunnel, toward the light and the way out. I shielded my eyes, and the light dropped. Mr. Tennin came into view, and the church light winked back on.

"What are you kids doing out here?" he asked.

I wanted to run to him and give him a hug. I wanted to tell him all about what we had seen. But I didn't. Instead I turned to Abra. "Hide the sword," I whispered.

"Mr. Tennin," I said when he got closer. My voice still shook from the close call with the Amarok. I coughed and tried to steady it. "Abra's mom was bringing me home, but she ran out of gas."

"Everything okay?" he asked. "You sound a little shaken up."

In the darkness, when I couldn't be distracted by his boring, humdrum physical appearance, I remembered that Mr. Tennin's voice was deep and beautiful. The deepness wasn't in the sound it made, but more in the way it seemed to lead to other things, long-ago stories or forgotten tales.

"Yeah, we're okay," Abra said, but her voice sounded as weak and unconvincing as mine.

"C'mon," he said. "Let's go find your dad."

We walked the rest of the way together, turning into the lane past the mailbox, walking along the garden and the growing-heavier-by-the-day apple trees. We came up to the barns and walked through the yard, past the lightning tree, to the front porch. Our feet made loud thudding noises on the boards. It was as if we had finally returned to reality.

We walked into the bright house. I could hear a baseball game on the television heading into its final stages.

"Mr. Chambers?" Mr. Tennin said. "You in there?"

"Yeah," my dad said.

"Abra's mother ran out of gas on the way here. You want me to drive back out there with a little gasoline to fill up her car?"

"Sure," my dad said. "Thanks, Tennin."

Soon Mr. Tennin and Abra headed back out into the night. I waved to Abra, and when she turned around I could see the bulge in the back of her shirt where the sword's handle stuck out. I hoped she would keep it safe. I hoped she would keep it secret.

All I wanted to do was go to bed. But as I got to the steps, my dad called out to me from the living room.

"Boy, Mr. Jinn was here earlier this afternoon. Said he expected to see you. He left a note for you in the kitchen."

"Okay," I said. I walked into the kitchen and there it was, a note written in scratchy handwriting on a small white piece of paper.

I wanted to come by and talk to you about that unfinished project and give you what I owe you. Make sure you're here

*tomorrow at one so I can talk to you about that. If you're not
here, I can always give your payment to your father.*

I knew what he was saying. He was angry that I hadn't yet
found the Tree of Life or gone back to his house to talk about
it. He wanted to feed me to the Amarok, or something worse,
and that's what he was going to do tomorrow. That's what he
meant by giving me what he owed me. And if I wasn't there, he
would do to my father what he wanted to do to me.

"You see the note?" my father asked, his voice from the next
room mingled with called strikes and balls.

"Yeah," I said, holding it in my hands, trying not to let fear
fill me up and knock me over.

"Well, make sure you're around tomorrow. He seemed pretty
intent on seeing you."

"Okay," I said. "I will."

———

I had another dream that night.

I'm playing hide-and-seek with my dad in the farmhouse.
I'm very small, maybe four or five years old. I hear him counting in the kitchen.

"One . . . two . . . three . . . four . . . five . . ."

He keeps counting as I climb the steps. I stop for a moment
in the hall and look at each of the doors: the bathroom door
at the end of the hall, the door to my parents' room right there
beside it, my door in the middle, the empty guest room to the
right. It's not day and it's not night. Dusk maybe. A whisper of
light drifts in the windows and under the doors.

"Twenty-three . . . twenty-four . . . twenty-five . . . twenty-
six . . ."

He keeps counting, and I can't decide which room to go into. I get scared. This is when I usually run to my mother, but suddenly I'm twelve again, no longer four or five, and I remember that my mother is dead. I don't have anyone to run to, and my dad is about to come looking for me. I don't like the feeling of not having a safe place, a safe person.

"Thirty-eight . . . thirty-nine . . . forty . . ."

I run into the spare bedroom and look out the window. The streetlight on the corner of the church building winks on and off. Then back on again. I look to the right, and the tree blows in the wind. It's getting dark, and lightning strikes over the eastern mountain.

"Forty-eight . . . forty-nine . . . fifty. Ready or not, here I come!"

Silence.

I wait. I picture my father searching the main level of the house. I can hear him calling out.

"Sam, are you in there? Sam, are you in here?"

I hear his feet climbing the steps, one slow step at a time. I look around the room for someplace to hide, but there's no furniture in there, not in my dream, so I stand by the door. I decide I'll have to let him find me, but then something strange happens.

"Sam, where are you?" the voice calls out.

But it's not my dad's voice anymore.

It's Mr. Jinn's.

I dash over to the attic door and pull it open. It doesn't make a sound and I wonder about that. I run up the stairs and hide among the boxes. I hear his voice again, and he's in the spare room.

"Sam, where are you?" he asks in a singsong kind of voice, and I know for sure that it's Mr. Jinn. "I'm here to give you what I owe you."

I tuck myself away in the back and hear thunder outside the attic. I hear his footsteps coming up the attic stairs.

Then, in the way dreams can change, I'm out in the lightning tree, way up high in the branches, and I'm reaching for a piece of fruit. I look down, and Mr. Jinn is climbing up the tree. He reaches up and grabs my foot, and I don't know how he managed to climb so high. He's so big and the branches are so small, and where his hand touches my heel I feel his nails claw a deep cut into my skin.

"That fruit doesn't belong to you," he says, and he turns into the Amarok. Then both of us are falling, falling, falling through the branches, the bright green grass rushes up at me, and as I make contact with the ground, I wake up.

"Finish feeding the lamb and come in for lunch," my dad shouted down from the upper level of the barn. I was down on the ground floor, sweeping the walkways. I heard him and Mr. Tennin walk out the back of the barn, where the second level was even with the hill. The massive barn door slid closed behind them, the sound of it grating and far away. It became very quiet.

I walked to the corner and leaned the broad broom against the wooden wall. My sweeping had stirred up dust, so the air was full of particles floating through the rays of light like a million planets. I stopped by the lamb's stall and picked up the fresh bottle full of milk. The lamb jumped over to the bars and bleated in a pleading voice. I smiled at it and patted it on the head. It tried to suck on my fingers, thinking everything was a bottle of some kind.

I leaned against the bars and fed the lamb. Its short tail wagged back and forth, and it jerked its head to move the milk out of the bottle. I thought about my mother and it made me want to cry again, and I got mad at myself for always wanting to cry. But still I thought about her. I remembered our last day together, how she brought me home from practice, how she stopped to let me pick up the cat, how she climbed up in the tree during the storm to save me.

The more I thought about her, the greater the ache. The more I thought about her, the more I found myself visiting old ground—I needed that Tree of Life.

Another thought lodged itself in my mind. I reviewed the previous days, and I knew who had the Tree.

Abra.

It had to be Abra.

Who else had access to it? Who else knew it was there? Only her.

That old familiar darkness simmered inside me, and I couldn't understand why I hadn't seen it before. Of course she had it! She must have realized what it was before I came back, picked the lock or used a spare key, and taken it. She either hid it or destroyed it.

Destroyed it.

The lamb wasn't quite finished, but in my disgust I yanked the bottle away and put it up on the shelf. Turning, I saw Mr. Jinn behind me, surrounded by the swirling particles of dust drifting through the sunlight. And standing beside him, leaning into the shadows and almost too big to fit into the barn, was the Amarok.

I saw a flash of movement at the opposite corner of the barn and glanced over in time to see Icarus slip through the bars and flee into the shadows.

I looked back at Mr. Jinn and the Amarok, but I wasn't scared. Why wasn't I scared? I didn't know, but I didn't care.

"She took the Tree," I said. "She hid it somewhere."

Mr. Jinn nodded slowly. "Doesn't surprise me," he said. "Doesn't surprise me one bit."

"She'll be here soon. Should we ask her about it?"

He thought about it for a moment. "No. Not yet. Let's leave it. Let sleeping dogs lie and all that."

He looked over at the Amarok. It hadn't taken its eyes off me, as if it still waited for Mr. Jinn to give it the order to attack. It took a step in my direction, saliva hanging from its lower row of snarling teeth.

"Don't worry," I said. "Mr. Tennin is going to help me find the other three things. Help *us* find the other three things."

"Is that right?" Mr. Jinn said, and he looked downright happy to hear it. "Mr. Tennin? Well, that's a pleasant surprise for sure."

He seemed very pleased with everything, which I couldn't understand based on the fact that Abra had the Tree. Why wasn't he more worried? I was very worried.

"We're not too late, are we? We can still bring my mom back, right?"

"Sam," he said, "if we can get that Tree of Life, it won't be too late for anything."

He turned and walked away. The Amarok backed away alongside him, ducking to miss the low crossbeams in the ceiling. But before it got too far away it became unrecognizable, blending in with the midday shadows in the corners of the barn.

"What should I do?" I asked, suddenly overwhelmed at what remained to be done.

"Keep doing what you're doing," he said loudly without turning around. "Find the remaining items and bring everything to me."

I heard the barn door opening. He shouted one more thing back to me.

"It's never too late!"

I sat down and realized I was shaking. I closed my eyes and put my head back against the wall. Why did things have to change so much? Why did my mom have to die? Why did I have to make all of these decisions on my own?

When I opened my eyes, I saw the door open at the far end of the barn. Abra came down the long aisle.

"Hey," she said.

I looked at her, and I wondered, did she have it? Was she the only thing standing between me and bringing my mom back?

"Hey," I said.

"Everything okay?" she asked.

"Yeah," I said. "Mr. Jinn came by."

"He did?"

"Yeah. He did."

"What did he say?"

"He said to get the remaining items. He'll take care of the rest."

"So he does have the Tree," she said.

"What?"

"Mr. Jinn. We were right," she said as if everything had been revealed to her. "He has the Tree. Why else wouldn't he be concerned about you not having it? He didn't even push you for it. When's the last time you had a conversation with him and he wasn't asking you over and over again for the Tree?"

I wanted to scream and shout and accuse her of being a terrible friend, a liar, someone who wanted to keep my mom under the ground in that cold, damp grave. But for some reason the darkness inside me felt stronger than ever, and it told me to remain calm. So I listened to it.

"Yeah, I guess," I said.

"My mom said she'll take us to the fair, but only for an hour or so," Abra said.

"Let's go find the stone bowl," I said, standing up and walking past her.

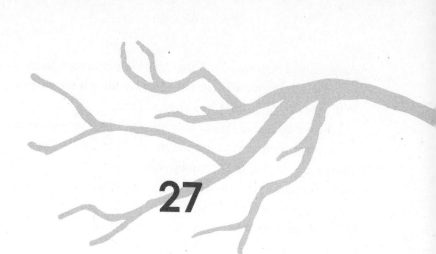

27

ABRA'S MOM DROPPED US OFF at the fair entrance and drove into town to run some errands, and as Abra and I walked onto the fairgrounds, I found myself feeling disappointed. At night, the fair seemed edgy and exciting. The flashing lights seared their images into my brain. The mirror maze and the haunted house felt like truly dangerous undertakings, and the shadows that drifted in the margins of the snapping tent flaps held mysteries and unknown terrors.

But during the day, the fair was ordinary. The gravel paths were filled with stale cigarette butts, and the toothless old man collecting the trash, who at night bore the appearance of a man who might steal little children, looked harmless. He even smiled at us as we walked past. Carnies lounged in their tents that lined the midway, napping or staring off at the horizon. They looked like real people during the day, not like the caricatures from fairy tales that they were at night.

When we had been at the fair after dark, finding the Tree of Life had felt like a distinct possibility. But in the light of a normal weekday, it all seemed too fantastic to be true. The Tree of Life?

An Amarok? A stone bowl? Three old women and angels and a sword that burned me when I touched it? All of it seemed hard to believe, like a dream I had awoken from.

Still, we wandered down through the various sections of the fair, past the food and the animals and the kiddie rides. The rides' lights were on, but they were bleached out by the sun. A few small children screamed as the rides whipped them around. A few of the carnies called out to us, encouraging us to try their games of skill, but their voices were ordinary and tired, and they weren't very persistent.

We passed the Ferris wheel and the large trucks parked just below it and wandered into the section of the fair where the carnies lived during the week. It was as boring as the rest of the fair, perhaps even more so because it was completely quiet. I guess they were all still in bed after a long night. A stale summer breeze wandered through the tents and RVs, rustling the canvas and tossing the long grass from side to side. A black and white dog, tied to a stake outside the entrance to a tent, perked up its ears as we walked past but must have decided it couldn't be bothered. It set its head back down on its paws and watched us pass without making a sound.

"There's the tent," Abra said, pointing down the hill to a green tent with a blue tarp over the door. I nodded. That was the tent the man had disappeared into with the bowl. Like everything else, it looked ordinary.

Could we just go in and take the bowl? If he was there, how long would we have to wait until he left? We only had an hour. We walked through the long, trampled grass and stopped outside the tent.

"Now what?" I whispered to Abra.

"Hello?" she said in not much more than a loud whisper. "Hello? Anyone in there?"

234

SHAWN SMUCKER

She took a deep breath, shrugged, pulled back the tarp, and looked inside. She glanced back at me with surprise on her face, then snuck carefully through the flap. I followed.

The first thing I noticed was a loud, raspy sound, so intense that I was surprised I hadn't heard it from outside the tent. I looked around, expecting to see some kind of machine click-click-clicking. I saw the man who had taken the bowl from the old women, lying on a mat on the floor, asleep.

The sound was him snoring. Each inhale caught and snagged like a door on uneven hinges, and each exhale swept out like a new start. Abra and I took a few more steps into the large tent and stood there for a moment, staring at him. Resting on his stomach, clenched by both of his hands, was the stone bowl.

It was the only thing I saw there that didn't seem ordinary. The stone was a gray white, and it had flecks of something in it that sparkled, the way sand glints in the morning light, or the way a granite headstone sparkles when the sun comes out from behind a cloud. It was about a foot in diameter and hollowed out, the shape of a contact lens.

"The dog?" Abra whispered and pointed, and I saw the man's pet lying beside him, on its back, paws in the air, tongue lolling off to the side. It was asleep too. I looked at her and shook my head. I didn't know what to do. We both took another step closer to the sleeping man and his dog. Then we heard the tent flap open just a few feet behind us.

A woman came in through the opening. She was one of those particular creations of the fair, someone you see nowhere else. Her hair was shoulder length, her face was as wrinkled as a balled-up piece of tissue paper that's been stretched flat again, and her body was skinny, a sack of bones. A cigarette perched between her purplish lips, and the watery whites of her eyes were more yellow than white. She wore a T-shirt three sizes too big for her, and it hung down around her knees. Her jeans were torn and dirty, and she wore work boots.

In one hand she carried a butcher knife, and in the other hand she carried a white grocery bag dripping blood from the bottom corner.

Abra leaned over closer to me, and I put my hands up, preparing to talk her out of murdering us. I kept expecting her to raise the knife and charge, or cry out to the man to wake up and bash us over the head with his stone bowl, or maybe she'd even wake the dog and tell it to attack us. But she did none of these things.

She fell to her knees, dropped the knife and the bag, and started crying.

"You're here," she cried out. "You're really here."

Abra and I looked at each other. I probably would have been less startled if she had charged at us.

"Thank God," she said, sitting back on her ankles before taking a long drag from the cigarette. She exhaled the smoke. It hung heavy in the tent, and the longer we stayed, the foggier the tent became.

"I'm sorry?" Abra said.

"You're here," she said again. "Those three old hags said you'd come."

"They did?" I asked.

She nodded. "They cursed my man with that bowl, and he's been asleep ever since."

I looked over at her "man." I found it hard to believe he was under any spell other than alcohol and laziness.

"He's been sleeping there ever since that night?" Abra asked her.

She nodded again. "Came in here and lay down, and I didn't

think he was ever gonna wake up again," she said, a fresh batch of tears flooding her eyes.

"So . . . now what?" I said.

"Take the bowl," the woman said. "Just take that bowl and get outta here. That's what those three old hags said, yes they did. 'When two children come here for the bowl, and when they take the bowl, this man will wake up.' That's what they said, they did."

I looked at Abra and she looked at me.

"What about the, um, dog?" I asked.

"Him too," she said, shaking her head, regret on her face. "Him too."

So I took a few steps toward the man, bent over, and lifted the stone bowl. His hands let go of it easily, as if he was relieved to give it up. It was heavy, with a texture like sandpaper.

When I first touched it, I thought I saw something in the bowl, like a shooting star traveling from one side to the other. But when I looked closer, all I saw was the shimmering of the stone. It had glints in it as if it were from another planet, another part of the universe. Or maybe another time.

Abra held open the tent flap for me, but the woman never got up. In fact, she leaned forward, then back on her knees, and it sounded like she was praying as we left, or saying something like a prayer. I heard the man shift on his mat, and the dog made a whining sound. We emerged into the light and I had to squint—the sun was bright outside the tent. We walked, the two of us, through that quiet, ordinary day.

Abra's mom was so happy we showed up on time that she didn't even ask us about the stone bowl, if she even saw it. We climbed into the back of the car without a word and put it on the seat between us. Once we got to Abra's house, Mrs. Miller rushed inside to relieve Abra's father of baby duty, and we were left staring at each other in the backseat of the car.

We decided to hide the bowl in the cave in the cliff at the end of the Road to Nowhere. It was a long walk and the bowl was heavy, but we made our way through the woods, always looking around, always waiting for the sound of the Amarok in the shadows.

We arrived at my mother's grave in the cemetery in the woods. My breathing came faster, and I approached the bare, brown earth that had so recently been put on top of her coffin. Someone had left a bouquet of tulips resting against her headstone. They were yellow with streaks of red from the stem to the end of the petal. It was a deep red, like the low, evening sun. I got down on my knees and read the inscription on her stone.

Lucy Leigh Chambers
Wife and Mother
Meet Me at the Edge of the World

I noticed something protruding from under the dozen or so tulips, so I picked them up and set them on top of the headstone. And there it was, small and bright green with its own white flowers.

The Tree of Life.

Someone had removed it from the log, brought it here, and planted it in a shallow hole. The green had faded a bit, and the flowers weren't so much white as they were ivory, a sickly version of off-white. The Tree was dying, that was easy to see. I felt the old darkness rise inside me.

"Who brought that here?" Abra asked, awe in her voice.

I didn't know what to say. We sat there in silence. I was relieved that Abra hadn't taken the Tree, and I was frustrated with myself for not believing her. What was happening to me that I was so suspicious of my best friend?

Yet, as I saw the plant right there in front of me, both my disbelief and my determination grew. On one hand, I found it even more difficult to believe that this small plant could somehow snatch my mother from the strong jaws of death. It was so tiny, so fragile. On the other hand, there it was—it just kept coming back to me. I thought that must mean something.

"We should leave it here," I said.

So we did. It looked too fragile to move again anyway, so I leaned the yellow tulips with the bloodred streaks over it, keeping it mostly out of sight. I took a deep breath and stood up. I set the stone bowl up on my mother's headstone, and I walked away.

I left Abra and the cemetery, drifting away from the rock cliff with the cave in it. I could feel Abra watching me. I could hear the river rushing out there somewhere in the trees. It was a never-ending sound, the sound of life. The roaring it made as it spilled into the valley and swept toward Deen was the sound of thousands of years of history, moving, carrying me away. I heard Abra walking along behind me, but I didn't say anything to her. I needed a minute to think.

There were three large granite crypts between the cemetery and the river, and I wondered why they were there, planted by themselves like some kind of strange orchard. I thought people had used crypts down there in case the creek overflowed its banks, to keep the bodies up out of the floodwaters, but I didn't know for sure.

I noticed that one of the crypts was covered in writing, a thin cursive script that stretched along the roof of the grave.

In Grateful Remembrance of Josephine M. Jinn

Going down each side of the crypt were the dates of her birth and death.

"Seventy years old," Abra said, and I was surprised to hear her voice. I hadn't realized she had trailed along behind me. "I wonder if she was related to Mr. Jinn?"

There was a small metal plate attached to the pillar, and there were words etched into the plate, faded words no longer legible.

I looked over at Abra. She stared at me.

"I don't think we should give the bowl to Mr. Jinn," she said.

"Not Mr. Tennin either," I said.

"I don't know," she said quietly. "I think I trust Mr. Tennin."

I didn't trust anyone. I realized I resisted choosing sides, resisted choosing between Tennin and Jinn, because I was the only person I could trust. I was on my own side now, getting as far as I could with the help of anyone who would aid me.

For a moment we stood there in the heat, and the river, still hidden off in the trees, sounded so appealing. I wished the summer had turned out differently. I wished we were boating in that river, floating down behind the church and winding our way toward town. I wished that when we finished swimming we could go back to my house, and as we went through the screen door we'd smell the chocolate chip cookies my mom was baking.

I wished. Instead we were sweating in a silent graveyard on a sweltering day, trying to figure out what to do with a stone bowl.

We walked back to my mother's grave, and I picked up the bowl again. It was heavy, but it didn't seem as heavy as when

I had first lifted it, as if my arms were getting used to it. Or perhaps it was getting used to me.

"Are you ready to put it in the cave?" Abra asked.

As far as locations went, I thought it was a good idea. It was past Mr. Jinn's house in a direction no one ever traveled. As long as he didn't see us coming or going, he would never suspect that we had hidden it there.

I carried the bowl to the small cave, only fifty yards away through the trees, where the cliffs came down from the mountains. Some of the rocks were wet and slippery from recent rains, making it hard going. At one point I got caught up in a few trees and we had to climb up a short outcropping of rock, so I had to pass the bowl to Abra. I imagined her dropping it on purpose, the bowl shattering against the rocks. I imagined her laughing at my sorrow. But she didn't drop it. She handled it as carefully as I did.

We arrived at the cave, and you could see the muddy river from there, moving fast with all the rainwater. The cliff was a huge piece of rock, nearly as big as a house, and it reached out toward the river. The cave was at the base of the cliff, about three feet high and two feet wide, and it was dark, like an empty spot where an eye used to be. I pushed the bowl in along the ground, and the weight of it made a divot, a short, hollowed-out path.

"One down," I said. "Two to go."

⌇

That evening after dinner I walked into the barn with my father and Mr. Tennin. The three of us stacked hay bales and cleaned out the barn. At one point my dad went down to the lower level for something, and Mr. Tennin and I were left alone, picking up the loose hay with our pitchforks and throwing it down through the hole in the floor.

"I found it," I said quietly. "I found the first item. The stone."

He kept working as if I hadn't said anything, and when he spoke he barely moved his mouth, as if someone was watching us.

"Good," he said. "Good. Now you have to find water."

"What kind of water?" I whispered.

"It's not water. It's blood. Innocent blood."

"What?" I pictured some kind of terrible sacrifice. An animal dying on an altar. A high priest raising a stone knife.

"It doesn't have to be much," he said. "Only a drop. Place a drop of innocent blood in the middle of the stone bowl, directly under the Tree." He stopped and looked at me. "Have you found it yet?"

"No," I said. The word came so quickly from my mouth that I didn't realize what I was saying. I lied before I knew I was lying.

He stared at me for a moment. He threw another forkful of hay down the hole, and it vanished into the dark lower level. A cloud of hay dust came whooshing back up and settled all around us.

"Remember your promise to me," he said, not looking at me as he plunged his pitchfork into the pile of straw, "because I won't forget."

The kindness in his voice was still there, but it was edged with force, and I knew he wouldn't forget. Not ever.

28

"INNOCENT BLOOD?" Abra asked, sounding nervous.

The whole long Friday afternoon stretched in front of me, chore free. It had always been something my mother insisted on. My father could have me working hard on the farm all week, but on Friday afternoon I got a break. I was free. No work, no responsibilities. "Just time to be a kid," she had said, messing up my hair and giving my dad those pretend pleading eyes.

"What does Mr. Tennin mean by innocent blood?" Abra asked.

"Innocent blood," I said, as if the two words explained themselves.

The two of us sat there in the lightning tree, one week after my mother had died. The tree itself was definitely dying. Its leaves were still there but were dry and brittle. Some of the branches that had been nearer to the lightning strike were charred, and those leaves were brown.

We sat in the flat area where the cat had been hiding, the palm of the tree's hand, the place I had been standing when my mother pulled herself up and told me to run inside. It might seem strange, but as I sat there with Abra on that Friday afternoon, it was the first time I realized how close I had come to death. I imagined the valley without me, Mom and Dad standing in the kitchen doing the dishes, my mom crying. My dad looked the same in my vision as he did in reality—tired and sad.

I wondered what Abra would be doing on that day if I had died in the tree. Would she be at her house, remembering me? Or would life already have gone on, seven days later? Time passes and people leave, and those of us who are left eventually move on in one way or another. Maybe that's the saddest part of death, the knowledge that when we die, we will eventually be forgotten.

The sky was low and gray and looked like rain, or at least a shower or two. But it wasn't stormy, and I didn't expect any lightning or thunder.

"Maybe he knows someone named Innocent and we have to get her blood," Abra said. "You know. Innocent blood."

"Do you know anyone named Innocent?" I asked her, shaking my head.

"I was kidding," she said. A breeze came through the lightning tree just for a moment, and all those dry leaves rustled against each other, a strange sort of shushing sound that made me eager for fall. Abra's blonde hair blew up around her face and she pushed it away. Her blue eyes looked silver in the light.

"So what's the most innocent blood we know about?" I asked.

"You're not touching my little brother," she said quietly.

"I wasn't even thinking about him," I said, which was completely untrue. Her baby brother was the first person who came to mind when I thought about innocent blood.

"What about your lamb?" she asked.

I didn't know if that would be good enough. I shrugged. "That might work. Mr. Tennin didn't say it had to be a person."

I thought back over the seven days since Friday when the lightning struck, and I wished none of it had happened.

"Well, should we go try?" I asked her.

"Sure," she said, but she didn't sound committed to it, and the more I thought about it, the less sure I became.

I reached my foot down for the ladder and climbed to the grass. Abra came scrambling down after me, and the two of us walked into the barn, back through the shadowy aisles, past the chickens, and into the farthest corner.

Something sprang from the dirty windowsill that let in filtered light, and I jumped. But it was just Icarus running away from us. I wondered where he was sleeping, what he was eating. I didn't have the heart to chase him, though.

We got to the pen at the back of the barn, and the lamb looked up at us, its little tail wagging back and forth. I think it thought I was there to give it a bottle.

"So," Abra said, "how do you get blood out of a lamb?"

The whole proposition had seemed so simple. All we needed was one tiny drop of lamb's blood. But there in the barn with the white lamb staring up at us, well, Abra's question was valid. How would we get blood out of the lamb? I didn't want to hurt it.

"What will we use?" I asked. I looked around. There was a shovel, a broom, and a pitchfork leaning against the wall, back in the shadows. I thought I could find a screwdriver if I looked hard enough. I'd have to go back inside for a knife, but if I saw my dad along the way, who knows what he would say. How would I explain why I was carrying a kitchen knife to the barn?

Abra reached around behind her and pulled out the small sword. I didn't even know she had it with her.

"We could try this," she said.

It made me jealous, seeing her with that blade. I wanted to be the one to hold it, to be the one with a weapon. I had found it—I should be the one possessing it, protecting us. But there she was, holding it, not being burned by it.

"Can I see it?" I asked.

"Okay."

I reached for it, and she grabbed it by the bottom of the blade, pointing the handle toward me. But as soon as I touched it, it burned me, and I dropped it. The sound it made as it hit the cement walkway was deep and heavy, as if it weighed ten times what it actually did. Abra reached down for it, and based on the sound it had made, I didn't expect she'd be able to pick it up. But she lifted it as if nothing had changed.

"I guess you'd better keep it for now," I said, rubbing my hands together, trying to get the burn out.

She held it in front of her and stared at the blade as if looking for hidden stories in its reflection. For a moment she didn't look like herself. She looked like some visiting angel, preparing to protect the entire world from an enormous evil. I was scared of her in that moment, and I felt small. I was scared of what she could do.

"Should we try?" she asked.

I moved toward the pen and the lamb came to the bars, trying to stick its head through. I stroked its soft wool. It felt like a great betrayal, what we were about to do.

"Where should I . . . you know?" Abra asked.

I wasn't sure. Lambs are all soft and white, but their legs and hooves are bony and hard, their skulls miniature boulders.

"Maybe on the leg?" I said. "There's not a lot of flesh. Maybe it would just feel like it was banging its shin on something."

She got down on her knees beside me.

"Wait!" I said. "What will we put it in?" We didn't have any containers with us, nothing for keeping the blood.

"Maybe if we get it on the blade, we can carry it to the bowl and scrape it in."

"Okay."

She reached the blade through the bars. Where it almost touched my arm, I could feel its heat.

"Watch it," I said. "That's hot."

I wondered if it would feel hot to the lamb, but when she propped the blade up against the lamb's leg, it didn't move. It didn't even seem to notice. It moved closer to me, and I held it tight so it wouldn't jump away.

"Go ahead," I said. "Go."

She grimaced and slid the blade slowly along the lamb's leg. Blood poured out.

"Whoa!" I shouted. "What are you doing?"

She screamed and there was fear in her voice, and horror. She inched backward, away from the lamb, and her eyes opened up wide and alarmed.

"I didn't try it," she kept saying over and over. "I didn't try it. It's just so sharp."

The lamb jumped away from us and ran to the back of the pen. It huddled there in the shadows, quivering, and I could see its leg was bleeding badly.

"We have to do something," I said.

Abra stared at the blade. It was wet with blood.

"Keep that flat," I said. "Don't let it run off."

She placed the sword on the floor and helped me climb over the bars into the pen. I took off one of my boots, then took off my sock and put my boot back on.

I crawled in close to the lamb, through the hay, talking to it all the time. "It's okay, little guy. You're going to be fine."

Its ears were limp on the side of its head. Its eyes were jumpy. "Wow, it's really bleeding," I said.

Abra couldn't keep her own cries quiet anymore. She sobbed right there in the barn. I remember her sobs, and now I know they were the cries of someone who has lost their innocence in one way or another, the cries of someone who has realized not only that there is pain in the world but also that they can cause it, that they will cause it. We all will.

I tried to wrap my sock around the lamb's wound. Abra had cut it on the back of its hoof, right where its heel would have been if it had one. It reminded me of my dream and how Mr. Jinn had chased me up the tree, burning or slicing my foot. For a moment I felt that same panic of trying to climb faster than him, of looking for that next branch. But that was just a dream.

I focused on the lamb. I kept trying to tie the sock on, but the crazy animal jumped and ran away from me.

"Come here, you." I reached for the lamb, but it kept running. "Abra, I need you to hold it still. I can't hold it and tie the sock at the same time."

By now my own hands were covered in blood and straw and dust. Abra came over the bars and got down there in the dirt with me, wiping the tears from her eyes and sniffing loudly.

"Here you go, little lamb," she whispered, and the lamb calmed. She walked toward it and got down on her knees. "It's okay." She reached out her hands. It walked slowly to her, and she held it tight. She put her face on its back, and I could tell she was crying into its wool.

I crawled over to where they were. "Hold tight. Here goes." I reached down and wrapped the sock around the still-bleeding cut. The lamb trembled, but Abra held it tight. I tied the sock in a tight knot and hoped it would stay.

"We'll have to clean it up later." I hoped my dad wouldn't see the state of the poor lamb. That would be a hard one to explain.

Abra nodded quietly, wiping her eyes again. We both climbed out of the pen and she picked up the small sword, always holding it flat. The blood sat in a straight line, one long run. And that's how we walked all the way from the barn, through the woods, and to the cave—carefully, eyes always on the lamb's blood.

"You'll have to put the drop in the bowl," I said. "I can't hold the knife. It'll burn my hand off."

She nodded, and she went inside and didn't seem scared, not at all. When she came out she looked somber, as if she had just come from another funeral.

"It's done." She bent down and wiped the blade on the grass, cleaning off the rest of the blood.

"Was there enough to go into the bowl?"

Her face crinkled up and she started to cry again, I guess at the thought of all the blood she had let out of the lamb. She nodded, leaned the hilt up against the rock, and put her face in her hands. I walked over and put my hand on her shoulder. We both took a deep breath.

"Only one thing left to find." I hoped that was the worst of it.

But Abra went back to a small patch of grass in the forest just beyond the cemetery, and she kept wiping the bloody blade on the green blades, as if removing every last stain would somehow mean she hadn't cut the lamb. A clean sword would somehow mean that none of this had happened.

I watched her, and I wished there was something I could

clean that would take away what had happened to my mom. I stared into the cave. It looked like a wound, and the darkness that seeped out was an infection, the same one I had inside me, the same one driving me forward, propelling me to do anything to bring her back.

I walked the short distance to a small pool that formed off the side of the river and washed my hands in it. The water seemed louder and louder every time we returned. Either the rainwater was finally making its way down from the mountains, or nature itself was beginning to roar at the thought of what we were bringing into being. The Tree of Life.

We were close. We were getting so close.

―――――

Abra and I walked back to the house. It still wasn't time for supper. The sun was well over the western mountains and the vultures were nowhere to be seen.

Something about the whole situation felt wrong. Even though I knew what I was doing and I wanted to do it, I still felt like I was being set up. But by whom?

Abra? What did she care about the whole thing, other than the fact that she thought it was wrong to bring my mom back?

Mr. Jinn? More likely. Now that I knew I was alone, taking care of my own interests myself, I realized I didn't trust that man for anything. Him and that Amarok of his. I wouldn't be surprised by anything he did, good or evil, heroic or heinous. Actually, that's not true. If he did anything heroic, that would have surprised me.

Mr. Tennin? He had started off being such a nice guy, so soft-spoken and polite. But each time I talked to him he seemed to grow sharper around the edges, as if some fake self was wearing away, revealing a harder core.

I said good-bye to Abra and she started walking home, the handle of the sword still bulging slightly from the middle of her back. She walked quickly, on the verge of a run, and even though we had both agreed she would be safe in the daylight, especially once she got to her property, I think we were both less than convinced. I took a deep breath as she disappeared down the road. I hoped she would be okay.

The rain had never arrived that day, and I wandered over to the lightning tree and followed the long, ivory scar running down it. I didn't know the exact nature of lightning, its power or its speed. Would my dad cut down the tree now that it was dead? Would we even stay here on the farm, with all the memories of my mother, or would we leave?

I didn't want to leave.

"Sam!" Mr. Tennin shouted from the barn. His voice contained an edge of panic. "Sam, where are you!"

"Over here, by the tree," I yelled back.

He came running as fast as he could, and he could run fast. I was surprised. Mostly I had taken him for a middle-aged balding man who knew how to work and wear boots but who didn't have much in the way of athleticism. But his stride was long and strong, and even in work boots his feet were light.

"Sam," he said, bending over and catching his breath. Perhaps his endurance wasn't so great. "It's the lamb."

I ran past him toward the barn. I thought maybe my dad had found the lamb and now I was going to be in big trouble. Huge trouble. I ran through the dark doorway and into the barn. I slid around the corner and ran the long straightaway to the back, past the chickens and the cows in their pens, to the lamb's stall. My dad was inside, squatting down beside the animal.

He looked over his shoulder at me as I climbed the bars and swung my leg over. I dropped down into the pen beside him.

"Dad, I'm so sorry," I began, but he interrupted me.

"I'm sorry, boy," he said. "We found him too late."

What?

I looked around him and then looked away. Could all of that blood have come from Abra's small cut? I didn't want to, but I looked closer. I had to see what had left that huge pool of blood around the soles of my father's work boots.

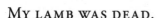

29

My lamb was dead.

My father's hands rested on the lamb's head, and his large, calloused fingers looked soft against the white wool. I noticed his wedding ring. He still had his wedding ring on, and for the briefest moment I comprehended the pain he must have felt when my mother died, the loss, perhaps even greater than mine. Yet he was moving on with his life. He was trying to survive without her. I felt selfish and small for wanting to bring her back.

He looked over at me.

"I'm sorry, boy," he said again.

I looked down at the lamb's leg, afraid of what I might see, afraid that Abra's cut had somehow opened up into a gaping wound. But what I saw immediately removed that fear and introduced a new one. The lamb's entire back half was gone, ripped off.

"What was it?" I asked. My voice came out in a hushed whisper, because I knew what it was. The Amarok.

My dad shook his head, pushed the ball cap back on his head, and rubbed his forehead. "I don't know," he said. "Might be the

253

same thing that made the tracks Mr. Miller saw a few days ago along the woods. Maybe some kind of crazy coyote, but the bite looks way too big for that. And the tracks they found by the Millers' farm, well, that wasn't a coyote. Too big even for a wolf, which we don't have around here anyway."

He pointed to a large arc that ran along the lamb's hindquarters, and I could tell he knew it wasn't a coyote. But we always try to fit the things we see into the world we understand, the world we can comprehend. Anything that doesn't fit into our tidy understanding brings fear.

"See that? That's a bite that didn't hold. Part of a bite." He looked at me. "That's a big bite," he said in a serious voice. "Bigger than anything I've ever seen. I don't want you wandering around anywhere from now on. You hear me? Not anywhere. At least not by yourself."

I nodded.

"You hear me?" he asked again, as if he wasn't convinced that I had actually committed to following his instructions.

"Yes, sir," I said.

And because he understood the wild heart of children and the ways they will convince themselves to disobey, he said it again. "I'm serious, boy. I don't want to find you like this."

"Yes, sir," I said again.

He sighed a heavy sigh that had more than a lamb's death in it. There was a tree and a lightning strike and a wife gone as well, and the fear that he might lose the only thing he had left. He stood slowly, the weight of it all trying to hold him down. He put his hand on the top bar and pulled himself over in one smooth movement.

"Tennin," he said. He had taken to calling Mr. Tennin by his last name only. "I'm going to go get some stuff to clean up this mess. You mind digging a hole in the corner of the garden? There's already a groundhog there. Might as well turn it into our own small graveyard."

He looked sad, sadder than he had been since the funeral, and I knew he was thinking of a different graveyard. He walked past Mr. Tennin, who grabbed a shovel from the wall and turned to follow him. But then Mr. Tennin stopped by the corner and turned back toward me.

"You'd better come with me, Sam. None of us should be alone, not for now."

Mr. Tennin asked if I wanted to dig a few shovelfuls, so I took the shovel from him and with my twelve-year-old strength dug some feeble bites from the summer earth. He took the shovel and clawed a little deeper. A small mound of earth built up there at the edge of the grass and the garden. Earthworms flailed as they were exposed in broken clods of dirt. The deep brown stood in contrast to the sharp green, and everything smelled alive and rich.

Above us, above the lightning tree, the vultures circled, perhaps drawn by the death of the lamb. Or maybe they were sent by Mr. Jinn to watch and report back. Whatever the case, their presence felt ominous. Their naked, pink heads looked greedy, and I wanted them gone.

"So where do I find the sunlight?" I asked.

"You got the water already?" He sounded surprised.

"Yeah."

"And you put it in the center of the stone?"

"Yeah."

He frowned and stuck the shovel in the earth. He looked at

me, his head cocked to the side. "You're serious about making this happen, aren't you?"

"Aren't you?" I asked.

He stared at me, and his stare evolved into a subtle nod, a determined yes. "Yeah," he said. "I am. I always have been. I just wasn't sure if that"—he nodded toward the barn and the dead lamb—"would make you change your mind."

I shook my head. "If I can bring my mom back, nothing will change my mind."

"Fair enough," he said. He looked around. "I thought it was going to rain today. Guess it's going to hold off now."

I looked up, but I was looking at the lightning tree and at the vultures high above us. Finally I scanned the clouds on the horizon. They were breaking up, and it looked like we might get a little bit of a sunset under the rim of those slate-colored clouds.

"Your father isn't going to be happy if you're off traipsing around the valley. Not after this. Not until they find that Amarok."

"Can they find it?" I asked. "Is that even possible?"

He looked at me, and I could tell he didn't understand what I meant.

"I mean, is it really real?" I asked. "Is it something you can see and hunt and kill?"

"Sam, what do you mean by real?"

He waited while I thought about that. Then he continued.

"All the myths you've ever heard, they're real in some sense. All the mythical creatures you've ever read about, they're out there, or at least they were at one time, in some form or another. This Amarok, of course it can be killed."

His words swirled around me, new and exciting. I didn't know what to say. I didn't know what to think.

"But beasts are mythical for a reason, usually because there's an aspect of them that you don't understand, something that doesn't fit with the rest of what you know about the world. The Amarok, it's part shadow. As real as you or me, but part of it lives in darkness."

I thought I understood.

"So, for someone to kill the Amarok, *the* Amarok—and there is only one, thank God—that person would have to figure out how to enter the shadow, at least partly, and hunt it there. And that may never happen."

"So it's old?" I asked.

"The Amarok? It's older than you even know how to imagine."

Mr. Tennin looked toward the house, and I looked back over my shoulder. My dad came through the door and walked down the porch steps. He didn't see us there at the edge of the garden, not right away, maybe because the light was dimming, or maybe his mind was elsewhere. Maybe it was because he was staring up at the lightning tree, searching for something. Someone.

My dad saw us then, so he changed direction and crossed the yard.

"The sunshine," Mr. Tennin said quickly under his breath, "is simply the light from a hot fire burning at night. It can't be too close to the Tree, and it can't be too far away. But once the Tree is in the stone on top of the water, and the fire is at the right distance, you'll know, because the blossoms will fall off and the Tree will begin to grow. Visibly."

He said that last word at the same time as he looked up and greeted my father. "Mr. Chambers," he said. "This look big enough?"

He gestured down toward the hole in the ground. It was dark, and for a second it reminded me of the cave holding the stone and the water.

My father nodded. "That'll do." He held up a host of old towels and rags and cloths. "You boys ready to do some cleaning up?"

We both nodded, and the three of us headed for the barn, but Mr. Tennin stayed back a little ways, held on to my arm, and kept me walking at his own slow pace. My father vanished into the barn ahead of us, and Mr. Tennin turned to me with serious eyes.

"Don't forget our deal," he said. "Don't forget."

~

I walk out of my room through moonlight that casts shadows all around me. I walk over to the fresh grave where Mr. Tennin and I buried the lamb just that night. I sit down beside it for some reason, and the grass is wet underneath me, I guess from the dew.

The dirt starts to move over the grave. I slide back, my eyes wide. First it crumbles, then it shakes, and soon it is being pushed away. Something isn't dead. Something is crawling out. I expect to see the lamb, and I'm terrified. A hand comes out. An arm reaches its way up out of the earth.

It's my mother.

I run to her and she hugs me tight.

Lightning strikes.

I wake up.

~

I looked at the small clock beside my bed. Just after midnight. I lay there for a moment and listened, but my dad had gone to bed long before and the television was turned off. I heard Mr. Tennin snoring in the neighboring bedroom. Outside my open window, an entire chorus of crickets and nighttime bugs chirped and screeched and hummed. I pushed my blankets down and got up.

In the backpack under my bed I had already packed a flashlight, matches, some newspaper, and an old pocketknife. I had also hidden a change of clothes down there, so I pulled those out and slipped into them as quietly as I could. My breathing felt way too loud. Every time my bed creaked under my weight, I held my breath, waited for the inevitable sound of footsteps in the hall.

But they never came. All was quiet in the house.

I crept across the room, and as I passed through the doorway I realized this was it. I would grow the Tree. I would finally see my mother again. There was no turning back from here.

30

I GUIDED THE SCREEN DOOR until it came to a quiet stop against the door frame and slid out into the warm, still air. It felt like I was the only moving thing on earth. I walked gingerly, as if the grass under my feet might explode into sound at any careless step, and I headed for the bright streetlight at the corner of the church. It was working again. I tried not to think about the night the light had gone out, the night the Amarok stood on the road and growled at Abra and me. I looked over my shoulder one more time to make sure no one had followed me from the house. I wondered where the Amarok was, which shadow it was clinging to. I didn't have to wait long to find out.

Somewhere between my house and the beginning of the Road to Nowhere, the Amarok ran past me, and I felt my insides turn cold. I knew it had devoured the lamb, and I knew it could have devoured me in that moment, but that's not what sent a shiver through my body. I grew cold because I realized there was a reason it kept me alive. It wanted me to grow the Tree so it could feed on it. Nothing that anyone could have told me would have dissuaded me from moving ahead with my plan to bring my mother back, but knowing that I was somehow on the same side as the Amarok made me feel lost.

Before bed that night, I had told myself I would go get Abra first. I had convinced myself that this was something we should do together—start the fire, grow the Tree, take off a piece of the fruit. But as soon as I woke in the middle of that Friday night turning to Saturday, I knew I had only been kidding myself. From here on out, I would have to do it alone. No Mr. Jinn, who might steal the Tree. No Mr. Tennin, who might destroy it. No Abra.

Only me.

My jog slowed to a walk, both because I was out of breath and because I didn't know what to do. I had told Mr. Jinn I would bring him Abra and the Tree. I had told Mr. Tennin the Tree would be his if he helped me find the stone, the water, and the sunshine. I knew I had to keep my word, but I didn't know how to do that when I had promised the Tree to each of them. What would they do to me if they found out?

But you can't tell them yet, I convinced myself. *Not yet. First I have to keep the Tree alive.*

I eventually passed Mr. Jinn's lane. I kept expecting the Amarok to double back and devour me, but when I looked into the shadows of my mind I couldn't find it. It wasn't anywhere close. So I disappeared into the shadows under the trees, down the Road to Nowhere. I walked through the dark toward the sound of the river and arrived at the old graveyard in the middle of the woods. I turned on my flashlight.

I didn't waste any time moving to my mother's grave site and gently prying the Tree from the earth with my pocketknife. The ground was soft and warm. My knife scratched against a few small pebbles in the ground, but most of the dirt was rich and clean. I picked up the Tree and stared at it in the darkness. I held it, and it felt like it was mine. I looked at the hole I had left in the loose dirt, and I thought, if I planted a piece of fruit directly over her grave, right there in that small hole, would that be enough to bring her back?

I walked over to the cave and looked into the shadows cast by the stones on that moonlit night, and I wondered what my mother would think of all this. It didn't take me long to come to a conclusion. I knew she would think I was being selfish, that I wasn't making a good decision. It hurt me to think she wouldn't be happy with me, but I still walked on. I didn't look back. I knew I could change her mind if I could simply have her there in front of me, with me.

I shone my narrow beam on the bowl where it sat at the back of the cave, and I placed the limp Tree inside, its tired roots barely held together by the dirt I had managed to dig up. I thought about the few drops of lamb's blood beneath it. The Tree looked pitiful there, sagging to one side.

It's nothing but a dying plant, I thought. *It's nothing but a hope that will never happen.*

And I laughed at myself. Why did I think this would change anything? Why did I believe?

But I did believe, no matter how silly the whole thing seemed. There was something spectacular about the small white blossoms that still clung to the tired green of the Tree. There was a smell about it, something that had come into the air when I dug up the roots. There was hope there, the kind of hope that makes anything seem possible.

I went to work making a fire, the sunlight Mr. Tennin had told me about. I gathered small twigs and leaves and pulled some paper out of my backpack. I peered into the shadows. I jumped at every sound, wondering if I had been found out.

I lit the match. A wind kicked up out of nowhere and blew it out. A small wisp of smoke twisted from the dead end of it, up through the narrow beam of my flashlight. I sighed and tried again. Match after match sputtered to life, only to be blown out. I was down to three matches when the flame managed to survive the transfer.

The fire grabbed at the paper and the leaves first, and a small stream of smoke rose. I blew lightly on the baby flame, and it reached up to the twigs and crackled, sending one or two sparks toward the sky. I scurried for a few larger twigs and small branches. At that point the fire was about three feet from the cave.

The Tree of Life started to look a little more withered, as if the fire was melting it, so I nudged the flaming branches a few feet farther from the cave with my foot and added some more branches. Light danced all around me, and I turned off my flashlight and put it into the backpack. I checked on the Tree again. It looked suddenly sturdy, and the small white flowers weren't drooping. They turned slowly, the way sunflowers lean toward the sun, and faced the fire. The blossoms opened wide, drinking in the light.

I sat down with my back against the stone cliff and stared into the fire. Every so often I glanced over my shoulder and into the cave, checking on the Tree, and each time it seemed a little healthier.

The warmth made my eyes heavy. The dancing light put my mind at ease. I leaned my head back against the stone. I had done it. Now all I could do was wait.

The shadows shifted like a hypnotist's locket. It was me and the fire and the stone behind my head and the Tree of Life and the changing shadows. I imagined there was an ocean on the other side of the trees, an ocean instead of a river that stretched out into eternity. And maybe, just maybe, if I sailed long enough and hard enough and didn't let the storms sink my ship, I could reach the other side, where I'd find my mother waiting, standing at the top of white cliffs, her hand shielding her eyes from the sun glaring off the crystal sea.

Because it was only me and the rock and the fire and the trees, it felt like the beginning of time. It felt like I was the first person and that all possibilities and hopes began and ended with me and that small Tree of Life in the cave behind me. The fire wasn't a fire anymore—it was our planet's sun, young and new. The trees weren't mature trees anymore—they were moments old, newly created. Even the shadows shed their strange nature and became young shadows, playful and harmless.

All of these thoughts swirled through my mind and I fell asleep, dreaming of the beginning of the world.

⁓

I woke up once in the night and the fire had grown low, so I threw on some more branches. As the fire rose back to life I thought I saw the Amarok moving among the treetops, its dark outline swaying with the movement of the highest branches. I ducked down and held very still, hoping it wouldn't see me pressed up against the rock. While it didn't come down from the trees, I thought I saw it stop and look at me, waiting for something to happen.

I saw the outline of a man as well, or something like a man but taller and somehow more beautiful, even though it was only a shadow. But as I threw more branches on the fire, the shadow man dissolved in the light.

I fell back to sleep.

I'm not sure what woke me. It could have been that my back had grown stiff from sleeping against the rock wall. It could have been the dim fog lit by a gray light that filled the forest or the distant rumble of approaching storm clouds. It could have been the realization that the fire had gone out, its dying breaths blowing smoke in my direction, a smoke that swirled and combined with the mist. It could have even been that I sensed someone approaching from the Road to Nowhere, their light footsteps snapping tiny twigs and breaking last fall's leaves.

Or it could have been the brief sighting I had of the Amarok, far off in the trees and the fog. I could barely see it, its black coat moving silently through the green. It padded off in the opposite direction, disappearing once again.

The sound of footsteps grew closer. I looked into the trees. The fog revealed only the outline of a person sneaking here and there through the shadows. A voice called out.

"Sam? Sam! What are you doing here?"

It was Abra, and I was filled with both relief and anger. Relief because I was scared of being there alone, with the Tree and the Amarok and the fog. But I also felt anger, because what was she doing there without me? Had she come to steal the Tree, only to find that I already had it?

Thunder rolled again, loud and close, and I could almost smell the rain.

"What am *I* doing here?" I asked. "What are *you* doing here?" My accusation didn't bother her.

"Everyone's looking for you!" she said. "They're all nervous after what happened to the lamb and the tracks they found. Your dad came to our house not long ago and said you were missing when he went out to do chores this morning. Everybody in the whole town is on the move, looking for you. My dad went searching in the mountains along the river . . ."

Her voiced stopped as she came closer. I saw her staring at the coals, still warm on the ground in front of me. They shone like small pieces of wet fruit. Smoke rose, a confession. She looked behind me and her face gave in to a weary sadness.

"Sam, what have you done?" she asked.

Various realizations flooded through my mind in that moment. My back wasn't resting up against the cliff wall anymore, although I hadn't moved. My hands, down at my sides, were holding on to massive tree roots so gnarled and twisted and large that they had to be roots from a tree that was thousands and thousands of years old. And even though the smoke from the fire still drifted toward me, I couldn't smell it. Instead, the sweetest fragrance surrounded me, the smell of new things, the smell of hope.

I turned and looked behind me. The Tree of Life had taken root, and it was huge. It had completely taken over the cave and grown up the side of the cliff wall until it stretched nearly as high as any of the surrounding trees. Branches spread out in every direction, each one drooping heavy with white blossoms the size of my fist.

Time seemed to stop as I examined the Tree. I stood up and touched the bark, surprised to find that it was soft like felt, and when I pressed on it my fingers left indentations. The leaves were large and almost oval, sort of like magnolia leaves, and they grew in an alternating pattern on the branches.

Some of the blossoms had yielded a lime-green fruit that blended in with the leaves. In fact, it was so close in color to the leaves that at first the fruit was invisible. But as soon as I saw one piece of it, I realized the entire Tree was covered with it. There was so much fruit that it weighed some of the lower branches down to where they almost touched the ground.

Lightning struck somewhere up in the mountain, and a few moments later it was followed by the growl of thunder. I walked over to one of those low branches and stared at the fruit. I could almost see inside it. Each one was like a tiny crystal ball, swirling with images and dreams and years. I reached up and touched the fruit, and it was as smooth as glass. I pulled my hand away, worried that I would shatter it, and that somehow the shattering of one piece would ruin the entire tree. When I pulled my hand away, one of the leaves caught in my fingers and stayed in my hand. I stared at it, stared into its waxy surface, but it didn't have the same quality as the fruit. There was nothing there to see, except perhaps the deepest green in the universe. I held it tightly in my hand.

Abra seemed to be staring at all the same things I stared at, and her eyes went from disappointment in me to wonder at that impossible Tree. She walked to a different branch and did the same thing I had done—touched the smooth fruit, felt the soft bark of the branches.

"This is it," she murmured. "This is the Tree of Life."

"What did you expect?" I asked.

"What did I expect? Sam, I helped you because I realized that if I was going to be your friend, I had to help you. But I didn't actually believe it. I didn't believe this would happen. And I thought that even if it could happen, you would still do the right thing."

Her blue eyes stared desperately into mine. "I never believed it," she whispered.

"And now what?" I asked. "Now that you see it's true?"

She pulled her hands away from the Tree reluctantly. "You can't do this, Sam," she said. "It's not right. You can't bring your mother back."

When she said those words, I felt that old darkness rise up inside me like a fire that had been fanned.

"Can't?" I pointed toward the branches above us, as if every single piece of fruit stood as a reason it could be done.

"Shouldn't," she said, shaking her head. "Shouldn't. She's at peace now! You want to bring her back to this?"

"What do you think I should do?" I asked, trying hard to control the anger I felt. "This is it! This is what everyone wants, isn't it? Death, gone! No more sadness! No more loss!"

My pleading anger grew into a rage, fueled by the more frequent lightning strikes and the pattering sound of the rain beginning to hit the highest leaves of the trees. A storm was brewing.

"Sam, you have to destroy it! This is the story Mr. Tennin was telling us about! This Tree isn't meant for us."

"Destroy it?" I said, almost laughing. "Destroy it? How could we destroy it now? Even if I wanted to, how could we—you and me, two kids—keep this from happening?"

She answered quietly, "With fire."

31

I SHOOK MY HEAD. I prepared to argue with her, to tell her all the reasons for bringing my mother back—that she didn't want to be dead, that she was waiting for me on the other side of the water, that she was fighting her way back up from under the ground. I tried to figure out how to explain the emptiness her absence had left inside me. But before any of the words came out, a huge shadow fell from the surrounding trees.

It was the Amarok, and it walked slowly toward Abra, baring its teeth and giving a growl that shook the earth under my feet, a growl that mingled with the thunder and the lightning. It felt different from when we had seen the Amarok on the road. At that point it had seemed curious. But there, in the shadow of the Tree of Life, the Amarok was different. It was angry, and it perceived Abra as a threat to the life of the Tree. Somehow it knew that she would destroy it if she was given a chance.

Abra looked tiny, staring at the Amarok approaching through the mist, its massive paws snapping branches and crushing leaves. She turned slightly away from me to face the Amarok, but I could still see her bright blue eyes flashing as they faced the east and the coming storm.

"You don't belong here," she said, and I was surprised at how little fear there was in her voice.

Even though the Amarok walked slowly, it covered a lot of ground with its long strides. Its eyes were black, two glittering pieces of coal, and there was a depth there, a darkness so deep that it didn't have a bottom. The Amarok's growl turned into a low, slow voice.

"That fruit does not belong to you," it said, and I shuddered, hearing the words from my dream.

"I don't want the fruit. I want to destroy it," she said, gritting her teeth with determination.

It growled again, so close it could have reached out and put one of its massive paws on her shoulder. She bent her knees slightly and reached around behind her, and I noticed the bulge at her back. She pulled the sword out from where she had been hiding it and held it out in front of her. The tip of it trembled, and I knew she was afraid.

The sword was definitely longer than it had been before, or maybe it grew after she pulled it out, because it was more the length of a normal sword, and it wasn't a dull gray anymore. It glowed a silvery white, like glass covered by a winter frost and lit up by the morning sun. The Amarok stopped moving for a moment. The sword changed things. It filled that early Saturday morning with all kinds of new possibilities.

The rain fell, heavy and clean. The drops disturbed everything, rustling the branches, causing the rocks to glisten, and making the dead leaves on the forest floor dance around. I guess that's what made Abra, the Amarok, and me stand out so much—everything else was moving, twitching, yet the three of us stood there completely still, unwavering, waiting to see who would make the first move.

The Amarok circled Abra again, and I found myself worried that the animal might somehow damage the Tree. That thought brought to the front of my mind how far I had fallen. I was more worried about the Tree than I was about my own friend.

"That fruit does not belong to you, to keep or to destroy," it growled at her, and I could barely understand its words. They were a combination of human sounds and animal growls. They spilled into being like vomit.

Without warning the Amarok lunged at Abra and she swung the sword, but the huge wolflike beast dodged her swing. It kept drifting around her from side to side. It darted at her, she swung the sword again, and the Amarok feinted to the side. She took one swing that knocked her off balance, and the massive black wolf plunged in and grabbed her entire body in its jaws, its mouth wrapping around her waist.

For one heartbreaking moment, I remembered the lamb, but for some reason the Amarok didn't bite clean through. It shook her viciously and she went limp. I felt a numbness spread through me, disbelief that all of this was happening, and the numbness slowly turned to horror and fear as the Amarok tossed Abra at me, knocking me over. She was completely limp, lifeless.

What had I done? First my mom, dead because I had to have a stupid cat. Now Abra lay on the ground, dying because I insisted on regrowing the Tree. Was my dad next? Would I lose everyone I loved, one by one, because of my selfishness?

Abra's body had knocked me onto my hands and knees, and the leaf I held from the Tree of Life was crushed. There was a stickiness inside it that oozed out onto my fingers.

"Now what about you?" the Amarok growled. "Whose side are you on?"

But the words came from a faraway place. The crushed leaf's thick, sticky sap was like the gel from an aloe plant, and it had a strong aroma. In the midst of that smell, the voice of the Amarok faded off to somewhere distant, somewhere far away, somewhere insignificant. I had the clearest vision of my mother's face that I had had since her death, and she was smiling at me. I realized that some of my visions had been true, that she actually was watching for me from the top of a tall white cliff on the other side of an eternally wide body of water, but she wasn't waiting for me to bring her back.

She was waiting to see what I would do.

And the smell of the leaf from the Tree of Life brought back so many good memories of my mother, memories of her taking me to the pumpkin patch in the fall when the shadows were long and cool, memories of the flowers we had planted together and of sledding down the small hill behind the barn when I was young. I even remembered things I couldn't possibly have remembered, like the way she looked at me when I was born, as if I was a treasure she would never give up, and how she fed me a bottle and sang me her favorite songs with her eyes closed and her voice clean and clear.

I remembered the songs, all the verses and choruses, the notes and the silence in between. They swirled around me in the fragrance of the broken leaf, and as those words and notes faded, the verse the preacher had read at her funeral service rose up through them.

On either side of the river is the Tree of Life with its twelve kinds of fruit, producing its fruit each month, and the leaves of the Tree are for the healing of the nations.

"The Tree is mine," I said. "I brought it here, and I grew it. Now I can do whatever I want with it."

The Amarok moved toward me, sensing my doubt. I think it knew somehow that I wasn't sure anymore, that I didn't know what to do, that I was as likely to destroy the Tree as I was to keep it.

"That Tree is not yours."

But I could see inside the Amarok, and in the midst of that darkness was a heart of fear and doubt. The darkness inside me was dying, withering under the influence of the broken leaf, and I could see clearly. I could see things for what they truly were.

I reached down and picked up the sword. There was no time to find something to protect my skin—I had to grab it immediately. It burned my hand, but I gritted my teeth and held it tight. The pain was excruciating, and I could feel my skin blistering, bubbling up and melting and sticking to the hot metal, but I knew I had to hold on. My entire arm went numb from the pain.

I cried out, a primal sound, as the physical pain mixed with my deep sadness.

Abra lay still on the ground behind me, and I didn't know if she was alive or dead. The Amarok stared me down, growling, saliva dripping from its glistening teeth. The Tree was still growing, slowly, and the movement it made as it grew was like a tree in the midst of a breeze, its leaves rustling, its fruit swaying. Lightning tore through the sky, followed by an immense explosion of thunder. The rain came down heavier.

Two flashes of light fell down in the midst of all this chaos. Those lights pounded into the ground and took form, and I knew right away that one was Mr. Jinn and the other was Mr. Tennin and that they were the two cherubim who had been fighting over the Tree of Life since the beginning of time. They shimmered and were of human form but were also something more, as if all my life I had seen humans only in a cloudy mirror until that moment. What I saw of them when they slowed was beauty and strength and power.

They didn't speak, but sometimes I could sense what they were saying to each other. It was as if their thought, their consciousness, was all around me, but instead of individual words, their communication was made up of streaming raw emotion and calculated movements. They streaked through the fog and the smoke like comets, and the sound of their rising was the screaming of jet planes or the roar of rockets.

They would stop for a moment, and that was when I saw their form, but mostly they moved and flew in a blur around the Tree and over the river, and sometimes their collisions with each other made loud cracks, like the snapping of an electric cable when it comes loose from the pole and strikes the ground. There were bursts of flame when they collided too, and the fire fell at the base of the trees on the far side of the river and licked at the broad trunks. Soon smoke from that fire mingled with the fog.

For brief moments I recognized them as two powerful men, and they wrestled there among the trees. Mr. Jinn's face was desperate and determined. His mouth was a firm line of desire, and it propelled him, strengthened him. He pushed Mr. Tennin to the brink of the river, and then they were in it, Mr. Jinn holding Mr. Tennin under.

I found myself holding my breath, wondering if he would come up. But I didn't have much time to worry about him—the Amarok roared, and the roots of the forest groaned in reply. It was like thunder in the earth, the sound of a thousand fault lines slipping out of place. I held the sword up again and glanced over at Abra.

Mr. Tennin rose out of the water, and when he did I recognized in him the quiet confidence of Truth. I could tell that he would stand not by the sheer power of emotion but in the conviction of someone acting simply out of love. I felt an ache for him, the same ache you feel looking out over a snow-peaked mountain range or walking through an ancient temple.

The Amarok came at me again, and I held the sword out toward it. It dodged off to the side and snapped at my face, but I moved and ducked and swung the sword like a baseball bat. The air around us crackled with the fighting of the cherubim, and the morning lit up as the sun prepared to rise over the eastern mountain, illuminating the back of the gray storm clouds. Abra still wasn't moving.

I held the sword in front of me, my arm still numb with pain. The Amarok circled. Behind it, Mr. Tennin and Mr. Jinn flew straight up into the sky like fireworks heading for their apex. Through the trees, through the smoke, and up into the low, gray clouds of morning. I tried to watch, but the Amarok growled. I waved the sword at it again.

The blade grew brighter and brighter. I wondered if it was getting ready to explode. Then two things happened at once: I took a swing at the Amarok as it snapped at me, and one of the lights fell from the sky so hard and fast that it sank down into the earth. Everything seemed to go completely still.

I realized the top half of the glowing blade was covered in blood, a dark blood almost black, and I looked at it strangely, wondering if somehow it was my blood. Was I dying? Was this the end?

The Amarok looked stunned, stopped in its tracks, and fell over dead—my last desperate swing had cut clean through its throat. I threw the sword to the ground and cried out as it tore the burned skin away. I held my hands palms up so they wouldn't touch anything, and I ran over to see which of the cherubim had fallen.

I think I was crying then, although I can't remember exactly why. Maybe it was the terrible pain from my burns finally registering in my brain. Maybe they were tears of relief that come after a terrible fright—the Amarok, after all, was dead. The great shadow had passed. Or maybe I was crying because somehow I knew who I would find in that hole in the ground. Maybe I sensed, even without seeing it, that something deep had shifted in the world.

I fell to my knees, my palms still facing up, and looked down into the hole the fallen cherub had created.

It was Mr. Tennin. And while it was the force of his fall that had caused the ground to rise up around him, for a moment it seemed the earth had done that of its own accord—had swelled up, maybe to protect him, maybe to hold him. It was almost as if even the earth itself knew what was taking place and wanted to help, wanted to play a part.

He wasn't bald and skinny anymore. It's impossible for me to describe exactly what he looked like besides this: he was beautiful and strong and there was power there, even after he fell. But I also had the sense that what power remained was leaving him fast, that he had somehow sprung a leak and everything that was bright and magnificent about him was growing dim. I wanted to reach out and touch his face, but my hands were so badly burned that I simply held them out over him, as if I was trying to hold down his fleeing spirit.

"Mr. Tennin," I said. "What . . . what happened?"

He turned a weary face to me, and all the words he said from that moment until the end came in a whisper.

"I fell."

There was weariness in his voice, but there were also tiny strands of relief.

"But what does that mean?" I asked. "Are you dying?"

He shook his head slowly. "No. It just means I can't stay."

"Where will you go?"

He looked me in the eyes, and I realized that he somehow knew my thoughts, that he had seen my visions or perhaps I had communicated them to him unknowingly.

"First I will go across the ocean, beyond the white cliffs, and then, who knows?"

I felt desperation rise inside me. "What if you can't come back?" But even as I said it, I knew what his response would be.

"Come back? Why would I care about coming back? Sam, if there's anything you should know, it's this: death is not a destination. It's a passing, a transition into eternity, the rest of time. When you leave this place, everything you have known will seem like only a dream or the memory of a dream. Dying is the shedding of one cloak and the taking on of another. Death is a gift."

I put my head down and wept. "I find that so hard to believe." I felt helpless, as if everything that had ever mattered to me was passing through my fingers.

"Life is not only made up of what you can see. This is the beginning of belief."

"It seems like so much," I said in a whisper. "So much to believe in. So much to give up."

"Samuel," he whispered. "Always remember this."

I could smell wood smoke drifting around me, the only slow thing in the midst of the gathering storm.

"Death," he said, then paused before whispering the last three words, "is a gift."

I looked at Mr. Tennin and had this sudden realization that he had been there for me all along. He had moved into our house to find the Tree, yes, but also to keep watch over me. He had protected me from the Amarok on the night we ran out of gas. He had helped me grow the Tree so that he might destroy it and keep me from yet another mistake. And now he was showing me that this path through death was one that could be traveled bravely, with dignity.

He shimmered like the flickering of a lightbulb nearly out. Then he was gone, and I stayed there, kneeling beside an empty hollow in the ground. I had so many more things I wanted to ask him.

A fire raged in the forest on the other side of the river. I thought it would cross over and consume all of us, leaving nothing. No one would ever know what had happened. The story would die with me and Abra. This was the end.

A shadow fell over me, the shadow of a person. I turned from where Mr. Tennin had fallen and looked over my shoulder. It was Mr. Jinn, not as the cherub who had just proven himself victorious, but as the dirty, straggly farmer still wearing that old brown overcoat, still walking with a limp.

"You killed my Amarok," he said, staring not at my face but at my blistered hands.

"Your Amarok? It wasn't yours," I said.

He waved his hand at me. "We have more important things to discuss," he said.

"Like what?" Pain shot through my hands again, and I let the cool rain fall on them, run over them.

"You're powerful, Sam," he said in a reluctant voice. "If, as a boy, you can kill an Amarok, well, there's nothing you can't do." He paused, and his eyes searched my face, searched for any signs of weakness. "You could bring your mother back, Sam. Think about it. You could bring her back. And you could be a prince among men, wealthier than Solomon, because you could sell what everyone wants: life. Forever life."

I shook my head, but the alluring smell of the leaf had faded and neither of us knew what I would do.

He pointed at one of the low-hanging branches above my head. "There it is, Sam! You did everything you had to do. You found the Tree, the stone bowl, the water, the sunlight. You did it all yourself. You even killed the Amarok, something no one else has been able to do, not for all of time. Now all you have to do is reach up and take a piece of fruit. Bury it deep in the earth above your mother's coffin. You can bring her back with it. Life from this fruit goes down deep. It's so close. Everything you wanted is here for the taking."

I stood up and looked at the fruit above my head, noticing for the first time that it came in various shapes and shades of green. Some were shaped like pears, the color of dark green grass. Others were round like limes, but so light green they were almost yellow. Still others looked like apples, but smaller and softer. The leaves hung heavy and thick, and I imagined all of that beautiful sap in each one. What people would pay for such healing power!

I would never have to die. My father would never have to die. And in my naïve youth, it all seemed so good. Living forever seemed like a wonderful fruit to eat.

I reached for a piece of it, then glanced at Mr. Jinn. His eyes followed my hand. They were hungry and intent and scanned the Tree as if he was looking for something. His tongue flicked at the edges of his lips, and the hint of a smile turned up the corners of his mouth. His hands came out of the deep pockets of his overcoat, and they were round and heavy and trembling. I remembered those hands from the room at the antique store, the way they had pounded the table.

I realized he couldn't see the fruit. He was waiting for me to pluck it and give it to him.

"Just imagine, Sam," he said. "Your mother here again, in the flesh. Welcoming you home from school and making you breakfast and tucking you into bed at night. Think of it."

Whether it was because of some special power he had or the recent sharp visions the sap had brought to mind, I could picture it all perfectly, what life would be like with my mother. I shook my head again, but my hand reached closer for the glassy fruit, and in each one I saw a vision of my mother's face, smiling.

That beautiful fruit!

"No," I said. "The Tree is mine. I found it. I brought it here. I grew it. It's mine and I won't give it to you."

The desire for it was too great, and I couldn't imagine sharing it, not even with Mr. Jinn, the one who had helped me find it.

"Yours?" Mr. Jinn's voice grew terrible and strong, and rays of the same glorious power I had seen in Mr. Tennin shone through the rags of his clothing. He was rising.

"You won't?" he asked, and this time his laugh filled the valley and the sky and made the trees bend away from us, trying to escape from some unseen power.

He shook his head, and I felt fear tremble inside me because something in his face switched from mirth to regret. He was about to do something to me that he didn't want to do. He reached his hand out, and my entire body clenched tight in an unseen vise. I couldn't move. It was as if he had drawn a circle around my soul. But then he dropped me in a heap and looked past me, toward the trunk of the Tree of Life, and surprise showed on his face, and disappointment.

I looked over at the Tree, and there was Abra. She sat beside the Tree, and the hilt of the sword stuck out from the soft trunk. A blackness had already begun to spread from where she had plunged the fiery sword into the Tree, and the branches had all begun to sink, as if it was deflating.

Mr. Jinn was overcome with anger. Multiple lightning strikes lit up the fog, shattering tree branches and exploding limbs, and were immediately followed by the sound of thunder. He ran at Abra, hands raised, coat billowing out and away from him, the light of a powerful, angelic glory streaking out in rays.

Abra stood up and pulled the sword from the dying Tree. It came out easily, like a knife pulled out of butter. She grasped it with two hands, raised it over her head, and threw it at Mr. Jinn. I was amazed at the force with which she threw it, and as it moved away from her, it seemed to increase in speed, as if it was obeying not only her physical will but also her emotional desire. It stuck into Mr. Jinn's chest as easily as it had gone into the Tree.

He stopped. He stared at her. He ripped the sword out as he fell, and it clattered onto the rocks.

The fruit all fell in one dropping motion, one thousand visions, and when they hit the ground each piece shattered and a strong wind blew through the valley. Every single shard of fruit was blown away into the sky. I closed my eyes and imagined those shards spreading out over an eternal ocean, then sinking into the water and dissolving. I imagined the waves rolling in huge breakers against a perilous, rocky coast, each wave carrying tiny glass-like pieces of fruit from the Tree of Life. I imagined the beach made up of sand from that pulverized fruit, and I could see the white cliffs rising out of the sand. And there, at the top of the cliff, I saw my mother smile one last time, turn, and walk away.

She was gone, and I couldn't bring her back.

Death is that ocean, filled with the dissolving shards of fruit from the Tree of Life. It is the sound of waves that crest but never break, a sound that rolls on forever.

32

ABRA CLOSED HER EYES for a moment, and I crawled to her, past the small depression in the ground where Mr. Tennin had fallen, past a fading Mr. Jinn, past the dead Amarok and the pile of ashes that had been the fire from the night before. We both sat with our backs against the Tree of Life, and we watched it die.

We leaned our heads back against the Tree, and I looked up at the top branches. The leaves had begun to change color, from that dark green to a blackish green, then to a reddish black, and finally to a deep, blood red. Autumn came for the Tree of Life in a matter of minutes. Seasons passing in a moment. Soon the entire Tree was waving crimson in the strong breeze.

The leaves fell and swirled in miniature twisters, and the breeze blew some of the leaves into the river and others into the flames or down the path to the Road to Nowhere. I caught a few as they fell and broke them apart. Too late. They were dry inside, and they crumbled in my hands. But even their dust soothed my skin. The blisters did not heal, but the pain dissolved. I grabbed more as they fell, and Abra rubbed them over her stomach where the Amarok had held her in its jaws. We were, both of us, in need of something to take our pain away.

Soon the entire Tree was leafless and old, and the branches clattered together like bones. The wind grew stronger and a few brittle branches fell around us. The fire rose like a wall up against the far side of the river, and a few of the trees that reached toward it from our side smoked and burst into flame. All that remained beyond the stream was ash and the blackened skeletons of tall, skinny trees still blazing, and among all of it the rocks that led up into the eastern mountain. The fire moved, devouring, looking for more fuel.

We were too tired to move, too tired to think through what had happened, but I knew we had to get out of the woods. Quickly. There was the pungent smell of smoke, the way it stung my eyes and burned in my throat, the glistening, black fur of the Amarok, the storm clouds passing over us, giving way to strands of wispy sky. The blue peeking through reminded me of the water in my dream, the eternal waves, and the white cliffs at the far side.

"My mom's the one who took the Tree to the cemetery," Abra said quietly, as if talking to herself.

"What?"

"My mom. She had wondered what we were doing over in the other side of the house, and she thought it was weird that the closet was locked, so she asked my dad to open the door. She found the Tree inside. 'It reminded me of Lucy,' she said, so she took it to her grave."

I started weeping, full of so many emotions. Regret. Sadness. Relief. Abra reached over and held on to my hand. It hurt, but I did not pull away. My own tears felt good on my face, as if some buried piece of me had finally fought to the surface, and something about those tears reminded me of the aloe from the leaves on the Tree. There is healing, after all, in sadness, and sometimes only tears will bring it. Abra's grip reminded me that I was human. I was here. I felt real again. I felt alive.

Mr. Jinn made a sound. He was laughing.

Abra and I stood together and walked toward him. Mr. Jinn reminded me of Mr. Tennin in the moments before he had vanished—he was weak, though not entirely powerless, but what power remained seemed to be easing its way out of him.

He moved only his eyes as he looked at us, and he kept laughing.

"What?" Abra asked, and we couldn't show him the contempt we wanted to because part of the glory he had shown earlier lingered there with him, like a mist within the fog. It was a wonder and a splendor, even hidden as it was beneath the curse he had carried for centuries. For millennia.

He shook his head back and forth, barely, and his laughing dimmed to a weak smile. "You don't even know, do you?" he asked. "You don't even realize what you have done."

That's when I recognized it. The darkness inside me was gone. After everything that had happened, I had given it up. I believed Mr. Tennin. I hadn't wanted the Tree to die, and maybe I couldn't have killed it if it had been up to me, but it was gone now.

I was free.

"What don't we know?" Abra asked.

"His mother," he whispered, staring at me. "There's nothing you can do to bring her back."

He looked over at Abra. "And you . . . You have only just begun."

He disappeared.

Abra retrieved the sword where it lay in the depression. It had returned to its normal color and size, and she held it tightly. But Mr. Jinn's words didn't fill me with terror anymore. I was okay, relieved even, that my mother could rest in peace. I looked around at the burning world, and I realized this was no place to bring her back to. The beach and the cliffs and the green fields beyond seemed like a wonderful place to be. Instead of anger or bitterness, I was filled with a sense of hope that I would see her again, that I could join her there. Maybe someday I could leave all of this behind.

"We have to go," I said, feeling the heat from the fire. We hurried back to the Road to Nowhere through smoke that filled the trees like fog, then continued on to where the road was paved with stones, past Mr. Jinn's house. We were both exhausted and coughing, our lungs burning. Abra put her arm around me and we stumbled down that road together.

I saw my father's car careening up Kincade Road, a cloud of dust billowing out behind him. As he got closer I could see him hunched over the steering wheel, a look of desperation on his face. My father was like an approaching storm.

"Look," I said to Abra, pointing west, away from the fire and the river, over the fields of deep green corn now approaching waist height. A long, straight line of vultures flew out of the valley and disappeared over the mountain.

My father took us to the hospital, but I remember very little about the drive. There was the rough road we bounced over, and the loose gravel pinging up under the car. There was the smell of smoke coming through the open windows, mingled with the heavy moisture of a wet July morning. There was the smooth hum of wheels on the highway, the gradual slipping in and out of sleep. There was Abra and me leaning against each other, exhausted, relieved.

The time I spent in the hospital was also a blur.

"Smoke inhalation," the doctors said. "Third-degree burns."

I guess the leaves hadn't healed me completely.

Abra was in worse shape, and the two of us had trouble explaining her injuries: a series of deep punctures in her chest, in her abdomen, and down her back. A broken rib. A sliced foot. In the end, our parents and doctors chalked it up to two children who had nearly been killed in a forest fire, who had injured themselves while fleeing the oncoming flames. We were okay with that. There seemed very little benefit in explaining the details of what we had been through, and even less chance that anyone would believe us if we did.

But I do remember one thing now. Something I had forgotten for many, many years.

I remember lying in my hospital bed that first night after everyone else had left. I knew Abra was in her own room, recovering. I was thinking about how close we had come to death, and I realized I was both relieved and disappointed not to have made that journey. I missed my mom, but I realized I loved life. I wasn't quite ready to die.

The doctor came in. I say she was a doctor, though in hindsight I have very little idea who the woman actually was. At first I thought I was dreaming because she looked so much like my mother. I thought I was having another one of my nighttime visions, and I settled into it, believing. I had come to enjoy those moments with my mother, even if they weren't strictly real. One of the machines I was connected to let out its rhythmic beep. Another hummed on into eternity.

But then she spoke, and I knew it was no dream.

"Sam," she said, and she even carried herself like my mother, so that I lifted myself up on my elbows and stared closer.

Could it be? I wondered if the Tree, during its brief time beside the river, had leached its life into the ground, enough that it brought her back. Maybe the roots of the Tree had reached far enough into the forest, all the way to the small cemetery and my mother's grave. Maybe this was the beginning of some new era, when all the once-dead people in our valley would come to life, walk among us, reunite with the people they loved. For a moment I imagined the celebrations, the surprise, the joy.

But it was only the late hour talking, or the medication, or my last hopes, because when she got closer I looked into the woman's eyes and recognized immediately that this was not my mother. The blue was not there. The humanness was missing. This person's eyes were dark and endless.

If you've ever looked into the eyes of one of them, you'll know what I mean. Her eyes were exactly like those of Mr. Jinn and Mr. Tennin—eternal, like the space between the stars.

I suddenly realized what she was.

"Why are you here?" I asked. I stared hard at her. She was dressed like a nurse, but she didn't have a name tag on. "Who are you?" Before, when I thought she was my mother, I had wanted to get as close as possible, but now I pushed myself backward in my hospital bed, as far away from her as I could get.

She looked sad for me, as if I would never understand.

"How are you feeling?" She held up a clipboard, writing a few notes on it, and for a moment I was confused. Maybe I was imagining things. Maybe she was only trying to do her job.

"I'm okay," I said. "It's the middle of the night. Can we do this in the morning?"

She nodded and scribbled a few more things on her clipboard. "Your appetite okay?"

I nodded.

"Are you feeling achy at all? Sick to your stomach? Trouble breathing?"

"No," I said. She made me feel tense, uneasy. It wasn't the questions she was asking. It was her. It was her presence.

"Exactly what happened in the forest beside the river?" she asked, eyebrows arched, as if it was a completely normal question for a doctor to be asking a patient.

"What?" I asked, confused.

"I believe there was a gentleman there with you in the woods?"

I closed my mouth tight, bit my lip.

"Isn't that right?" She bent closer. "I believe he worked for your father."

"Mr. Tennin?" I whispered, and for a moment it felt like I didn't have any control over my mouth. It felt like my lips and tongue were going to say whatever information was in my brain. She would ask, and my mind would tell her whatever she needed to know.

I shook my head. Maybe I was trying to clear the cobwebs. Maybe I was trying to wake up.

"What happened to Mr. Tennin?" she asked, and I could tell that for her, everything rested on the answer to this question.

"He fell," I whispered.

She sighed, but I could not tell if it was a sigh of sadness or relief, or the kind of sigh when someone tells you something you already thought to be true but didn't know for sure.

"Do you have it?" she asked, and I knew she was talking about the sword.

I couldn't help it. I shook my head, hoping that would be enough to protect me.

"Do ... you ... have ... it?" she asked again.

"No," I said.

"Does your friend have it?" she asked.

I shook my head again. I remembered seeing Abra retrieve the sword after Mr. Jinn disappeared, and I remembered that it had seemed suddenly small, almost insignificant, like a pocketknife, as she tucked it back in her waistband. It took a great amount of willpower not to answer the woman's question. It was like trying not to respond to someone who says something untrue about you. Words started escaping, but instead of holding them in, I turned them into my own question.

"Who are you?" I asked again.

I sensed a great tension rising in her, and it spilled into the air between us. It was a cloud of anger and resentment, and for a moment I thought she had been sent to avenge Mr. Jinn.

Whose side was she on?

"I need to talk to your friend Abra." She said the words as if explaining something to a very small child who might not understand.

But I shook my head once again. "Who are you?"

She leaned forward and whispered her name. Her breath was ice-cold against my ear, and she lingered there a moment longer than necessary, seeming to enjoy how uncomfortable she made me. Her name was one I had never heard before, but it filled me with darkness, the kind that you can feel closing in around you.

I slept.

When I woke up the next morning I couldn't remember

exactly what had happened, though her name was etched in my mind. I doubted for many years if it had actually even happened.

I never told Abra.

Koli Naal. That was her name. Koli Naal.

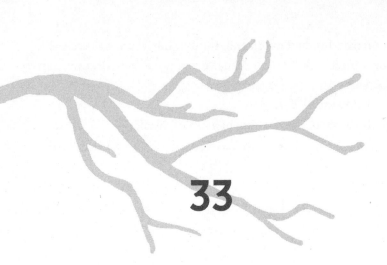

33

IT WAS A SUNDAY MORNING in the fall. The fire had ravaged the valley. The trees that lined the eastern ridge of mountains had been scorched all the way along the river, all the way down to Deen. The town had nearly caught fire as well, but the townspeople had fought it, and the wind had changed, and that storm had finally come in. Mr. Jinn's farm was reduced to ash, as were our house and barns and most of the fields. It was a fire unlike anything anyone had ever seen, and even the green things had caught.

But small signs of life reappeared: tractors had dug out new foundations, and structures rose from the desolation. My father had decided to rebuild, and the new farmhouse was taking shape. It seemed like my father knew more than he was letting on—there was no other explanation for his lack of questions. Why didn't he ask about my injuries? Why didn't he talk about Mr. Tennin's sudden disappearance? In any case, it looked like our new home would be finished before winter. The leaves of the trees on the western mountains, unaffected by the fire, had turned red and yellow and orange, as if the whole mountainside was ablaze.

Abra came to the partially rebuilt house as she had been in the habit of doing on Sunday afternoons. Sometimes we would walk out to the Tree of Life and sit there with our backs against the hard wood, surrounded by the blackened poles of burned trees and the smell of an old fire. But every Sunday that we went out, we found more and more signs of life. The animals returned, creeping through the barren trees, and the tiny green plants created a haze over the gray ash. The trees would be replaced. Life would come up out of that dead ground in the spring.

Everything felt like recovery. Everything, that is, except the Tree of Life. It somehow looked even more lifeless than the other burned trees.

We never said much when we went out there. Mostly we just waited for something, although we weren't sure what.

On that particular Sunday afternoon, about three months after the day the angels fell, Abra and I looked through Mr. Tennin's box again. We sat on the porch and examined all the articles, paged through the atlas. We tried to find the pattern in the appearance of the Tree of Life, but it all seemed so random, those strange trees that sprang up all around the world and then were killed or died under mysterious circumstances.

"Look!" Abra said, pointing toward the church.

Icarus meandered along the road, his tail tall and curling.

"The cat," I said, and the strangeness of that entire summer seemed somehow summed up in those two words. We watched as he disappeared behind the church, walking slowly through the decimated forest toward the river.

"Maybe there isn't a pattern," Abra said, her attention back on the articles and the atlas. "Maybe there's no way of telling where it will appear again."

I shook my head. "But Mr. Jinn knew. He knew it was coming here."

Mr. Jinn's farm was a mystery. When no one showed up to claim it, he was officially declared dead and the farm was eventually auctioned off. We never found out what had happened to the real Mr. Jinn—the man, not the angel who took his name. New people moved in, strange people nearly as private as Mr. Jinn had been. But their neatness extended outside the house, and as the years passed, the grounds of the farm eventually looked immaculate. Silent and lonely, but immaculate.

We studied the contents of Mr. Tennin's box and made maps and charts and long lists of numbers, but we didn't get any closer to figuring it out.

I walked with Abra all the way out the lane. My dad must have been burning debris somewhere, because there was smoke in the air—the smell of fall, the warning of winter. It took me back to the day the angels fell. The smell of wood smoke always did after that.

"Let's go say hi to Lucy," Abra said. In those months after the fire, she had taken to calling my mom by her first name, and something about it seemed right, as if she was one of us, a friend, walking right there beside us.

So we went up Kincade Road, into the forest, all the way to the cemetery, and as we meandered among the stones, Abra let her hands rise up from her sides as if she was flying.

At my mother's grave, we sat down. I told Abra all of my favorite stories about my mom, and she listened, even though

I had told them all to her before. I felt that sense of peace again, a peace I couldn't explain, that what had happened would be okay, and anything that wasn't all right would be made right before The End.

I remembered Mr. Tennin's words, and I tried hard to believe them.

Death is only a passage.

Death is just the exchanging of cloaks.

Death is not a destination.

Death is a gift.

I grabbed a red leaf and held its stem in one of my scarred hands. The wind had blown it all the way from the western mountain, where the trees were still alive and in their full autumn glory. Suddenly, a cloud of those leaves from the other mountain swept into the woods and swirled around us, red and yellow and orange, like fire.

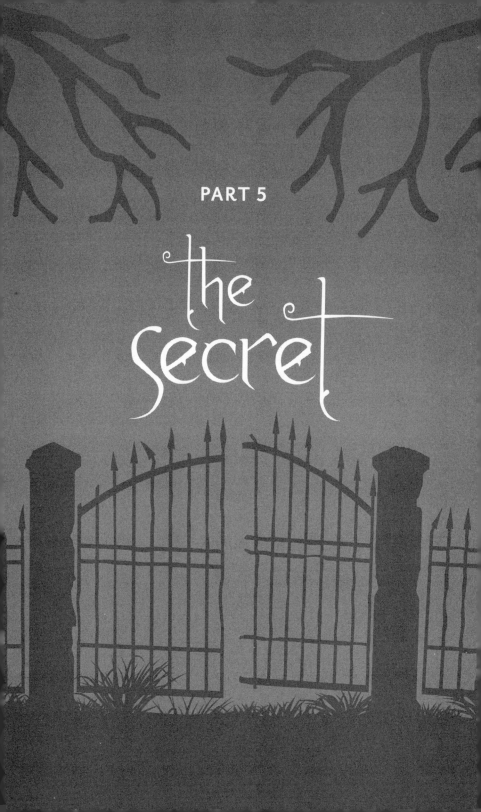

PART 5

the
Secret

Do not be afraid; our fate

Cannot be taken from us; it is a gift.

DANTE ALIGHIERI, *INFERNO*

34

"WAIT," I SAY TO JERRY. "Keep driving."

He looks over at me, confused. "But there's nowhere to go from here," he says.

"Just keep going. Please."

The word "please" sounds strange coming out of my mouth. I can't remember the last time I used that word. Jerry drives straight past the lane to my farm, past the old cemetery on the right, the one that used to have a church right beside it. He drives all the way back to the Road to Nowhere, as we used to call it. He passes the lane to Mr. Jinn's old farm, then stops the car when he can go no farther.

"Okay. Thank you," I say, getting out of the car with my cane and the box Abra's husband gave me.

"Should I wait here?" he asks.

"No, no, I'll manage."

"Where are you going? There's nothing back there. No road. No path. Nothing."

I push the cane down into the soft ground and look over my

shoulder through the open car window. "Things aren't always the way they appear. I'm going to see an old friend."

Jerry and Caleb glance at each other, and I know that look. They think my mind has wandered off without me. But it is the privilege of old age not to care when people look at you as if you're going crazy. And anyway, who knows, maybe I am. I turn away from the car and pick my way through the trees, my cane in one hand, the box in the other.

The old path is gone. It's as if it never existed. But I know the general direction, even after all these years. Everything is green and overgrown, and it makes me feel old that I have been alive long enough to witness the regeneration of an entire forest, one that was, in my lifetime, charred and lost. It says something, I think, about the heaviness of patience, the power of waiting.

The ivy snags at my cane and it's slow going. I push branches away from my face and walk through spiderwebs.

Eventually I come to the cemetery where my mother was buried. The old iron fence still surrounds the small space, though it's rusty, like an orange weed, and leans over so far in some places that it looks like it might topple. The gate is stuck open. Someone must have opened it a long time ago and never closed it. Some of the headstones have fallen over—broken teeth—but others are still in one piece, drowning in weeds.

My mother's gravestone still stands, and I wonder why it has been so long since I've come this way. I remember her funeral. How long ago that day seems! It feels more like something I read about in a book than something I saw with my own eyes. I place the box on top of her grave, then put my hand on the stone and close my eyes. It's warm in the summer heat.

I have never forgotten the verse the preacher read in the

church. I looked it up many times as a child until the words were etched in my mind.

Then the angel showed me the river of the water of life, as clear as crystal, flowing from the throne of God and of the Lamb down the middle of the great street of the city. On each side of the river stood the tree of life, bearing twelve crops of fruit, yielding its fruit every month. And the leaves of the tree are for the healing of the nations.

How I hope that is true.

But I haven't come here to stand at my mother's grave site all day. No, this is not my destination. I turn away and walk through the narrow gate and continue back through the woods. The going is even more difficult, and for a minute I'm not sure if I can make it over the rocks and the roots, through the weeds and the soft earth. But I get there, my black shoes pinching my feet.

I see it. It's still there.

The Tree of Life.

The outside of it is smooth like worn leather, and it's the color of a cloudy sky, a slate gray that's just beyond white. The bare branches are tangled in the leaves of other, living trees. I sit down with my back against it and lay my cane down on one side of me, the box on the other. I lean my head back against the old trunk and close my eyes. I can still feel the amazement I felt that morning when I looked up into its branches and saw all that glistening, almost-clear fruit. I feel a burning in my hands, or imagine I do.

I wonder what would have happened if I had taken a piece of that beautiful fruit and planted it in the loose earth of my mother's grave.

Would she be with me today?

Would we have been able to save the Tree?

Would she go on to live forever as I wasted away and eventually died, leaving her here alone? Or would I have eaten from the Tree too, sealing our fate, forcing us to roam this old world forever, never to see the other side of that vast water?

In the midst of all these thoughts, I hear the river.

I open my eyes and lift the box up onto my lap. I remember the other box, the one from the attic, the one I had kept for so many years without looking inside, the one that is now inside Abra's coffin and will soon be buried under the ground. And now another box, another mystery.

What could Abra have left me?

I lift off the lid and am not surprised.

The small sword is sitting over to one side, the same dull gray color of unpolished metal. I reach toward it carefully, but when my finger glances against it, it is still terribly hot. It would burn me again if I held on to it. Again, the burns tingle in my hands. I can see the Amarok again, and the fire raging in the forest, and the angels streaking through the sky.

I look beside the blade and see a kind of leather journal tied closed with a thin leather strap. I lift it out and untie the knot and gently ease it open. A breeze blows through the trees and flaps the pages. A few leaves drift down to the ground. It's the sound of fall in the middle of summer.

Then, there it is—something like a title page, written in Abra's childhood scrawl.

*The Adventures of
Abra Miller:
My Many Quests to Destroy
the Tree of Life*

I sigh. So many years have passed. So many things have been lost. Where will we find the courage we need?

I turn to the first page, and I can almost hear her voice reading the opening sentence to me.

After the death of the Amarok, I went to New Orleans. It is a city surrounded by water, a city full of magic. The sword took me there.

LOOK FOR

SHAWN SMUCKER'S

NEXT ENTHRALLING

NOVEL.

COMING SUMMER 2018

"I didn't speak with Abra for many years, you know," I say, trying to sound convincing. "Many years. We grew apart."

I pour two cups of coffee, my nerves on edge. The porcelain spout of the coffeepot chatters against each of our porcelain mugs like the teeth of a cold man. Steam rises, swirling, and the smell calms my nerves.

"Yours is here on the counter," I say as I make my way to the table, holding my own scalding mug.

I had forgotten the very particular feeling that comes when sitting across the table from someone like him, someone who is what he is, but when he returns to the table and settles in, it comes rushing back: the sense that you are not sitting across from a person as much as you are sitting across from an era, an epoch. Looking at this man was like looking at the Grand Canyon and seeing all those lines in the rock, all those different ages of the earth.

"Did you know anything about what she did after your mother died?" he asks.

"How do you know about my mother?" I ask.

"Everyone knows about your mother," he says with a hint of

impatience. "Your mother was . . . What do you know about what Abra did after your mother's passing?"

"She was my best friend. I gave her some things. Our friendship died. No, it didn't die—it wasn't that dramatic. We grew apart."

"You could have helped her, you know," he says, sipping his coffee, glancing at me over the rim.

I shake my head and look down. "No," I murmur into my coffee. "I was never strong enough."

"Come now. That's not true?" he says, but his voice turns the words into a question.

I look at him. "Apparently you know the story," I mutter. "I don't have to tell you about it."

"Our weaknesses are poised to become our greatest strengths. If we are patient and if we believe, the switch will often happen when we most need it to. Weakness"—he pauses, tilting his head from one side to the other—"to strength."

"I don't think that switch ever happened in me."

"Maybe you haven't needed it yet," he says. "What did you give her?"

"She ended up with the box. With everything."

He nods. He knows about the box. Of course he does. Mr. Tennin had it—they probably all wanted it after what happened at the Tree.

"Recently. Did you give her anything recently? Or did she give you anything?"

I stare into the black depths of my drink, and it feels like I'm still staring into this man's eyes. His eyes are everywhere.

I picture the box I put into her coffin.

The atlas.

The notes.

I envision the sword and the journal given to me by her husband. This was the moment. It was why this man was here.

I look up at him. "I can't help you. I don't know you."

I say these things in a voice that I hope will communicate that it's time for him to leave. I have been kidding myself thinking I can perhaps climb back into that adventure from my youth. I am too old for this. I have nothing to do with whatever real or imagined saga is going on around me, behind the curtain.

That phrase sticks in my mind: "behind the curtain." That's how Abra and I used to talk about the strange things that happened, as if normal life was on one side of a veil, and the other things—the Tree, the angels, the Amarok—were behind it. If we looked hard enough in those days, we could see the rustling. But not now. Not for many, many years.

"I appreciate your . . . discretion. But there is something Abra had that we need." He waits, then speaks again in a careful, insinuating tone. "I think you might have it. Here."

My heart pounds in my chest. I have no way of knowing which side this man is on. I have no way of knowing if he is a Mr. Tennin or a Mr. Jinn. I look in his eyes, desperately searching for something. Kindness, maybe.

"There's nothing here for you," I say, nerves stealing my breath.

He nods. His dangling earlobes sway. He reaches up and strokes his eyebrow with its seven small piercings all in a line. The space between them is the space between stars, which means that he and I, across the table from each other, must be light-years apart. How long is it taking his words to reach me? How many worlds have fallen in the time it takes me to refill his coffee?

"Do you have time for a story, Mr. Chambers?" he asks.

"I have as much time as I have." I shrug. "Look at me. I have no friends. I have no family. I have very little money. Time is all I have."

He smiles a sad smile. "You have less time than you think. This is a long story."

I take a long drink of coffee.

"It's about Abra," he says.

I nod, and the sadness rises again, this time without the apprehension.

"Let me put it this way," he says. "It's primarily about Abra, but there are others involved. It took me time to gather all these stories together. Decades. There were large gaps. Recently, I had to reopen doors that were not meant to ever be opened again. I sat in the shadows for years, looking for answers, always looking, never finding. Always seeing, never comprehending. I went very close to The Edge."

His voice fades. The wind kicks against the door. The windows rattle. Sleet falls for a minute or two, tapping against the glass, but it turns to snow, a swirling cloud of thick, hypnotic flakes.

"Do you know about her trip to New Orleans?" he asks.

"Only the basics," I say. "She mentioned it in her journal, but it was only a few paragraphs. Something terrible happened there, something she didn't want to write about. She was different after that. Her journal went from descriptive and flowery to matter-of-fact."

He sighs and nods. "How about Egypt?" he asks. "Jerusalem? Paris? Rio? The South Pole? Sydney?"

I am stunned but try not to let it show. I had no idea.

"Those are only the major journeys she took. There were smaller trips. Side trips, you might say. New Orleans was . . . unexpected. For all of us. And we only knew about the Tree

growing there after Tennin fell. By then Abra held the sword.
The Shadows were rising everywhere. People like me were turning. No one could be trusted. Two Trees at once! Who could
have ever imagined? Jinn's replacement was . . . ruthless. Her
name was Koli Naal. She wanted it all." He shakes his head. "She
wanted every last thing. Not only the Tree. Not only everything
and everyone here."

The name shoots through me like the memory of an intense
pain.

Koli Naal.

I had never spoken that name to anyone.

He stares hard at me to see if I understand what he's saying.
"You've heard that name before," he says, and it sounds like he
feels sorry for me.

I nod.

"She wanted every last thing," he repeats. "Those who came
before her, the Mr. Jinns of the world, wanted all of this." He
raises his arms to take in the walls of the house, the ends of the
earth. "Those who came before her wanted all of you—all of
humanity and all of this earth. But Koli Naal wanted even more
than that. She wanted everything."

When it's obvious I'm not catching on, he says something
in a whisper, something I can barely hear. He says it as if it's
blasphemy.

"She wanted Over There too."

"Over There?" I ask.

We stare at each other there in my little farmhouse, frost on
the windows, the snow sliding along the hard ground. We stare
at each other over mugs of coffee that are cooling. We stare at
each other over eternities and galaxies, cities and friendships,
swords and shadows.

He shrugs as if it will all make perfect sense to me at some point. "There was no one else who could go inside and do what needed to be done. Only Abra. Those were dark times."

"They must have been," I say in an even voice, "if you had to turn to a young girl to rescue you."

When he speaks again, there is something tender there, something that begs me for understanding. Or forgiveness. I wonder if he can be trusted after all. Perhaps.

"She was the only one who could go," he insists. "I would have gone. I hope you understand that. But it had to be her."

I wait, and the steam from our mugs rises between us like spirits.

"The story starts four years before the Tree appeared in Deen. Four years before the two of you killed Jinn and the Amarok and Mr. Tennin fell. Four years before your mother died."

"I didn't actually kill Jinn, you know," I say in a quiet voice. "Abra took care of that."

It feels a cowardly thing to have said, as if I'm trying to pawn all the dirt of that summer onto Abra, trying to save my own skin in case this man has come for revenge. I have a feeling that he knows far more about those events than I do, even though I was there and he was not.

He keeps talking as though he didn't hear me. I stare past him out the window. The snow is really coming down now. It looks like a blizzard is on the way.

"This is what happened," he begins, "the day Ruby vanished from the world."

This is the story he told me.

Acknowledgments

MANY, MANY YEARS AGO, a skinny kid sat on a farm-house porch under the reaching arms of two large oak trees, shooing away the flies, putting off his chores, and devouring any books he could get his hands on. His greatest dream was to someday write a novel.

That boy was me, and this book is the realization of that dream. So many of you played a part.

Ruth Samsel, this wouldn't have come about without your encouragement and patience. Thank you.

Sarah Hoover, you (very rashly, I might add) forwarded my email to your literary agent, and without that one quick click, this would not have happened. Thanks for your friendship and your belief in my writing.

Kelsey Bowen and the rest of the team at Revell, your vision and kindness and enthusiasm have overwhelmed me. Thank you for reading the manuscript of an unknown novelist and believing.

Bryan Allain, thanks for the many years of breakfasts where we talked writing and built huge dreams for ourselves.

Jeremy Martin, your long friendship and kind words have led me through many a dark place, including a time in my life when discouragement nearly stopped me writing fiction.

Thanks to DC for all of your constant friendships.

There are many families who embraced this book and continue clamoring for a sequel, including the Harveys, the Schneiders, the Haineses, and many others. Thanks for welcoming this child of mine into your own families.

Andi and Philip, God's Whisper Farm is a haven. Thanks for letting me do a reading there and for welcoming my family so often.

Thanks to those who made special contributions to the initial self-publication of this book, including Tim Lapp, Scott Bennett, David McCarty, Tamara Perry-Lunardo, and Gwyn McVay.

I also owe a huge debt of gratitude to those of you who supported my Kickstarter campaign and helped make this book possible. I'm going to list you all here because you're awesome: Steve Goble, Carl and Fan Smucker, Leanne Shirtliffe, Ryan Haack, Meghan Diller Glick, Dave Stoltzfus, Merrill and Verna Smucker, Dan and Jamie Smucker, Brenda Lee Sieglitz, Andrea Cumbo-Floyd, Dianne Yuninger, Jessie Buttram, Tor Constantino, Bryan and Erica Allain, Jesse and Sarah Hoover, Stewart Conkle, Christine Niles, Gordon Delp, Tammy Turney, Laura Stocker, Jim and Suzy Ogle, Ben and Shar Halvorsen, Susan M. Andrews, Deanne Bullock, Matt and Suzanne Silva, Brian and Angie Schmidt, Noah Martin, Jon Martin, Jay and Dena Riehl, Diana Trautwein, Preston Yancey, Robert and Bethany Woodcock, John and Kim Sanderson, Jason Boyett, David McCarty, Milynda Foushee, Jon

Fisher, Jon Hansen, Jason McCarty, Patricia Gibbons, Corri Gross, David and Orpha Longenecker, Sean McCarty, Joshua Samuelson, Todd Adams, Ryan and Janae Dagen, Brandon Fisher, Rich Hartz, Samantha and Lauren Good, Justin and Cindy Smucker, Mark and Heather Buckwalter, Rob Stennett, Roxanne Stone, Jim and Sharon Silva, Alicia Sierra, Tamára Lunardo, Dustin Sangrey, Jill and Brad Kane, Sharon Osielski, Matthew and Jessica Turner, the Arthurs, Joel Cornett, Michelle Woodman, Anna Haynes, Arne Radtke, Chris Davis, Susan Pogorzelski, Kevin Hostetter, Paula Aamli, Eric Wyatt, Evan and Laura Brownstein, Paul and Julie Peachey, Janice Riley, JR Forasteros, Gabe and Michelle Harvey, JJ Landis, Jeanne Befano, Chuck Blair, Patrick and MJ Miller, Samuel Gray, Blaine Houger, Robyn Pretorius, Nissa Day, Alexandria Gilbert, Seth and Amber Haines, Clay Morgan, Marilyn Coblentz, Caleb McNary, Allison DeHart, Daniel Fedick, Tamara Thompson, Paul Heggie, Doug and Shannon Schneider, Burnie Smucker, Donna Coleman, Gregg and Lize Landis, and Ashley Smucker.

To the entire family of Peter Perella, for enduring such a difficult loss and bearing it with grace and hope, and then supporting a book that made the audacious claim that "death is a gift." I thank you.

To Jason Darity, my friend.

Aunt Lin, I wish I could hand this book to you. And number six was a girl, but you probably already know that.

Mom and Dad, thanks for all the books. And everything else.

To my sisters, Sharalee, Angela, and Ashley, for putting up with me for so many years.

To my children, Cade, Lucy, Abra, Sam, Leo, and Poppy. You helped me create this story around the dinner table one spring evening in Holtwood in the middle of our forty-acre wood. Your imaginations inspire me and remind me to stay childlike.

And to Maile. We actually did it. We did it! Without you, my life would be unrecognizable. Without you, this book would not exist.

Shawn Smucker lives with his wife and six children in Lancaster, Pennsylvania. *The Day the Angels Fell* is his first novel. You can find him online at www.shawnsmucker.com, where you can also sign up for his newsletter if you would like to be notified when and where the Tree of Life grows once again.